CW00865005

DARK HYSTERIA

CYBORG SHIFTERS #8

NAOMI LUCAS

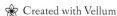 Created with Vellum

To my husband, Justin, and our baby dragon boy, Jesse. They are the loves of my life and my entire world. Thank you for giving me meaning.
And to my dad.
I miss you every day.

Alexa has one purpose in life, and it's to take down the war machines called Cyborgs. Specifically the one known as Hysterian, also known as the Tormentor, the Twitch, the Jumper. The Cyborg killed her father in cold blood, and she's determined to see the same thing happen to him.

First, she needs to get close to Hysterian.

Second, she needs to get him to trust her.

But the closer she gets, the stranger and more fascinating he becomes. He's in every shadowy corner. He's in her dreams. He's even stoking a desire in her that she's long kept buried. There's no turning back while stranded on a ship in the middle of outer space.

There's nowhere to run.

There's nowhere to hide.

He's her father's killer.

Whatever happens now, however the Cyborg makes her feel, she's determined that only one of them will make it off the ship alive...

ONE

ALEXA STARED at the Cyborg on the other side of the airfield.

The one creature in this universe she'd spent years chasing. The bastard who murdered her father. She knew she was being conspicuous—she wasn't shy about staring—but she wasn't the only one. The rest of the crew watched him too.

Hysterian.

Cyborgs were uncommon, relics of a past that everyone wanted to forget, but still lived with everyday. Products of a war that devastated two species.

But the crew didn't watch him the way she watched him.

They didn't have the burning hatred for Hysterian like she did. They didn't have a history with him.

She squeezed the rag in her hand then wiped it across her brow. She was sweating like crazy, and it wasn't even that hot. It was a mild day near the end of summer. Even though she'd been doing manual labor all morning to prep the ship for takeoff, the heat shouldn't have affected her like this. None of her other crewmates were as hot as she was.

Alexa glanced at them. Some glanced back, and she averted her eyes.

All of them were men. She knew they would be but had *hoped* there would be at least one other woman on the ship with her. That was a lot to hope for in her field. Getting a degree in space systems technology, space law, and ship management wasn't something a lot of women did, though there had been a handful in her classes on Elyria. Elderly women especially.

No one wanted to retire on Elyria. It was a glitzy metropolis with the seediest underground in all the cosmos. It was cheaper to get a job working on a spacecraft for a woman than going through the application process to move to a different planet, even with the looser restrictions for women who hadn't been born on Earth.

Old folk wanted to retire on Gliese, or Kepler, but not Elyria. Even retiring on Earth was better than a place that gave no rights to the elderly.

Turning back to the task at hand, Alexa lifted her case and headed for the hatch. Her gaze slid to Hysterian as she walked up the ramp.

Covered from head to toe in a black mesh and cloth suit, he stood out.

Speaking to several men in business suits out on the tarmac, Hysterian was devilish and enigmatic. His dark eyes lightened to gray when numbers skittered across them. If that didn't command attention, then it was his height, or the way his uniform hinted at the manmade muscles beneath it.

The muscles were hidden, though. His suit covered him from toe to...eyes. Alexa averted her own eyes when he looked in her direction.

He'd been speaking to the men most of the morning.

She tried to find a reason to get within earshot of them earlier, but nothing had come to mind. Whatever they spoke of would remain a secret.

If I was a higher rank, I could maybe find out...

She wasn't. She was high enough to be on a Cyborg's ship, but she wasn't an officer. She wasn't military. She wasn't even bridge crew.

She was one of two people to oversee the ship's laboratory and requisitions. She wouldn't be in Hysterian's neck of the ship.

Alexa wanted to be closer, needed to be closer. After he killed her father, she'd only wished to get as close to Hysterian as possible. To kill him. To do to him as he did to her father.

Elyria had been hot that day too. She'd sworn the planet was trying to cook her.

It was a hungry planet, after all. Elyria, always insatiable. Cooking her would be the kindest thing the planet could do. She hated the heat. Almost as much as the man she now worked for. Though, back then, she didn't even know Hysterian existed. His kind had been nothing more than a distant nightmare. A prickling memory. One she hadn't experienced since she was a child.

Regardless, the day her dad was murdered, her blood boiled under the sun... *Skin melting in the summer heat...*

Alexa shook her head, clearing it. It'd been a hot day.

She entered the ship.

Earth was just as hot as Elyria on its worst days. And with it being midsummer on the human planet, she'd already experienced a few. She checked her grip on the case, bypassing the ship's menagerie and making her way to the storage facility attached to it.

The door opened for her as she neared.

A blast of cold air hit her, and Alexa paused, enjoying the chilling relief. It was enough to take the edge off. She placed her load on a shelf and locked it into place, scanning the barcode attached to it.

Inventory updated.

It wasn't something she needed to do. The ship was high-tech enough to have an artificial intelligence programmed into it to keep inventory on everything up to date, but she did it anyway. She moved to the other resources and scanned them as well.

She didn't trust anyone else's data. They were often wrong. Her lack of trust had saved her ass on several occasions. If she trusted Elyrians, she'd still be in the slums. If she trusted the police on her home planet, her father's death would go unavenged.

Why else did women not get degrees in her field of study? Because they were discouraged—sometimes aggressively—to do so.

Women, and only women, were welcomed within the Trentian-controlled space sectors. If a woman owned and piloted her ship, what would stop her from leaving Earth's jurisdiction and cross over? What would stop her from smuggling other women across?

Trentians suffered a breeding disease—their society had few women left because of it—and those who remained had trouble reproducing. Trentian males and females could reproduce with humans, though, and with the lack of Trentian females having babies, or even being born, Trentian males sought human females to replenish their ranks.

Human men don't like the competition, especially not

from a species that had warred with them for over a century.

The Earth government couldn't afford to lose women to the aliens. *They want to have the biggest dicks in the universe.* Keeping women landlocked was what the government sought to do instead.

There was talk that the Trentians grew their young now in labs, but that was speculation and rumor. No one actually knew. She didn't. Breeding politics meant nothing to her. She had no interest in having kids with a human man or an alien.

Hysterian's demise was all she cared about.

Which was Alexa's driving force to degree-up because she didn't have access to money any other way. If she was going to kill a Cyborg, she had to be competent, smart. She had to know more than what she could learn in the slums. She knew Hysterian wouldn't remain on Elyria forever. Traveling through space was *expensive*.

Though Elyria was different from most Earth territories. It was easier to do as you pleased, even as a woman. Breaking the law was commonplace.

Yet another reason why she didn't trust easily.

The medical examiners said her dad died of a drug overdose—their equipment verified it. They were wrong.

Dad hadn't overdosed on drugs. There were no needles, no marks on his flesh. There was no sign of vein bulge from Elyrian Sky, or excessive sweating from Scarlet opioids.

He was murdered.

All they found was an abnormal substance on her dad's hand, nothing more. The substance neutralized all their tests—it responded to nothing. Benign, they decided. They took a sample of his skin and put it in a container to cryopreserve it. But when she followed up with them, the sample had miraculously gone missing.

It wasn't missing. Someone stole or destroyed it. Why else would it have gone missing?

She scanned another container. Words flashed above her wristcon telling her what it was: grain.

"There you are."

Alexa saw her coworker walking into the room. Raul, her menagerie maintenance partner. Middle-aged and muscled, Raul was a decent-looking human man. With thick black hair that was cut short and curled around his head, he always appeared as if he'd spent his morning sitting in front of an industrial fan. What with his five o'clock shadow covering his jaw, Alexa was certain he had.

He could've spent that time shaving instead. He was dressed in the same form-fitting uniform she wore. Unlike hers, his vest wasn't zipped to his neck, which left a peek of his white undershirt showing underneath.

His name tag was displayed prominently on the right side of his chest. Raul Gilmartin.

All of her crewmates were well-built. One had to be in peak condition for a job such as theirs.

With a pallet under his arm, Raul moved past her and set his load down, locking it in place. She went to his side and scanned it.

Tranquilizers.

A lot of them. Alexa licked her lips. When she looked up, Raul was watching her curiously.

"You do know there's more to load, right? You can scan them in later," Raul said. "It's not like we'll have a ton to do between requisitions."

"I needed to get out of the heat for a bit." She held up her rag still scrunched up in her hand.

Raul laughed. "If you think this is hot, you should head south to Texas for the summer. This heat isn't anything compared to that."

She headed for the door. "Right."

A hand grabbed her arm. "It's him, isn't it?"

She tensed and looked down at Raul's hand on her. "Release me." Her eyes snapped up, realizing what he just said. "Him?"

"Our captain, the boss man, the scary Cyborg fucker we now work for. You're in here because of him, aren't you?"

"I—"

"It's okay. I won't tell anyone. He gives me the heebie jeebies too."

"I'm not here because of him. I'm not scared of our captain," she said. Oh, how she lied.

"You heard what he is, right?"

She shook his hand off. "Besides a Cyborg?"

"He's one of those shifter ones."

"I knew that." She did know that. She'd known that since before he killed her father. People whispered about him back home, saying Hysterian could bring you bliss or death with a single touch. She didn't know of an animal in all the universe that could do that.

She didn't know what kind of animal Hysterian was, and it wasn't for a lack of research.

That type of information about a Cyborg was heavily guarded. Besides several old articles about Hysterian's time during the war, there was virtually nothing about him anywhere. There was very little about any Cyborg.

It was frustrating. It made tracking him hard, at least at first.

What made them so special? It wasn't fair how they were given things that normal people weren't. Most humans would give their souls to be born into the kind of power Cyborgs possessed. *Killing machines with unlimited freedom...* It wasn't fair. They needed to pay for what they'd done.

Unlimited freedom, unlimited strength, unlimited wealth and power.

Alexa was desperate to ask Raul if he knew Hysterian's animal. But that would reveal that she cared enough to know more about the Cyborg. Could she trust Raul? Trust wasn't her thing.

"Although, I hear he's messed up," Raul said. "Bad design or something. It's made him mad, really mad. Being defective. Heard he only took this job because there's a possibility the EPED could fix him."

"Messed up?" *Bad design? Wait?* "Defective?" She'd never heard of Hysterian being defective. She'd also never heard of Hysterian having a problem with his mecha side, but then again, the only information she had about him came from people who used to work with him.

And those were some shady individuals. Anyone who worked for the crime boss Raphael at his club, Dimes, wasn't someone you wanted to know. Which was who Hysterian used to work for.

Traffickers, drug dealers, murderers, rapists. Raphael surrounded himself with shit. And since Hysterian had been working for him, Alexa assumed he had done all of that and worse.

Shit breeds shit.

"Yeah," Raul continued. "Daniels, his second-in-command, was given a briefing by the big guy, Nightheart. We're not supposed to get close."

"What do you mean 'get close?' I haven't heard anything."

"He probably hasn't come to talk to you yet. You know how it is." Raul shrugged.

"No. I don't know how it is. Is it because I'm a woman?"

He let out another laugh that made her bristle. "Woman? Not at all. We're all stoked you're here. What I meant is that—" Raul stopped and looked at something over her shoulder. She watched as Raul squared his shoulders.

Someone was behind her in the doorway.

A feeling of foreboding had her inhale a breath and hold it. Alexa stiffened, knowing exactly who it was behind her. She prayed Cyborgs couldn't really read minds, and that was all a rumor too.

"Captain," Raul said and genuflected, briefly catching her eye in warning. "What can we do for you?"

She twisted and locked eyes with *him*.

Her captain.

Hysterian.

Though his suit came up to cover everything below his eyes, she would recognize him anywhere. Those dark irises, the sharp brows framing the tops of his eyes, and his incredibly pale skin were unmistakable. She was pale herself, but Hysterian was unnaturally so. Like at any moment, he'd go translucent and slip into thin air.

But it wasn't his skin and eyes that were so recognizable, it was his hair. It was shock white, pulled back from his face and gathered behind his head, falling to an arrow-point at the base of his neck. It was always perfectly kempt, and she didn't know how he did it.

She couldn't imagine an indomitable war machine using hair gel.

Hysterian stepped forward, his hair brushing the top of the door frame. He was tall, and built too, because what Cyborg wasn't muscled? Hysterian wasn't like a wrestler.

He had a ripped, lean way to him. His neck and arms were long, and what she could see of his facial features were sharp and piercing, giving them the appearance of elongation without the uncanniness.

He was one of a kind.

He clearly looked down at them.

Pushing her sudden hatred and curiosity deep within her, she greeted him. "Captain," she said thickly, nodding her head. His eyes went to her, and she nearly choked on her heart.

"Ms. Dear, Gilmartin, you're needed in the menagerie. Now."

"Yes, sir," both she and Raul said at once, breaking the tense moment.

Hysterian remained in the doorway when Raul tried to leave, refusing to let him pass. Awkwardly, Raul waited for him to move so he could obey the order. Alexa remained behind. She was immobilized under the Cyborg's gaze.

His cold, black eyes were hard to be under, and Alexa tried not to balk. She summoned her courage and clenched her hands.

It would be better if Hysterian didn't know she existed. The longer she stayed under his radar, the easier it would be to destroy him. If he saw her coming...she was as good as dead.

His heavy stare bore into her, and as it did, her anxiety grew. Could he read her intentions? Did he see through her mask? Did Cyborgs really read minds?

Alexa's fear spiked. This was too much, too fast. She wasn't ready. Her fingers trembled.

No one should be subjected to this murderous Cyborg's intimidation.

Hysterian stepped aside, breaking eye contact with her, startling her out of her rising panic.

"Raul, you can go now. We'll meet you in the lab," he ordered.

"I think—" Raul began.

Hysterian scowled at Raul, and she never saw a man cower so fast. Alexa was sure she'd been cowering a moment ago. Raul gave her an apologetic look as he fled.

It was just her and Hysterian now.

For nearly twelve years, she dreamed of this moment. She was sixteen when she'd discovered her dad's body. This moment, in her head, was her getting justice, with Hysterian on the floor, waiting for the final blow, unable to stop her.

This moment *never* had her recovering from a near panic attack.

"Captain"—she swallowed, trying not to wither when his gaze returned to her—"what can I do for you?" His pupils jittered, but it happened so fast she couldn't be sure.

"It's nice to finally meet you, Dear," he said, reaching out his hand.

Alexa stared at it.

'We're not supposed to get too close.' Raul's warning fluttered through her head.

Hysterian's hand was gloved, covered like the rest of him. She recalled rumors about his skin on Elyria... *One touch: bliss or death.*

This is a test.

Holding back her need to wipe her palm on her suit, she clasped his hand. His fingers wrapped tightly around hers, and his thumb pressed down into the back of her hand, trapping it so thoroughly that fear zipped up her spine.

Their hands shook once before she jerked it out of his grasp.

"Nice to...meet you, Captain," she managed, pressing her nails into her palm. "Are you okay?"

Hysterian's head cocked.

Alexa wished she could read his expression, but his mouth was covered.

She didn't even know what Hysterian truly looked like. It bothered her. She liked to imagine he was the ugliest motherfucker there ever was, but she knew that wasn't true. She had a picture of him facing away, looking at something outside the frame, in the lining of her bag. Just the contour of his face proved he was handsome.

All Cyborgs were uncannily attractive.

Fuck them. A lot of people are attractive and are evil.

"I run hot, Dear."

"Is that why you cover yourself up?" she asked before she could think better of it.

"Do you always ask so many idiotic questions of your superiors?"

Her lips pursed. "No, sir. I apologize. You startled me, that's all. I'll get out of your way and head for the menagerie." She needed to get out of here before she asked or did something really dumb. Getting fired before they even took off would hurt her chances of success.

She couldn't let her dad down, not after everything she'd been through, everything she risked.

She tried to leave, but he stepped in front of her, blocking the exit again.

"I am teasing," he said, further confusing her. "I don't mind questions. Raul told you I was a shifter, and he's right. I just run hotter than most, but it's not why I cover myself, Dear."

The way he said her name made her uncomfortable. "You were listening to Raul and me?"

"Yes."

She was suddenly very thankful she didn't grill her coworker for information.

"I'm sorry," she said, hoping he'd finally move out of her way.

He didn't.

He took a step toward her. "Why are you sorry?"

"I—" Her mouth snapped closed as she craned her neck to meet his gaze.

"You're not sorry, are you?"

"No..."

"Don't ever lie to me, I will know. It's my job to know."

Tension filled the space, and the ability to breathe left her. She was afraid of him, she realized, truly afraid. This was her dad's murderer. She'd never been afraid of him before. Only the ending...

He now knows I exist.

"Yes, sir," she said, keeping her voice level. "I won't do it again."

"Good to know." He moved out of her way.

Alexa slipped past him as quickly as possible. Like she was moving under the watchful gaze of a gargoyle. One waiting to strike out for blood. She stepped out the door, her heart lodged in her throat.

"Alexa." His voice was ominous.

She stilled.

"Don't ever try and get close to me. You won't survive it. Defective doesn't come close. That was the briefing you missed."

Alexa fled, taking his warning to heart.

TWO

Alexa entered the menagerie to the sound of a crash and men yelling.

The whole crew was surrounding a large, wooden box on a robotic lift as she neared. Screeches were coming from the inside of it. Something banged within, and the box shook hard, rocking just enough to one side that it almost fell over.

She ran over to help the others keep the box in place.

"Keep your hands on it! Don't let it fall," Daniels barked. He caught sight of her. "Where have you been, Dear?" Frustration edged his tone.

"With me," Hysterian said, joining them around the crate and saving her from yet another reprimand.

She was getting a lot of them recently.

Daniels went back to what he was doing. "Very good," he muttered.

Hysterian grabbed the back of the box, promptly stopping whatever was inside from overturning it. "Restart the lift. We need to get it into the enclosure. Now!"

Like ants, they all scrambled. The shrieks of what was

within grew by the second. Alexa rushed to the enclosure that the lift was heading for and signed into the adjoining computer. She unlocked it, and the glass door to the enclosure rose up. Hysterian lined up the wooden box to the opening, latching it. The enclosure's door lowered to align with the crate.

His arms were straining, tense and spread wide to keep the box from falling. "Dear, when the beast enters the cage, shut the panel. You may only have a second to do so. If the locust gets out, we'll have blood on our hands." He grunted.

Locust? Whatever was inside didn't sound like a bug. It sounded like a monkey—a large one.

"Yes, Captain."

Raul and Daniels readied tranquilizer guns.

"Everyone ready?" Hysterian called.

"Yes," they all said to varying degrees. Pigeon, the ship's EPED liaison and mechanic, wiped his mouth, and Horace, another member of the bridge crew, placed his hands on his hips. Alexa poised her finger over the door's trigger.

Hysterian let go of the box, jumped a top, and unlocked a mechanism. The part of the crate lined with the enclosure swung open.

Something big shot out, slamming into the back wall of the reinforced glass cage with a howl. Alexa initiated the panel door shut. Hysterian jumped off the crate and pushed it out of the way as the door came down. The creature spun around, nostrils flaring, and four meaty arms rose only to slam down onto the ground with a resounding bang.

Two large black wings popped out from its back.

It rushed for the door, crashing against it. Alexa stepped back. The glass panel held, and continued to hold as the beast pounded away. When it realized there was no escape, it lifted its head and roared.

Alexa flinched before setting the perimeters on the enclosure to muffle the sound.

Silence filled the space when the primate's roar was cut off.

The alien creature coiled into a ball and rolled, hitting all the sides. It gained speed upon its second roll. The glass wobbled but miraculously held.

"What the ever-living fuck is that thing?" Raul asked.

"An Atrexian locust," Hysterian answered, the only one of them completely unfazed. He moved to the enclosure's computer, and Alexa shuffled to the side. He typed something in and a mist poured out from the top, shrouding everything inside and hiding the primate from view for a moment.

"That's not a fucking locust. I've seen locusts at the zoo," Daniels said.

Hysterian stepped back. "On Atrexia, it's known as a locust."

She and the rest of the crew circled the enclosure and stared at the creature raging within. Claws came out to swipe at the glass. Its wings hit the sides.

"They swarm areas destroying everything in their path, consumed with a breeding rage when entering adulthood. Their strength is beyond any animal borne of Earth, their rage indomitable. The males, like this one, will go from one female and to the next, forced to copulate as much as possible. They're the only beasts we know of that are continuously in heat after they mature. Everything we know about them is in your requisition files."

"Great," Raul muttered, glancing at Alexa. "Guess we'll have our hands full?"

She shrugged.

Hysterian glanced down at her. "It's your job to keep them alive and contained."

Hysterian's abysmally dark eyes twitched again, and her brow furrowed. When he looked away soon after, she stared after him, confused.

Was it just me, or did his pupils bulge? His words came back to her, warning her of getting close. *He's right beside me.* She stopped herself from taking an extra step away.

Her eyes narrowed. *Is he testing me? Again?*

She fisted her hands at her sides.

"And why is it here, on Earth, and in our possession?" Horace asked. "I thought we were picking up and delivering resources, taking the odd jobs the EPED is known for?"

Raul hmphed. "We're delivering this, obviously. Why else would the *Questor* have a menagerie and enclosures like these"—he waved his hand at the space around him—"if it wasn't for animals like that?"

"That wasn't mentioned in the job description."

"Maybe because it has nothing to do with the bridge crew."

"I want to know if there's dangerous creatures confined in the same space as me," Horace quipped.

Raul laughed. "What did you think odd jobs stood for?"

"Enough," Hysterian barked. Raul and Horace glowered at each other. "We have several more to onboard before we can take off. We can talk after we're in the sky."

"Yes, Captain," Raul muttered.

"There's more?" Daniels asked, sliding his tranq gun into the waist of his pants instead of setting it down.

Daniels wasn't nearly as handsome as Raul, but was built all the same. With a closely shaved head and stocky features, the bridge officer looked more like infantry than someone who sat all day in front of a computer.

The doors to the lab zipped open behind them, revealing another, smaller crate and several tarmac servicemen.

"There's always more. This is the job. If you don't like it, there's still time to leave." Hysterian said, heading for the incoming crate, shooting Horace a look.

She watched him walk away, giving orders to the servicemen. He was the only one who wore a black suit, unlike the rest of them, who wore gray. Hysterian's suit was devoid of metals, straps, or even buttons, and only had his name tag pinned to his right breast and a belt that had a gun attached at his hip.

His suit was strange, tight, leaving nothing to the imagination, unlike what she pictured he would wear. She'd never seen material like the one Hysterian seemed so comfortable in. Because when it came to revealing everything...it did; the bulge of his crotch, his physique, the play of his powerful muscles as he moved. She tried not to check him out each time she saw him, but it was hard not to.

Was vanity his weakness?

He'd been the object of her vengeance for so long; she still couldn't believe how near he finally was. Before this, she'd only glimpsed him from afar on several occasions, and had her one picture of him.

One truth Alexa realized this day was that Hysterian was fucking intimidating up close, even to other men. She knew killing him was going to be hard, but this just made it all the more difficult.

"Fucking hell," someone said behind her. "Poor Alexa."

"Don't call me—" Alexa faced the enclosure and came face to face with the primate. She jumped, taking a step back.

Daniels and Raul laughed.

"Was wondering when you'd stop eyeing the captain. Looks like the primate likes you, Dear," Raul teased.

"Seems the monkey knows who the females are in the room," Daniels added.

Alexa gritted her teeth. The primate stared at her, drool pouring out of the sides of its mouth. Her skin prickled under her uniform. Awareness shot through her. When she finally tore her eyes away from the animal, she discovered her crewmates watching her.

Her spine straightened. "Seems to know who the real boss is," she said, feigning indifference, trying not to look back at the salivating ape.

"More like it knows who it wants to mate with," Daniels said.

Alexa pursed her lips. "It and the rest of the males in this room will soon realize they'll be dead if they tried."

Raul laughed again and clapped his hand on her shoulder. "We're just teasing you. Don't need to get yourself worked up. We're family now. Don't you know that?"

"Are you going to do your jobs, or do I need to fire you all?" Hysterian said, shooting them all a withering look. "Keep your hands to yourself, Raul."

Raul dropped his hand from her shoulder. "Yes, Captain."

Her crewmates went to help Hysterian with the new crate. She moved to join them when Pigeon, the ship's manager who'd also lagged behind, stopped her.

"Ms. Dear, if you ever feel uncomfortable, please don't hesitate to come to me," he said as if to make her feel better. As if she didn't know what she was getting herself into. "I've been on many ships, traveled through space most of my life, and I know how hard it is to be a female in this field, alone with men for long periods of time."

Pigeon was the oldest among them. Nearly wizened with gray whiskers and white hair, he had the appearance of exactly what he said he was: a lifelong crew worker. His face was thin with shallow wrinkles, and his nimble hands barely hid age spots and their decreasing elasticity, Pigeon looked like he'd spent years working hard, yet hardly in sunlight.

"You come to me if anything happens, even if you're unsettled. It'll come to an end, I promise. I may be old, but I've championed many women in my time." He smiled. "And our Captain made it a point to look out for you, knowing your unique situation."

"My unique situation?" she asked, not sure she should be offended. Men like Pigeon, feeling as if they needed to help the poor females in their industry, were all too common. Alexa couldn't count them on two hands. Whether in training, or in the field, there were always a few.

And why had Hysterian asked someone to look out for her? Did he think she couldn't take care of herself?

Alexa shook her head. It didn't matter. His opinion was less than nothing.

"That this is your first job. It's not easy, spending long spans of time in space. Your circadian rhythm gets all jacked even if you follow the health guidelines, you'll see. Your feminine cycle—"

"Is none of your business," she snapped. Alexa stopped Pigeon again when he grew flustered and tried to apologize. "I don't need your apology. I appreciate your concern and will come to you if something should happen that I can't take care of myself, but this is hardly my first time traveling through space. I can watch my own back."

Pigeon smiled. "Good to hear."

"You two coming or what?" Raul called.

With one last glance at the locust, whose creepy gaze followed her every movement now, she joined the others at the new crate.

The rest of the afternoon went on without incident, and by nightfall, Alexa was certain that her first meeting with Hysterian and the crew wasn't something that would often be repeated. She could still manage to make herself relatively invisible.

Except to Raul, who was always where she was.

He'll be a problem, she mused when she hauled a bushel of leaves to the male locust's enclosure. It was feeding time, and even though the creature had calmed down after the tranquilizer spray from earlier, it was still very much alert. It'd only acted up again when he saw the female locusts being placed in their enclosures.

The females, unlike the male, were less aggressive. After their initial fear, they settled easily into their spaces. It gave their enclosures time to replicate a small, simulated habitat for them. Raul was feeding them while she took on the male.

A stream of drool fell from the side of its mouth as she placed her bushel into the drawer. Whether it was hungry for food or her, she had no idea.

She didn't care to know.

She didn't like the locust either way. Alexa closed the drawer and let the food drop into the space. The male grabbed it with its four arms and tore into it, crushing chunks of bark with each bite.

If they could see it now... She thought of Horace and Daniels. As she stared at the locust feasting with a violence that didn't make sense, since there was nothing it needed to fight to keep its food, she thought Horace had the right of it.

I'd want to know if I was sharing the small confines of a

ship with a monster like that. But she knew when she applied for the job that she'd be working for animals and creatures from around the known universe. It was in the description.

The locusts aren't the only monster on this ship. She frowned.

The ping of the ship's intercom went off, and Daniels's voice came through. "Take off commencing in fifteen. Lockdown initiating in five. Say your goodbyes to Earth, everyone. We won't be back for months."

Raul grunted in response. "Earth needs no goodbyes."

Alexa agreed.

"Come help me if you're done." He pointed to the third female locust. "She still needs her bush."

With one last glance at the male, who rolled its jaw as it finished the last of its food, Alexa grabbed the remaining female's bush and dropped it into her drawer. Raul came to stand beside her. "Thanks."

"You're welcome."

"They'll need to be fed once more before shift's end. Then we'll finally be able to take a load off."

"Yeah."

"You okay?"

Her eyes shifted his way. "Why wouldn't I be?"

"Captain wanted to talk to you alone. I didn't want to leave you, wasn't sure if you were in trouble. Sorry about that."

Alexa wiped her palms on her pants and turned toward the menagerie's central computer panel where her workstation was. Raul followed her.

"I wasn't in trouble," she said. "He wanted to formally introduce himself to me."

Raul sat down in his station and strapped in. "Odd."

"Why odd?" she asked, doing the same.

"He never formally introduced himself to me." Belt buckles clicked. "Whatever. Maybe it's because you're..."

"I'm what?"

"I was going to say a woman then thought better of it," Raul said. "I have no problem with your sex, but who the hell knows what our captain thinks? I shouldn't have assumed."

The lights flickered, lowered, indicating takeoff lock-down. *Questor's* AI listed off safety measures, which were all redundant. When it was over, Alexa sighed and sagged into her seat. "It doesn't matter what he thinks or what anyone else thinks. Let's just do our jobs, okay?"

"You're not a talkative one."

"No. I'm not."

"Fine by me. Though I'll crack you open someday, Ms. Dear. It's not like we'll have much else to do to occupy our time between missions. Crew becomes family, ya know? Maybe it doesn't seem that way at the start, but you'll see. The people you work with—*survive* with in space—when there's no one else for billions of miles to rely on, they become your family real fast. Some of the best people I've met were on previous jobs."

Family? Right, she thought dryly. She had family once, but it was taken away from her. The lights lowered further, and a whizzing sound filled the space. The locusts were curled up in balls, probably responding to the thrusters. There were anxiety supplements added to their bushels she and Raul fed them. She hoped it was enough.

Daniels's voice came over the intercom again counting down from five. Alexa closed her eyes and counted down with him in her head.

Earth needs no goodbyes.

She'd been on it a little less than a month, and had no plans of ever returning.

In fact, she was certain she wouldn't. It was more likely she would be dead after all was said and done. Killing Hysterian—if she managed it—would be tricky to walk away from. There'd be an investigation, and she wasn't an idiot. Cyborgs recorded everything they saw, keeping it within their databases.

No, if Hysterian didn't kill her first, and she managed to do the deed, it would take more than a miracle to survive what came after. She knew what she signed up for.

The ship shuddered; internal gravity shifted. She clutched the armrests.

There was no turning back now.

THREE

Two days back in space, and he was already pent-up. Hysterian clasped his hands behind his neck and stretched, cracking the metal joints in his back and neck.

In that time, he'd firmly established himself as captain, gaining the respect of the two men he worked the closest with—Daniels Waller, ex-miner freight co-pilot, a man who had years of experience maneuvering large, obnoxious behemoth ships through space, and had a keen desire to prove his manliness, and Horace [*Redacted*], his navigator and stand-in for when Hysterian wasn't around to deal with the locals they would eventually encounter. Horace had been to more places throughout the universe than even Hysterian had. The direct knowledge that his navigational specialist had was something he grossly lacked.

He'd picked them for a reason. Neither Daniels nor Horace liked interacting with people. Besides the occasional joke, they kept it business between them. It didn't mean they were always serious; he'd overheard them conversing with a beer after the end of the second shift in *Questor's* lounge. They laughed, talked about him, the job.

There was always someone talking about him. Hysterian was used to it.

Captain. Fucking captain of a ship.

Hysterian dropped his hands and stood. How had he ended up back here after a half century of avoiding such a fate? He left the bridge without a backward glance and went straight for his quarters.

He hadn't captained a ship since the war, and even then, it had only been for a short time.

Hysterian wasn't built for it. He hadn't had the material programmed in his systems when he was created. He'd been built for something else.

The night shift ended two hours ago. He waited that long to leave the bridge; he didn't want to run into the others as he wandered. By now, his crew should all be in their quarters and asleep. Just in case, he seeded into *Questor's* security cameras and pinpointed everyone's whereabouts.

Pigeon, Raul, and Horace were in their quarters. Daniels was in the lounge.

Alexa was in the laboratory.

If she wanted to work late, that was her prerogative. Perhaps she was studying. He didn't give a damn as long as she did her job and stayed away from him. That went for the rest of the crew as well.

The captain's quarters were located near the bridge so he didn't have to walk far. His was the only quarters that weren't shared. Horace, Daniels, and Pigeon shared a room down the corridor while Alexa and Raul had specialized quarters attached to the menagerie, which was on the level below him.

They had no reason to come up here, and he had no reason to go down there—unless it was for a job. He would've preferred to have the rest of the crew roomed below as well, but the ship wasn't laid out that way, and so he'd have to make do. Everyone slept near where they worked to optimize efficiency.

A crew of five... He hadn't thought five people would be a crowd, having been around crowds for the past fifteen years, but in a space as enclosed as the *Questor*, it was beginning to feel that way.

Hysterian strode into his room. When the door closed, the tension in his muscles eased.

Reaching up, he pulled down the top of his suit and opened his mouth, relieved to have fresh, cool air again. Rolling his jaw loose, he tugged off his gloves and set them down. He unbuckled his belt, rolled it up, and placed it on his bed beside his gloves, making quick work of his suit next. He stepped out of his nano-sewn clothes, checked them over for moisture, then stuffed them in his laundry receptacle, where they would be sanitized.

When naked, his restraint eased.

He pressed the pads of his fingers together, then ran his fingers through his hair. Hysterian eyed the blanket on his bed.

He craved warmth more than anything. More than immortality, strength, power. He craved it so badly he'd spent the majority of his manmade life chasing after it. But it wasn't the warmth of a blanket, clothes, or an environment that he wanted. He had tried all that. No, he craved the warmth of contact. Living, breathing, human contact.

He was fucking desperate for it.

Hysterian glanced at his bunched-up gloves with disgust.

How long has it been since I touched someone, something with my bare hands? How long had it been since he'd touched someone who wanted it? A year ago, Zeph had torn Hysterian's suit in a fight, swiping the skin off his face. The touch had been violent, but the kiss Hysterian gave Zeph hadn't been.

Hysterian laughed. *My last warm touch was with a cold-blooded bastard. A brother.* It was almost funny, in a sad, pathetic way. At the time, a kiss was the only way Hysterian could subdue the other Cyborg without killing him.

He rubbed the back of his hand across his lips. Still, that fleeting touch had been warm, even more so with blood gushing from the wounds he sustained from the other Cyborg. He felt guilty for nearly killing Zeph, but there were innocents needing protection, and Nightheart promised Hysterian the thing he'd wanted most by playing mercenary for him.

Which was why Hysterian was here now, working for Nightheart and the EPED, and no longer selling his services to the richest crime lord on Elyria. Raphael hadn't been thrilled to lose him, but there was nothing his ex-boss could do to make him stay and Raphael knew it.

There was nothing Hysterian cared about enough for Raphael to use against him.

And they had come together more as friends and less as boss and subordinate. Hysterian often refused to do Raphael's bidding, and Raphael dealt with it because he enjoyed the bragging rights of having a Cyborg bodyguard.

If it weren't for Zeph and his misadventure in Hysterian's neck of the universe, then Hysterian wouldn't be here now, feeling a modicum of hope.

Nightheart promised me warmth, contact.

He promised a cure. He has money.

More money than anyone else as far as Hysterian suspected.

Raphael promised the same thing when Hysterian first entered into Raphael's employment, and he delivered, but not in the way Hysterian needed.

His ex-boss used his connections to look into a drug or a cure, but when all avenues failed, the inquiries stopped, and the encounters with random humans picked up instead. It'd been the only way for Raphael to pay him...

Raphael delivered to Hysterian victims, drug addicts who were just as desperate for a fix as he was. His ex-boss gave him the warmth he craved in small fucked-up doses. For a while, Hysterian took them willingly, killing and doping up whoever Raphael wanted him to.

Hysterian crouched, pressed his head between his knees, and wrapped his arms around his body.

Glazed eyes, raspy coughs, pale spotted skin flickered through his mind. Stringy hair, urine-stained clothes, bulging purple blood vessels. Hundreds of faces flashed behind his eyes. Ghosts. Demons. They were always there.

Did they matter? Back then, he would have said no. If these people ended up in his space, they got there because they were stupid. Anyone who came to Raphael for help was an idiot... Killing was second nature to a Cyborg made for war, but cold-blooded killing was something else entirely...

Everything had slowly changed. It was like a genetic code rewrote itself within him. What made him so good as to be dubbed the name *Tormentor* no longer computed.

Hysterian had started to care.

When? He had no idea. It no longer mattered because any warmth he'd stolen from these idiot humans diminished, and he was jonesing for a new fix. He couldn't turn to tranqs or hallucinogens because of his mecha nature and the nanocells that were like a disease throughout his whole body. They'd nullify the effects as soon as they entered his body. He'd need a great deal of alcohol to get any effect from it.

Hysterian hated and envied the druggies he had spent so much time with.

The pulsing bass of the music at Dimes rang in his ears. Hysterian hissed through his teeth.

He remembered everyone he touched. He wouldn't allow himself to forget. Wiping his mind clean of the memories would be cowardly. His jaw locked. He was far from a coward.

But then Zeph ended up at Dimes, and Nightheart made contact with Hysterian to take him out. Was it fate? Probably not. Fate didn't factor into Cyborg coding.

Nightheart made him an offer Hysterian couldn't refuse.

"I'll find a way to cure you, to stop your body's reaction to contact, but in return, you'll work for me. You'll contract as a new retriever for the EPED. You'll stop working for that fat fuck and get some fucking dignity back."

Hysterian had laughed at the time.

Raphael hated being called fat.

Unlike most Cyborgs who saw humans as inferior—especially human males—Hysterian saw them as useful. Their randomness and lack of calculation made them fun. Their ability to touch and hold everything—to *feel* everything—made him envious. And they were warm. Always warm.

He had always been this way, but it wasn't until the war ended that it became an issue.

Perhaps being an interrogator and executioner for the military had something to do with it. They spliced his human DNA with an unusual creature for that very purpose.

The cybernetic doctors spliced him and then didn't give him the ability to shift.

Raul had the right of it.

Hysterian *was* defective.

He rose to his feet and stretched. Though he couldn't fully shift, he hadn't lost all parts of his other half. The cybernetic doctors had given him some quirks that they thought could be useful.

Thank the devil they gave me my tongue. Hysterian rolled his eyes.

Self-pitying piece of shit. He strode to his lavatory and turned on his bathing unit. He may not have had an animal he could unleash when pent-up, but at least he could seek relief in other ways.

Microscopic pores opened up all over his skin, undetectable to the human eye, and his body slickened with oil. Toxins. Boiling water sprayed down upon him from overhead, hiding his secretion. The clear substance his body produced vanished with the water. He rested his arms on the wall and bowed his head. Hysterian stared at the water pooling at his feet being sucked into the drain. In another minute, the lavatory would be filled with steam, blinding him.

The ship's recycling systems would never encounter his secretion either. By the time they made it to the ship's normal water unit, the nanocells within his toxins would have destroyed it. He made sure of it when his ship was being redesigned. The water gathered in a separate tank to be scanned, and only released back into the ship's normal systems when it was deemed pure.

His crew would never know their captain poisoned the water supply nightly...

Hysterian slid his right arm off the wall and grabbed his cock. It hardened in his hand.

Thank the fucking devils who created me for giving me a dick. Hysterian squeezed his shaft as hard as he could without crushing it. Pain zipped through him for an instant. He kept squeezing, praying for the release he really needed.

Boiling water would never be enough.

His hand would never be enough.

The phantom of a willing woman, one open to his desperate affection, took shape in his mind. A lithe creature he fantasized about every waking second of every day. A female who was immune to him. Not only immune, but one who also wanted him despite his past.

His hand slid up and down his length.

He'd never had a woman before. There wasn't anyone alive who could survive long enough for him to take. Trentian women could, if he was willing to seek one out. But they were exceedingly rare due to the biowarfare his kind released, all but wiping their fertility out to the point that Trentian numbers sharply declined over the past several generations.

It'd been a terrible measure humans took to make sure the aliens would never rise up in the future and restart the war. They couldn't if their numbers were low.

The Trentian females who remained lived on their home planet, protected by their God Xanteaus and his chosen Knights. A place no human was allowed to go near, especially a Cyborg.

Hysterian hadn't encountered a purebred alien woman in over forty years, and when he had, his codes urged him to kill her.

Hysterian squeezed the tip of his shaft and rolled his palm.

The woman survived, of course. His urgings weren't like some of his brethren, who couldn't resist. Not to mention she'd been very old back then, having lived for over a century. An elder, a diplomat for her people, she had still been very beautiful. His lips twisted, remembering her. He hadn't wanted to fuck something warm so desperately back then either...

He pictured the alien female's face and thrust his dick into his hand.

A Trentian female was out of the question. Even if he sought one out—actually procured one—she'd be terrified of him, more so than any human female ever would be. Cyborgs had killed their kind by the thousands after all...

And what would stop him from killing her anyway on accident? Battling one's own nature was hard, and would be much harder if he was fucking. Fucking the way he wanted to fuck.

Hysterian groaned and leaned his brow against the stall wall.

No, he needed a damned cure.

A devil-damned blocker.

The water began to cool, and his thrusting increased. His need ramped as the shadowy female in his head arched her back, stuck out her ass, and screamed for him.

Scream for me.

He was going to burst.

He gritted his teeth. His tongue shot out to lick the wall.

Hysterian reached down with his free hand and thrust into both of them at the same time.

Phantom lips pursed, a head flung back, and he fell to his knees gripping his cock. He released all over the wall, exhaling hard. The water turned frigid as he stared at his cum where it trickled. Thick yet slick, it didn't take long for his seed to mix with the water below and vanish into the vents.

He reached up and turned the bathing unit off. He'd released enough of his toxins to breathe easier—for a time. With a modicum of ease, Hysterian rose and stepped out, letting the lavatory's drying system suck out the humidity. Less than a minute later, he was dry except for his hair. It had fallen forward and tangled around his face.

He stared into the mirror, his eyes were bright teal but dimming. He watched through the white strands of his hair.

Picking up a comb, he brushed his hair back until it was straight and precise.

His appearance was something he could control. The day he stopped caring about it was a day everyone should fear.

He might not be able to shift, and he may not be as big or as vicious as other Cyborgs, but he was still a force of nature. With just a touch, he was deadlier than most.

Hysterian dressed and placed his gun back into his utility belt. He glanced at his empty bed once before heading for the door.

The first requisition was in a couple of days. The *Questor* was due to arrive at Luxor Port soon, a moon that circled Gliese and was a corporate mining base for EonMed. Many of their processing plants were there.

EonMed also ran drug trials on Luxor. One such trial had proven great results in curing G Fever, an infection brought on by exposure to a rare fungus that grew on ships with aging life support systems.

He was to pick up a case of the prized vaccines and

bring them back to Earth. Vaccines worth millions, wanted by thousands.

The door zipped open as he neared and he came face-to-face with the last person he wanted to see.

A woman with fake black hair and bland brown eyes. Eyes he was certain he'd seen before but couldn't place.

There were no direct matches for them in his memories.

"Dear," he said, stilling.

She jerked back as if she wasn't expecting him. "I'm sorry!"

His brow furrowed. *She's supposed to be on the lower level, in her quarters or the menagerie.*

"What brings you to my room?" he asked. "It's the middle of the night shift."

His nostrils twitched as he got a whiff of her scent. It wasn't pleasing; she smelled like chemicals. She used dye in her hair, the cheapest stuff on the market, he'd bet.

Black. Jet black. It was so unnatural against her pale skin that it made her look sickly under the bright ship lights. And the way she kept her hair cinched tight in a bun made her features sharp, cold.

Her gaze skidded away. "I was looking for the lounge."

Lie.

His eyes narrowed. *Why is she lying?*

"You passed it," he kept his voice level, stepping out of his room and pointing down the hall. "It's the first room on your left coming up the stairs."

The door to the lounge was always open... The lounge was impossible to miss coming from the stairs. So why was she in front of his cabin?

And how the hell had he not known? Hysterian bristled.

"Yes. Right," she coughed, straightening her uniform.

He couldn't help but notice how it conformed to her curves, or lack thereof. He asked for a woman to be on his crew, hoping for a veteran, or a matron to soften the male dynamic. Studies showed that having a feminine presence did well for keeping morale up on the long flights. When he saw Dear's picture, he hired her without reading her resume. Her severity was perfect, her plainness almost comforting. He'd never be tempted to touch her. If someone on his crew wanted to pursue her, that was up to them, though he wouldn't be thrilled having a couple on his ship.

"I knew that," she muttered. "I'll head there now." She scurried away.

"Dear, is there a problem? Something you want to tell me?" he asked.

She stilled.

Is that why she's here?

She turned back to face him. Brown eyes met his. Eyes that didn't belong on such a frigid woman. For a moment, he thought he saw anger creep into her features.

"There's no problem. I just got caught up in my head and missed it. It's been a long day. Thank you for your help, Captain." She turned to leave again. "Goodnight."

He wasn't buying it. He always knew when someone was lying. It was what made him so good at interrogation... *Torture.*

He stepped toward her, and the door closed behind him. "I'll walk you there." He didn't like being lied to. Whatever Dear was searching for, he was going to find out.

"There's no need. I didn't mean to bother you," she said.

He joined her anyway. "It's fine."

"Captain..."

But he continued to walk and she went silent, following him.

He knew everything about the *Questor* and its specs, its layout. Every detail of his ship was in his head, permanently in his memory banks. If Alexa Dear was searching for something, it had to be in his quarters or the bridge. There was nothing else this far down the hallway.

Nothing pertinent was accessible. She'd have to be a genius hacker or a spy. He couldn't even hack his ship or the systems Nightheart set in place. So, why else would she be standing in front of his cabin? Only someone seeking death would spy on a Cyborg in his domain.

Dear didn't seem the type to do something so idiotic.

Hysterian stilled. *She was looking for me.*

The shadowy phantom female in his mind, the one he pictured screaming his name earlier, morphed...

Without glancing her way, he eradicated the picture of her in such a state. It wasn't safe. For him but especially not for her. *And she's not my type.*

He usually fantasized about supple women with soft curves. Women with sun-kissed skin that were warm and inviting. He imagined sunspots he could kiss, tan lines his tongue could trace. A female who'd never spent any of her life in the dark cold of space, and had never been hurt by death, drugs, or violence.

An unattainable woman. One he had yet to encounter. Someone happy, perhaps naïve, and loyal.

All too soon, they were outside the lounge. Daniels was gone.

Hysterian stepped aside to let Dear pass through.

"Thank you," she muttered without meeting his gaze.

"You're welcome."

When she walked by, he got another whiff of her hair dye. His systems flushed it out but not before he winced.

She stopped in the middle of the room and turned to

face him. For some reason, he stood there and stared back at her. She was a sliver of darkness in an otherwise white and gray room.

She cleared her throat. "I'm good now. I really am sorry. It won't happen again, Captain."

Hysterian shook himself, nodding. "Make sure it doesn't. Goodnight."

"Goodnight."

He turned and made his way back to his quarters, deciding he was going to need another shower. Hot or otherwise, because in the back of his mind, Alexa had come to see him.

And he wasn't sure why...

FOUR

SHE WATCHED from her station as Hysterian waited for Horace in the hallway outside the menagerie. He checked the battery of his laser pistol then attached it to the belt at his hip. From where she sat, she could see the open armory behind him.

They'd landed on Luxor thirty minutes ago.

It had been three days since the encounter with Hysterian outside his quarters.

Alexa curled her fingers where her hand rested on her thigh, trying not to tap her foot. Hysterian looked at her, and her eyes shot to the screen in front of her. When Alexa peered up a moment later, he was staring at her.

She stiffened, nodded once, and turned away. Whether he continued to watch her afterward, she had no idea. All she knew was that she'd been on edge for days, kicking herself for being so stupid.

I knew better.

I shouldn't have approached his door.

She had anyway. She'd been on her way to the bridge—

a nightly stroll, she called it—but had paused when she came across his quarters.

Part of her wanted to see if her wristband would give her access if she neared, but a bigger part of her wanted to test fate. She was finally close to her target, after years of chasing him, and that other little part of her, the piece that couldn't believe her luck, wanted to see him. Alexa shook herself.

They'd been in space for days since then, and she hadn't been in the same room as him once.

Cyborgs are supposed to be heroes, but they're fucking villains. To an entire species, Cyborgs are devils incarnate. But up close, Hysterian looked like a normal man. A strange, albeit tall man, with dark, twitchy eyes, but a man all the same.

A man with a body of metal. A being ran partially by code.

Still, she had to chance upon seeing him. She needed a reminder for why she was here.

Because she'd been focused on doing her job, and doing a good job at that.

That, and there wasn't any place on the ship the crew was told to stay clear from. The armory and medical chambers weren't accessible without a manual punchcode, but they were allowed to use the spaces when needed. She wanted to see if that was true.

Fortunately, the armory and medical chambers weren't places she cared to go to. If she had a choice, she'd stay clear of the medical facilities entirely. Her medical files were on record, but they'd been forged. She paid a lot of money to a doctor on Elyria for that. Almost a year's worth of wages due to the law they were both breaking. She had to make it worth it for him, though she was certain the doctor had done the same things for others.

How else had she obtained his name?

There was no way she was going into the medical rooms on this ship unless she was dragged, kicking and screaming.

Feeling Hysterian's gaze on her, Alexa stared at her screen, wishing she had something pertinent to do to keep her from storming up to Hysterian and asking him what his problem was.

Yeah, I went exploring... Alexa wanted to snap but thought better of it.

She planned on knowing every corner of this ship before long. But the other night was just a stroll. One where if she happened to be on the bridge, trying to hack into the captain's panel, she couldn't be blamed for it. Or any of the myriad concerns in her head.

Because she was just familiarizing herself with her new surroundings... Right?

Alexa wiped her palms on her pants.

Horace's voice came down the hallway. She kept her head down. She didn't want to know if Hysterian still watched her. Because although she hadn't encountered him since the other night, he'd made sure to catch her gaze and keep it until she was forced to turn away. She knew who the alpha on the ship was... She didn't need him to remind her.

"Ready, Captain," Horace said. "How long do you think this'll take? I just got a missive from Mia about Atrexia."

Mia?

"Minutes if we're lucky, hours if we're not," Hysterian answered him. "Let's get this over with."

They walked away, the opening of the ship's back hatch and the quarantine chamber sounded soon after. When the hatch closed, and a vent of pressurized air filled her ears, Alexa knew they were gone.

She sagged.

"You okay?"

Alexa peeked her eyes open to find Raul staring at her from where he sat to her left.

She straightened. "Yes. Only taking a moment."

"Riiight. Is there something up between you and the captain? Something you're not telling me?"

"You're implying I tell you anything," she snapped. What had he seen? Was she being that obvious? "There's nothing between me and the captain. I don't like what you're insinuating."

He stood and shrugged. "Whatever you say. If you're up to mischief, I'd recommend against it. If you make enemies with someone out in space, there really is nowhere to go to get away from them. Especially on a ship like this. It's sizable until you try living on it, then it's a fucking prison. Come join me and Pigeon for a drink at the port bar? Pigeon's meeting me at the hatch in five."

"There's a bar here?"

Raul's lips turned up into a smile. "Oh, Dear... There's a bar on every space terminal. You're so green it's almost cute. Alcohol in space is top-notch, and the gravity shifts play with your head. Getting wasted every time you make a landing is tradition for people in our field."

"Are we allowed to leave the ship during a job?"

"Sure, we're not needed right now. He doesn't give a damn what we do in our free time. The ship isn't taking off until tomorrow morning—the reactor needs to cool down—so as long as we're all here and doing our jobs, our time is our own. You really are new to this whole space traveling thing, aren't you?"

One thing Alexa learned growing up, especially with the childhood she had and the world she lived in, there were far more things to worry about than being offended over the small stuff. A drink sounded great, but she couldn't let her guard down.

Alexa leaned forward anyway, an idea forming in her head. "Is Daniels going?"

If the whole crew was leaving the ship, then she'd have free rein. For the first time since take off, a real opportunity presented itself to search for information. Real information. The kind that could either destroy Hysterian or give her a lead in how to kill him.

Raul pressed his hip to her desk and crossed his arms. "He might be going. Why?"

"No reason," she said. "Curious, that's all."

"He's not your type."

Her lips flattened. "Really? How would you know?"

Raul laughed. He always laughed. It was annoying. "Dear, we've been working together, practically sleeping together for the past week. Daniels is harder, colder than you, and that's saying something. You two together would be like glaciers colliding. There'll be a lot of ice, a lot of sharp edges, a lot of noise, and a lot of pain. You need someone softer. Daniels is fucking miserable. I think I might hate him."

What was it with the crew thinking she needed someone to hook up with? Not even in the academy had men asked after her. Was there something about space and companionship she wasn't getting?

"Like you?" she muttered, suddenly finding her screen fascinating. It only took three days in space for Raul to make his move.

She'd told him off. Told him there's no way she was

going to bed with him. She couldn't risk growing attached to anyone.

Companionship wasn't in the cards for her.

Last time she loved and cared for someone, he was murdered.

Raul stretched, undisturbed. "I'm up to the task. I'm pretty soft when I want to be. Very soft, actually. Hard as hell too when the need arises."

"Hey, you coming?" Pigeon called from outside the menagerie.

Alexa could've kissed him for his perfect timing. It was easier to ignore Raul's advances than to actually interact with him. And sadly, she didn't know if he even wanted to be with her. He could be teasing her for all she knew. She had no idea. Flirting and the interplay between a man and a woman was something she was sorely ignorant about. No one had ever wanted her.

"Trying to get Alexa to come with us!" Raul yelled back as Pigeon entered the lab.

Alexa stood as he approached.

Pigeon's face wrinkled when he smiled. "If anyone needs to take a load off, it's you. Join us. For one drink at least."

"Not today." She was already backing up to her cabin door. "I think I'm going to catch up on some sleep. Raul snores."

"I don't snore," Raul grumped. "Maybe a little. They're affectionate snores, the robust kind. My body's natural way of attracting a mate."

Pigeon laughed. "Next time then. Being cooped up on a ship isn't good for anyone. You'll look forward to these port visits once you've been in space for a few months."

"Next time," she agreed.

"Taking that as a promise," Raul said as he followed Pigeon out.

When she heard the pressurized sound of the hatch go off, Alexa stood there on the precipice of her quarters for another minute to make sure she was alone, twirling her wristband.

She glanced around the space and the giant glass cages that were lined on either side of the menagerie, most embedded in the walls. Some were small, some huge, like the ones the locusts were using. Each had its own habitat, own computer system, all linked up to the main panel she and Raul sat at.

In the last week, she'd explored every inch of the space. The rooms off the sides created for plants, the empty cylinder capsules filled with chemicals to transport corpses, and the biodomes for microbes. The plant room also could grow food—like the leaves the locusts consumed.

They'll need to be fed soon... That reason alone was good enough for her to stay behind. She grumbled for having not thought of it. She and Raul could set them up to be manually fed, but the locusts were finicky with the machines and so they did it themselves.

A *thump* sounded, and her gaze snapped to the male locust. Its four forearms were braced against the glass, framing its large, fanged face, and between its furry legs was its rigid cock, purple and meaty. *Hell.*

Its eyes were on her.

Like Hysterian's.

The male locust watched her constantly. It made her skin crawl.

The locust was almost worse than Hysterian. She didn't know if the locust wanted to eat her or to do something far more horrific. Considering its bulge, she had an idea... She did her best to ignore the beast as much as possible, only approaching it when necessary. Even Raul noticed how much the alien creature was interested in her. He offered to do its feedings.

She appreciated his concern but refused him. If she couldn't handle the first alien animal to be transported, then she wasn't qualified for this job.

Which amused her to some degree since she only took the job for one purpose only: to get closer to her target. Still, she didn't want to do a bad job in case it took a while for her to figure out how to achieve her goal.

Getting fired is out of the question.

It was perhaps also hope that she'd survive destroying Hysterian and that she'd have a real future someday.

After all was said and done, she'd go to Gliese or another world like it, get a quiet position, and live a quiet life. If she could help it, she'd never return to Elyria.

Alexa made quick work of feeding the locusts then stepped out of the menagerie. She looked at the armory but kept going, leaving the weapons for another day. Passing the medical chamber and the side passage that led to the reactor and the ship's bowels, she made her way to the stairs beyond them that led to the upper level of the ship. Sleek silver and white walls surrounded her on every side. Tubes of light ran across the ceiling as well as the floor, embedded into the ship.

The *Questor* was gorgeous, brand new, completely remodeled from a previous EPED ship. The remodel was obvious, even if she wasn't already privy to that information. Alexa had never seen a nicer ship.

She was lucky—real lucky—to be here.

Just need a new captain... Then the job would be perfect.

Getting to travel around the universe, seeing exotic faraway places that others couldn't because of travel restrictions, tasting new food, meeting new people... It was a dream.

Someone else's dream.

Coming upon the lounge, she peeked in to see if Daniels was within. He wasn't, which meant he was either in his room, the gym, or in the bridge. She'd have to be careful. Excuses ran through her mind, in case she was caught lurking.

She lingered on the lounge for a moment, eyeing the cleaning bots lasering the floor. There was a round table in the center and two booths to the left. The rest of the room was covered in food replicators of different varieties and activity stations to relieve boredom. It was the far wall that kept her rooted in place, though, where there was a porthole.

Outside, she could see Luxor Port, and the vast wasteland-like moon sprawling beyond. Huge, industrial buildings littered as far as the eye could see. From them, smoke plumed into a hazy pink sky like spiraling pillars. Drones and skiffs flew between them.

Luxor was a dreary place. Most moons were.

Alexa turned from the lounge, glanced at the gym across the way, and kept going. Ahead, she could see the hatch at the end of the hall that opened to the bridge. Before that was a series of closed doors that were more rooms used for housing the crew. Including one filled with dormant androids if the need for them ever arose.

All the doors were closed except one.

Her brow furrowed.

Hysterian's room was open.

Alexa glanced behind her. She was alone.

I saw Hysterian leave. There's no way he got past me. Why is his door open? Is it being cleaned?

She heard shuffling within. Instead of turning back and fleeing to the laboratory like she probably should—because it could be Hysterian and then she would have to explain herself again and he probably wouldn't believe her. Alexa quietly tiptoed to the room.

She heard a bang followed by cursing.

"Fucking hell, where is it?"

Alexa stepped into the doorway to find Daniels rifling through cabinets at the back of the room.

"What are you doing?" she accused.

Daniels jumped, fear exploding in his eyes. When he caught sight of her, he straightened, stepping away from the drawers he'd been digging through. "Dear."

"What are you doing?" she asked again, looking around the room pointedly. Multiple cabinets and drawers were open. Cabinets and drawers she would die to scrounge through herself to discover the secrets within.

But instead, it was Daniels doing it. Her lips pursed as her curiosity skyrocketed. Straight through the roof and into outer space.

"It's not what it looks like." He raised his hands. "Captain asked me to fetch his glock."

She wasn't buying it, not at all. "He needs another gun to pick up vaccines?" She'd seen Hysterian leave with a laser pistol.

"Don't ask me why our captain wants another weapon. It's not our place to question him."

Fucker. I caught you red-handed.

"Right," she agreed. "So he sent you into his quarters to retrieve it."

Daniels scowled and pushed past her, striding out of the

room. The door didn't close behind him. Alexa turned, not wanting to lose sight of him. He was sneaking, like she was, but she didn't know why he would be.

And that posed a problem. A big one.

If Daniels had an agenda, then they were bound to tangle. Why did he have an agenda? Was he looking for something of Hysterian's or was he after the Cyborg like she was?

Alexa's heart thundered. Were there others Hysterian had wronged? There had to be. She just never thought about it. Did everyone on the ship have an agenda?

Her eyes watered, staring at Daniels, unable to blink. *Impossible.*

But now Daniels had been caught, and cornered prey was the most likely to strike out. She finally blinked.

Daniels was halfway down the hallway toward the crew quarters when she spoke. "Aren't you forgetting something?"

He stopped. "I'll fucking kill you if you tell him," he said, not turning back.

It wasn't what she was expecting, but Alexa wasn't surprised. "Tell me why you were really in his room."

Shoulders stiff, his empty hands clenched at his sides. "None of your business, Dear. If you know what's good for you, you'll keep your mouth shut and stay out of my way. What I'm after doesn't concern you." He started walking again and went into his quarters, leaving her alone outside Hysterian's room.

Alexa stood in the corridor for a few minutes, replaying what had just happened. Was there really someone else who had an ulterior motive? Though whatever Daniels was after, she had no idea whatsoever. *If he wants Hysterian dead...then I might have an ally.* Alexa shot down the thought the moment it went through her head.

I have no allies.

She couldn't trust Daniels, not for a second. He could turn on her, use her, offer her up as a scapegoat if things went sour. And if Daniels had no intention of killing the Cyborg, she was practically putting herself naked on a platter if Daniels betrayed her.

For all she knew, her crewmate was just curious, snooping on a being who was viewed as a God to many people. Maybe he was looking for something to steal and sell to the highest bidder.

Maybe he was a Cyborg hater, seeking a way to undermine him.

Whatever Daniels was doing, it was best she kept out of it. Safer if she did so. The last thing Alexa needed was someone out to silence her when there was no possible escape.

Suddenly, the *Questor* got a little smaller. Alexa shook herself, forcing her body to move. She'd fallen into her head, waiting for Daniels to come out of his room and threaten her again, to see if he did something else. Fight or flight wasn't something she dealt with often. Now that her curiosity was waning, all she wanted to do was run.

But...

Hysterian's room's open. She turned back to the Cyborg's quarters.

Stepping to the threshold, she peered in, shaking with fear, but unable to let this opportunity go to waste.

Cabinets and drawers remained opened, but from where she stood, she couldn't get a good look into any of them. And entering the room, with Daniels at her back, wasn't something she was keen to do anyway.

He'll know. Hysterian will know if I invade his space.

She wasn't dumb. She was willing to take risks, but she wasn't an idiot.

Though her coworker was. Daniels spelled his doom right before her eyes.

Our doom. If she didn't play it safe.

Her fingers twitched with curiosity. There was a big, unused bed off to the left up the short steps in the back of the room. Up those same steps, in the second half of the room, was Hysterian's personal lavatory on the right, same with a glass desk devoid of knickknacks, and a metal dresser with drawers attached to the wall.

In the front of the room was a seating area with a glass, oval table positioned before it, and a wall of shelves, also empty.

Nothing. Nothing was incriminating. At least nothing out in the open.

Alexa took a step back and jumped when two cleaning bots moved past her and into Hysterian's room. One went straight for Hysterian's drawers and closed them. She didn't know why but she was relieved when the bots began cleaning the space.

It was time to leave.

She opted to skip the bridge. Every second she meandered was more of a risk than the last. Heart thundering, she darted past Daniels's door, and once she made it to the lounge, she was breathing easier, wondering if the ship had cameras.

She wondered if Hysterian already knew everything. He could... There was no limit to what Cyborgs could do.

She also feared not knowing what Daniels was up to and if she needed to watch her back.

When she returned to the menagerie, the ship's hatch

opened, and the blast of pressurized air filled the room. Her pulse ratcheted up, and she wrenched her eyes closed to calm down.

They'd come back much sooner than she expected.

Calm escaped her. Booted feet drew closer. And she knew by the way one of them walked that it was Hysterian and Horace returning, not Pigeon and Raul.

"Thank you for your help, Horace," Hysterian said.

Horace grunted. "Just doing my job."

"Are you going to join the others at the bar?"

"And spend money on drinks I could just make for free here? Fuck that."

Alexa scurried to her desk and sat down just as Horace and Hysterian appeared. His eyes went straight to her, and she looked away, down at the briefcase in his hand. Palms slick with sweat, she twisted her hands in her lap.

"Understandable," Hysterian murmured. "I'll see you at the start of the next shift. Get some rest."

"Have a good evening, Captain," Horace said. He continued down the hall, leaving her and Hysterian alone.

Her face heating, Alexa wished she hadn't taken so long upstairs. Still feeling the need to run, she thanked whatever god or devil ruled the spiritual plane that she had turned back when she did.

Hysterian made his way toward her, and she scrambled to her feet and hated that her computer screen was blank behind her, obviously unused. *He knows. He has to know.*

I didn't do anything wrong.

If he doesn't know now, he's going to know soon that someone was in his room.

He saw me outside it.

He'll think it was me...

A thousand more thoughts soared through her head as Hysterian came to a stop in front of her.

Keep your mouth shut. Alexa tore her eyes from the briefcase and looked up to meet Hysterian's. "Captain," she rasped in greeting.

He cocked his head, and her belly twisted. "Is something wrong, Dear? Your face is flushed. Are you getting sick?"

"No, Captain. I, uh..." She glanced around the room looking for an answer. Why wasn't there anything when she wanted there to be something? "Just finished feeding the locusts." It wasn't quite a lie. She had fed them.

He stared at her.

Much longer than a normal person would.

Alexa hated Daniels more than Hysterian at that moment for putting her in this position.

"Are you sure you're not sick?" he asked, his eyes narrowing.

She felt like a bug under a magnifying glass. "I'm pretty sure."

She wasn't ready to be caught. Or burned. Burned would be worse.

"Your heart is beating rapidly," he stated as if it was normal for him to know that standing several feet away from her.

"The male locust scares me," she said quickly. Also not a lie.

He finally took his eyes off her and looked at the creature. "Why?"

"He watches me," Alexa said before she can stop herself.

Hysterian's eyes returned to hers and the awkward silence that followed made her feel way worse.

"He can't hurt you," he said.

She swallowed. "I know." Desperate to change the subject, she reached out. "Are those the vaccines? I've prepared a freezer slot for them."

Slowly, far too slowly for Alexa's comfort, Hysterian handed the briefcase to her. "Yes," he said, eyeing her curiously.

When she had the briefcase in her hands, she held it to her chest. "I'll take care of this."

"You do that."

Alexa turned and stiffly walked away, her joints suddenly glued together. She made quick work of securing the vaccines into their slot and prayed that when she turned back Hysterian would be gone.

Please be gone.

Please. Be. Gone.

When she turned, he was behind her.

Alexa startled. If today couldn't get any better...

This was it. He was going to confront her about her snooping. She had to decide now if she was going to tell him about Daniels, lie, or come clean and hope Hysterian didn't kill her.

To her shock, he didn't say a word. Instead, for the second time that day, she was left in stunned silence.

Because Hysterian's eyes weren't dark, but bright and turquoise, unlike anything she'd ever seen, and his brow was beading with...

Sweat?

"Captain?"

Hysterian straightened, turned, and walked out of the room, and Alexa, once again, was rooted to the spot in confusion.

FIVE

Hysterian rested his head on the wall, pumping his cock. Warm water dribbled down his skin, washing his secretions away. With every thrust, the water was a little milder, with every pump, the water chilled ever more. His phantom female had jet black dyed hair.

He thrust faster. The water iced.

Fucking Nightheart. The Cyborg knew some of what Hysterian's problem was, but not the full extent, just enough to pay the cost and develop a way to cure him. Still, it was enough to make sure the *Questor* had ample hot water. What kind of ship couldn't keep the hot water going?

With another hard tug, Hysterian jerked away and leaned back against the bathing unit's wall, glaring at the lack of steam filling the chamber. He turned the faucet off all while fucking his hand. The pressure was too much. *Too much.* His tongue snapped out of his mouth to hit the far wall. He drew it back in.

Disgusted, he came, spurting seed over the wet floor at his feet. Then it was gone, sucked into the drain. Breathing hard, he glowered. His cock remained hard in his palm.

Already, his systems were replenishing his seed, his secretions, everything. His body absorbed the moisture. He stopped ingesting liquids decades ago for that very reason. He squeezed his shaft as the bathing unit went awash in blue light.

He blinked, and the light diminished.

I need to upgrade the fucking water unit.

Hysterian leaned back again with a sigh, rolling his head to gaze at the ceiling. *What I need is a sauna.* He had one at his apartment in Oasis City. At the end of every cycle, he used it to sweat the day's sins away.

The day's druggies, the day's vacant eyes of the enviable reaping that followed.

He pumped his cock slowly, thinking about it. The heat. The endless steam. The woman he imagined sucking him off within it, because he couldn't see *her.* She swallowed his cock until it was lodged in her velvety throat, and from there she inhaled, squeezing him beautifully. She drank him down as if she were starved, dehydrated, needing only what he could give her.

He had so much to give. Too much.

His phantom female, that woman he craved, was always, always thirsty.

Hysterian closed his eyes, squeezing his shaft again. He could probably keep a woman alive on his body alone if he weren't poisonous.

Black hair filled his head. Wet and long, plastered to dewy flesh. He pumped faster.

She was on her knees, gripping his root. He couldn't see her face. He needed to see her face.

"*Captain,*" she moaned around his length.

Hysterian's eyes shot open and cut downward. "Alexa?" It was her voice that rang in his ears.

Only his cock and his hand greeted him. Gritting his teeth, he got off one last time and fled from the lavatory.

Naked and dripping, he stood in his quarters, banishing Dear from his mind. He toweled off and dressed before he had a chance to grab his cock for another round. A half-dozen times was enough. It had to be. The day shift was starting soon. He didn't know how he was going to focus on getting any work done. They weren't due to land anywhere today, but his next job was only several days away. He was meeting with Titan's ambassador about a problem with the local wildlife.

Giant bug-like beasts were killing locals who oversaw the mines. Titan requested allowance from the government to eradicate the bugs and clear the mines, but the government wouldn't allow the locals to kill the creatures without first ensuring killing them wasn't going to fuck up the ecosystem, or the resources they valued so much.

It was now *his* problem to assess and decide what was to be done. Including capturing and bringing back a female and male of this bug species for Titan's scientists to study.

Hysterian shoved his collar up over his mouth and strode to the door, needing freedom from his space. But when he got to the barrier, he paused before allowing it to open.

If she's standing outside my door again, I don't know what I'll do.

He already knew she wasn't, but that initial surprise at seeing her there several weeks ago hadn't left him. He was rarely surprised, and lately, he'd been surprised a lot.

There were secrets some of his crew were keeping from him.

Daniels had been in his room when Hysterian was picking up the vaccines with Horace.

Hysterian was also aware that Alexa had been here as well.

The ship's cleaning bots could hide a lot, and if he'd been human, he might have missed the signs. When his door was triggered, he'd known immediately. He'd watched the whole thing from the security camera feed channeled into his head as it happened.

Daniels was a problem.

Hysterian hated problems.

Especially ones he couldn't deal with adequately because he was stuck in the middle of space with witnesses. He'd planned to let Daniels go and force him to disembark on Luxor but had forgotten, losing himself in what was even worse...

Alexa Dear.

His mundane, worker bee stationed to oversee his living requisitions.

She blushed.

Her pulse had drummed in his ears the moment he'd returned, across the fucking room. He scented her fear, her anxiety.

Worst of all, he'd felt the heat her body gave off from those emotions. She was normally cold. It had stunted his mind long enough to forget about Daniels. His focus had been on Alexa.

Now his phantom woman had black hair.

Hysterian squeezed his brow, allowing the door to finally open. No one stood on the other side. He wasn't sure if it was disappointment or relief he felt. A mixture of the two perhaps.

The bridge was empty. If he went there now, he could read his correspondence and review his new requisitions without watchful eyes. He could contact Titan and let them know he was several days away.

He could study the layout of the mines and the footage taken of the bugs.

Hysterian turned away and went in the opposite direction.

Reviewing the ship's feed in his head as he walked, his crew was all where he expected them to be. Horace and Daniels were sleeping in their bunks. Pigeon was in the lounge ahead of him—the smell of cheap coffee in the air—and Raul and Alexa were in the menagerie.

Except Raul was already up and at his desk, and Alexa was still in bed.

I want to see her.

He crept past the lounge and descended the stairs toward the laboratory. A soft, gasping moan pricked his ears.

Hysterian stiffened, listening. The moans built then slowed, followed by a rasping breath. It sounded like sex.

Alexa and Raul? Angry, he strode into the lab.

He half-expected to see Alexa bent over her desk and Raul atop her. Even though he knew she still slept. His fingers twitched to tear the image in his mind and beat Raul's head against the wall until there was nothing left. For a microsecond, it was real.

Finding Raul jacking off to porn, was, to say the least, a fucking relief.

With his back turned to Hysterian, Raul had no idea that his captain stood behind him watching him yank his cock, itching to shatter his skull.

Hysterian tamped down his anger as Raul's arm jerked. Disgust filled him for the second time that morning. It wasn't because of what Raul was doing—so out in the open as he was—but that Hysterian had been doing the same thing not a few minutes prior.

That, and Alexa was mere yards away and could stumble upon Raul in the act.

That she shared a room with him.

Co-ed rooms—with locked privacy screens—had never mattered in the past, but now it pissed him off. A screen wasn't enough. Alexa shouldn't have to worry about her crewmate. Hysterian swallowed the need to throw Raul against the wall and punish him for being a disgusting creep and stalked to his and Alexa's quarters.

Had they fucked?

He needed to know. It was his right to know. He was the captain, after all, and if his crew were fucking, it was good to be aware of it. That's what Hysterian told himself as he neared the room. He and his brethren all had an annoying trait where they needed to know everything that was happening around them at all times. It was embedded in their codes.

Control. It was all about control. When dealing with animal DNA, control was precious, priceless, sanity.

But this wasn't about control... This was about something else. Something he couldn't quite put his finger on.

Annoyance? Envy?

Jealousy?

He couldn't have his one female subordinate become pregnant on her first requisition cycle. At least not by Raul... And *fuck*, not with a cock as small as the one he saw in Raul's hand.

Hysterian inhaled deeply, scenting the air.

He smelled Raul's musk and the chemical aroma of the lab, but he needed to scent the room. His jaw ticked. He was going to throw Raul in the brig if Hysterian found out the man had fucked Alexa. The idea alone made him want to turn back and make his presence known.

He couldn't smell sex.

That didn't mean it hadn't happened.

Without Raul noticing, Hysterian opened the door to the quarters and walked in. The door slid silently shut behind him.

His eyes went straight to Alexa's bunk and the privacy screen securely in place. Was she asleep? The cadence of her breathing and her heartbeat indicated she was.

Sex was the last thing he smelled in the small chamber. Alexa's hair dye—and only her dye—filled his nose. The stuff was shit incarnate but so fucking welcome when the alternative could've been dried cum, sweat, and moldering arousal.

Raul gets to live another day.

Hysterian knew he should leave but stared hard at the privacy screen blocking Alexa from him.

In his mind, Alexa was two different entities. On one hand, he saw her as the frigid, quiet, subordinate that she presented to the world. With her hair tightly pulled back into a bun, no makeup, and wearing a uniform devoid of the merest wrinkle. If he didn't know she was flesh and blood human, she would've passed as one of his kind.

A Cyborg. A damn good one.

On the other hand, her other entity, the one he'd glimpsed on occasion, was entirely different. *I didn't fucking hire this other one.*

So why had he heard her voice in his head last night?

Hysterian glared at the privacy screen between them, willing it to dissolve into dust.

I like it when she calls me captain...

He reached down and squeezed his aching shaft,

already feeling the pressure building again. Torturous pressure. Pressure he shouldn't have to be dealing with because he'd spent half the night cycle draining his body.

I'm a Cyborg, and this is my fate?

Disgusted, he dropped his hand and turned away. He'd gone too far. It should be Raul throwing *him* across the room and bashing his head in. Hysterian was just about to slip out when he heard a moan.

He paused.

Bedding ruffled behind him, followed by the dreaded swish of a privacy panel being opened.

In a blink, he pivoted and pressed his hands on the other side of the privacy screen to stop it from opening farther.

Alexa sighed and pushed harder. He kept it in place.

"Oh, come on," she grumbled.

Hysterian closed his eyes and cursed.

If she pops her head out, she's going to see me. He had no explanation whatsoever to give her—or Raul—if Hysterian was discovered in their room. Alexa jerked at the screen again.

"Not today, please, not today," she begged.

His brow furrowed.

Then she jerked the screen closed and Hysterian took the chance to hide. In a flash, he jumped up and into the unused bunk above Alexa's, rolling to the back. He heard the screen opening back up below him just as he quickly closed his.

He did something he'd never done before. He fucking prayed. He prayed to every god and devil out there to be anywhere else in the universe than where he was right now.

Alexa moved out from her bunk with a mumble, and Hysterian's body tensed as if readying for battle. He tempered his systems to keep quiet. He'd never hidden from anyone or anything in his long, mechanical life. The room's private lavatory door opened, closed, and he slumped with relief. When the bathing unit turned on, he shoved the screen open.

Then Raul walked in.

Their eyes met.

Raul came to a halt. "Captain...?"

Hysterian calmly climbed from the bunk and straightened out his suit.

"Raul," he responded.

Raul couldn't look more confused or shocked to see him, but to Hysterian's relief, having Raul find him was a lot less embarrassing than Alexa finding him.

"Umm... Can I do something for you? Do you need something? How did you..." Raul trailed off, his face going red. He glanced at the bunk Hysterian just climbed out of.

"Yes, you can. You can keep this between us," Hysterian said. "In fact, I order you to keep this between us."

"Yeah, of course. Wait. What am I keeping between us?" Raul's eyes drifted back to Hysterian.

"That you saw me here at all."

"Are you and Dear—"

"No."

"Then why are you here?"

Hysterian wished he'd surrounded himself with a crew that didn't give a fuck what anyone else was doing as long as they were doing their job.

But Raul stood in his way, and didn't look keen on moving, so Hysterian had to give him some fucking answer to his question. And soon. Alexa wouldn't be showering forever.

Showering...

Hysterian paused, adjusting his audio to listen to the spray of water through the wall. The water was cold. He'd used it all. He didn't sense a temperature shift in the small room beyond.

He refused to imagine the soaking wet female under it... How close he was to her. How cold she must be...

"Captain?" Raul stared at him with wrinkles deepening between his brows.

"I insist you keep this between us." Hysterian shut Alexa and what was happening behind him from his mind. Wet, cold, or not. Her comfort wasn't his problem. "I have a tendency to... wander when I'm seeded into the network. I don't pretend it isn't a problem, but it shouldn't affect you or anyone else in my command," he lied.

"You wandered into the empty bunk above Alexa's?"

Hysterian glowered.

The bathing unit turned off.

"Yes."

Raul's lips twitched, and to Hysterian's dismay, Raul smirked. "Riiight."

"Get out of my way," he ordered.

"If you're not here for Alexa, are you here for me, Captain?" Raul crossed his arms, mischief in his eyes.

"Get out of my way, or you'll be spending time in the brig."

Raul stepped to the side, grinning now. "Yes, Captain."

Furious, Hysterian stormed past him. Raul followed. Hysterian made it halfway across the room when his twat of a crew hand opened his mouth again. "So, Captain, if you're not here for Alexa, you don't mind me pursuing her?"

Hysterian was across the room in an instant with Raul pinned up against the male locust's habitat. Murder. Hysterian was on the brink of committing murder.

Raul's eyes bulged as Hysterian slid him up the glass by his neck. Raul grabbed Hysterian's hand, struggling to get out of his grasp.

He kicked and squirmed, coughing.

Hysterian watched him struggle. Sputter, spittle, saliva, he enjoyed it all. Raul's face went beet red, and when his kicks slowed, Hysterian dropped him.

Raul fell to the ground, clawing at his neck. Hysterian looked up and came face-to-face with the locust. Its four large arms thumped the glass.

Raul coughed and gasped in equal measure.

"I don't give a fuck what you do with Dear. You can have her. But if you ever get in my way or question me again, you're off this ship, and I don't care if you have a way to get home. Are we clear?"

Raul nodded.

"Good. Now get the fuck up and clean yourself. I can smell your cum all over you. It's stinking up the entire lab," Hysterian spat. Without waiting for Raul to rise, Hysterian stormed out of the menagerie.

His tongue pushed at the inside of his lips.

His mouth twisted into a sneer.

What the fuck am I doing? How the hell had he ended up in this situation?

Alexa wasn't for him. She ticked none of his boxes. And above all, she was his subordinate.

He wiped her from his head and vowed to keep her from it and his fantasies going forward. Because if he didn't, and he didn't find a better outlet soon, he was going to lose his mind, and someone was going to die.

SIX

Alexa stared down at her coffee. The muddy brown liquid had cooled since she'd gotten it from the food replicator, but she couldn't make herself get a fresh cup. Tension had sunk into her bones, and it worsened with each day.

Raul had barely looked at her over the last two days. She had emerged from their shared quarters to find him flushed, coughing, and rising from the ground by the locust's enclosure.

"I think I'm getting sick," he'd told her.

She had rushed toward him, thinking the locust had hurt him somehow. "You need to get to medical!"

She hadn't wanted to get sick herself, but she also cared for her coworker's wellbeing. If he'd been sick, she'd have to pick up the slack, and with all that had happened, she was already bogged down.

She hadn't made any progress on getting closer to Hysterian. At least in the way that could gain her the information she needed to destroy him.

Twice now, she'd missed her opportunity to explore the bridge. Alexa kicked herself for not taking advantage of

Daniels's snooping and searching Hysterian's chamber when she had the chance. Nothing had happened to Daniels afterward, so he'd gotten away with it. She felt like a failure.

She'd been in the same space with her enemy for a while now, and nothing had happened. In her mind, she'd always thought finding a way to hurt Hysterian would be easier.

"No," Raul had grunted his reply. She'd tried to help him, but she could neither convince him to get checked out nor get him to talk to her further. Raul hadn't looked her way since.

Something must have happened.

Raul being quiet was strange.

Alexa swirled her cup.

She missed the company. She can't believe why. *I don't even like Raul.* But now that she'd spent the last cycle in silence, she missed noise, missed the sound of a human voice, missed conversation. She glanced around the lounge, hating that even here, she was alone.

Pigeon was right. Space takes a toll.

There's no noise, no *life*, out in space. The sounds of air pressure and steam vents were all she had to keep her company. Maybe she should play music in the menagerie during the day... Maybe music would help. Alexa thumbed her vitamin D pill before putting it in her mouth, swallowing it down with her cold coffee.

She was even braving running into Daniels for company. She wasn't afraid of him—they hadn't spoken since the incident—but she also didn't want to rehash the threats. As for Hysterian, Alexa was certain he wouldn't be wandering into the lounge.

She hadn't encountered him either since he had

returned with the vaccines. Their strange interaction replayed in her head often. The terror of almost being caught, the way he'd studied her, and the confusion she felt when his eyes glowed and his brow slickened with sweat. It had all happened so fast.

The whole encounter had been unusual.

His eyes... In all the years she chased Hysterian, she had never seen his eyes glow teal. He'd always had dark, glistening, malicious eyes in her imagination. She recalled one of the strippers she'd questioned outside Dimes mentioning his eyes...

'They glow bright when he's worked up.'

Alexa sighed. What had worked him up? She didn't think she'd given herself away. *My heart was pounding but that wouldn't affect him. Would it?*

Cyborgs were calculating beings. His eyes left her with questions she was afraid of answering. *Raul said he was defective.*

Alexa chewed on her bottom lip and then cursed for caring at all. If he was defective, that was good for her. She was more than willing to put the *defective* thing out of his misery.

Defective might make it easier for her to find a way to kill him.

But his eyes had been beautiful in that moment. So beautiful that she couldn't stop thinking about them, and why they'd become that way. She wanted to see them again, and she hated it. When she dreamed last night, it had been about his eyes, and how mesmerizing they were, not the cold-blooded killing machine that needed to be unplugged.

She ran her hands over her hair. *If only it was that easy!*

At least it's not hot. She couldn't suffer being in a space bubble that was warm on top of everything else. Alexa gathered the loose strands of her hair and redid her bun.

"Morning," Pigeon grunted as he walked into the lounge.

Alexa dropped her hands and sat up, excited to see Pigeon. Pigeon was her favorite. "Morning."

He yawned and grabbed a cup of coffee, joining her. His presence brought her comfort.

"You getting used to this life yet?" he asked.

"Yeah."

He laughed, taking a sip. "Not convincing at all, Dear, but still good to hear. I'd be better off myself if Daniels and Horace didn't snore all night long. You'd think they're trying to power the damned ship at night."

"I'm sorry to hear that. Raul snores too."

Pigeon peered at her over his cup. "You look like you could use better rest too?"

Idle talk. Any other day, Alexa would've shut it down or found a way out of it, but today she welcomed it.

"I'm plenty rested," she said. "The coffee is terrible, though."

"Isn't it? I call it barely drinkable scum. You're lucky you've managed to get some rest. The transition can be brutal."

"I guess so." Alexa looked down at her drink.

"You okay?"

"Yeah, I'm just waking up."

Pigeon set down his cup. She glanced up to find him scrutinizing her. Alexa stopped from shrinking away, afraid that he saw through her lies and to the secret she kept so close. That if he stared at her long enough, he'd see what she really was under her fake hair, fake...everything.

Suddenly, she wanted to tell him. She wanted to blurt

out everything. She wanted someone else to share her burden. Alexa shook, stamping down her wants. She couldn't afford to trust anyone, especially someone she barely knew. One small mishap and her life—her quest for vengeance—was on the line. Years and years of patience...over.

She'd also be putting Pigeon's life at risk if she came clean. She couldn't do that.

"You know you can come to me if something happens. I'm not like these young men. I've been there and done that, and found it tiresome. You remind me of my daughters."

Alexa perked up. "You have daughters?"

"Three, in fact. They're on Earth living their lives." He waved his hand. "They're grown now, have families of their own. My ex hates that I no longer have to pay child support. She hates it even more that I won't return to Earth and be with them where I'm an easily accessible cash cow. I took crew work to pay for my children, and now it's all I know." Pigeon shrugged. "They're better off without me."

"How can you say that? Do you know?"

"I'm a geezer. I'd just be a burden to them."

"I would kill to be with my father. If they want you home, you shouldn't assume they're lying."

Pigeon's face shuttered. "Is he gone? Your father?"

Alexa dropped her eyes to her cup again. "Yeah."

"I'm sorry to hear that. I lost my parents a long time ago, and I still miss them to this day."

"It's fine." Alexa swirled her coffee some more. "I'm sorry for your loss as well. I miss mine too, though I never knew my mother."

Why had she said that? Alexa sucked in her lips. She never talked to anyone about her parents.

"Makes sense."

Her eyes snapped to Pigeon's. "What? What makes sense?"

"That you're here, doing a job like this, when you could be anywhere else in the universe." Pigeon smiled, and it almost brought a smile to her own lips. "My ex would never have let our kids leave Earth."

"That's a shame. Earth sucks."

"Yeah," Pigeon laughed. "It does."

Someone cleared their throat, and Alexa and Pigeon turned in unison. Standing in the doorway was the last being she wanted to see. Hysterian's black eyes—the ones she knew—were watching them.

How long?

"Captain," Pigeon greeted. Both he and Alexa stood, straightening out their uniforms.

"Captain," she said as well, nodding.

"The day shift is about to start," he warned, making her stiffen. "You should be at your posts."

"Yes, sir," Pigeon agreed, walking to the door; Hysterian moved to the side. Pigeon turned back and met Alexa's eyes. "It was good talking to you, Dear. Come with us to get a beer next time. It'll do you good. I'll make sure you get back to your bunk safe afterward." He smiled and left, strolling past Hysterian before she could respond.

Silence filled the lounge as she listened to Pigeon's footsteps recede, wishing she could escape just as easily.

"Sorry, Captain," she mumbled, dashing for the exit.

"Stop."

She came to a halt. Tall and stiff, and ever watchful, Hysterian glared at her when she met his eyes. Now she remembered why she never left the menagerie if she could help it.

Hysterian sucked the energy out of her every time she encountered him, and she always left him bewildered.

"Yes, Captain?" she asked hesitantly.

His eyes shot over her, and she bit down on her tongue from his blatant perusal.

"You do know we're landing on Titan tomorrow, right?"

"Yes, sir."

"Have you prepped the habitats?"

The ones she and Raul spent all day yesterday preparing? "Yes. They're prepped."

"I want to see them."

Her heart dropped into her stomach. "Of course."

"The creatures that the Titan people want will only be on our ship for a short time, but they must receive intact, unharmed specimens to study. This is our first real job, and we want to do it right. The specimens can't be introduced to anything that doesn't meet Titan's code of standards for their wildlife. That includes tranquilizers."

Alexa nodded. "Raul and I—"

He waved her off. "Show me."

"Yes, Captain. Follow me."

She led him out of the lounge when all she wanted to do was punch him in the face. Alexa glowered, glad Hysterian was behind her. Maybe it was a good thing she couldn't see the Cyborg's face either. One scowl or sneer her way and she was going to the brig. Today was not the day for games.

She was going to fucking punch him if he talked down to her. She might even try more.

This is good, she told herself, trying to calm down before her body reacted in a way Hysterian would surely notice. She needed to spend more time with him to glean information.

Because hell, she wasn't finding anything out about him elsewhere.

She wasn't on a timeline, but she knew her clock was ticking. Someone was going to discover her secret eventually. And staying employed by the very creature that killed her father made her want to vomit. She couldn't get comfortable. If she did...

Alexa inhaled. The guilt would kill her if Hysterian didn't kill her first...

They walked past Raul's station—she waved at him when he lowered his headset and sent her a questioning look—and headed for the habitats in the back. The male locust thumped on the glass and perked up as she glided by.

"We chose the habitats nearest the loading hatch. We figured since these critters aren't staying long, loading and unloading them with ease was the best course of action," she said to fill the silence.

The thumping of the male locust grew louder when she came to a stop at the habitats she and Raul calibrated. Turning back to face Hysterian, he was gazing at the empty glass cages like they were the most interesting things in the universe. Alexa glanced back to see what he saw. Nothing. Nothing but empty space.

There was literally nothing.

When her gaze returned to Hysterian, his eyes were teal.

She blinked. His eyes remained teal.

Hysterian continued to study the habitats like she wasn't standing right beside him waiting for his response. She studied him while she waited.

He wasn't at all like what she thought he would be. He wasn't a robot monster like how she'd pictured him, cold and unfeeling. What stood next to her was a man. A beautiful, dangerous-looking man, but a man all the same. Why couldn't he be deformed and hideous?

After a minute she gave up. "Is there something you want to know, Captain?"

"Why do you dye your hair?"

"I—"

He faced her.

What to say? Fear zipped through her. "I like the color."

"It doesn't suit you."

"I think it does."

"You're too pale. The black washes you out." He cocked his head and reached up. Alexa stilled as his gloved hand vanished behind her head.

What is he doing?

She felt a tug.

He pulled her bun loose, and her hair fell in a crimped wave down her back.

She swallowed thickly hoping her heart wouldn't jump out from her throat. Hysterian held her hair band between his fingers.

"You're naturally blonde," he said.

How did he know that? "I... Yes..." she stammered.

"Blonde would suit you better."

"How do you know I'm blonde?"

"I searched the network for pictures of you just now, prior to the dye. You've worn it black for a long time, it seems. There were very few of you blonde, and you're very young in them."

He just scanned the network while she stood in front of him? Prying into her past like he had a right too? Blood rushed to her face. "You have no right."

Hysterian shrugged.

"I'm allowed privacy. Even from my captain."

If he searched too deep into her past, he'd find out a lot more than she would ever want him—or anyone—to know. Yet he didn't seem to care. He pocketed her hair band instead of giving it back.

"You are, and I wouldn't snoop on any normal occasion, but I've been curious. Most women change their looks to enhance themselves, and you may think you are going black." He indicated her hair. "But the dye you're using is cheap. It smells."

"I haven't dyed my hair in weeks. There's no smell anymore."

"Maybe to you. To me, it reeks."

Alexa reached up and pulled her hair behind her, stepping away. "I'm not changing my looks to suit you, Captain," she spat. "That's beyond protocol. I'm sorry you don't like the smell. You're going to have to get used to it."

His brow arched. "I'm not asking you to change. I'm insisting you use better dye from here on out. I'll have the replicator make some. Though it would be easier if you stripped it out and went natural."

His eyes roved over her hair, and she wanted to gather it back into a bun more than anything but couldn't. It made her uncomfortable, how much he had noticed about her.

"No more of the shit you're using. It doesn't work for me."

The audacity. Her anger took over. "No."

His eyes finally met hers. "No?"

Alexa stood her ground. "No. You don't have a say in my appearance. I'll use what I've always used."

"Not many people have the courage to tell a Cyborg no."

"That's a shame. You need to hear it more often."

"I'm your captain."

"And I'm a woman, unowned by any man, including you. Do you want to hear about the habitats or not? Because you're wasting my time."

His eyes flashed, making her wince. Somewhere behind her the locust banged on the wall of his habitat. Alexa refused to back down, meeting Hysterian's gaze head on.

He took a step toward her.

She strained her neck but didn't back away. If he was going to hurt her, so be it. He could not possibly force her to change her hair, in this life or the next. He'd have to hold her down and do it himself...

Pulse racing, she was afraid that might just happen.

He leaned down. She clenched her hands. Cloying heat plumed from him to envelop her. It made it hard to breathe.

When his face was before hers, he whispered, "I'm not a man."

Her lips flattened.

"I'm a Cyborg," he continued.

"Are you trying to scare me? Intimidate me?"

"I'm correcting you."

He was so close they were nearly touching. Every fiber in her body was tense, waiting for the moment he would reach out and make contact. Death or bliss? What would he give her? Her belly danced, and her toes curled as he only stared at her instead, sending her into a tailspin.

Fear? Anger? She didn't know what she felt anymore. All she knew was that she wanted him to touch her. She wanted to find out.

She needed to know how she'd react to it. Because right now, she wasn't convinced she'd hate it. She wanted to believe she'd fight him.

"Cyborg or not," she breathed, "you can't tell me what

to do." But she took a step back, putting her spine against the glass. She pressed her hands flat against it at her sides.

It was an invitation.

One she'd given without first acknowledging it. Her cheeks burned.

Do it. Touch me. Remind me that I loathe you. I'm ready. But her sex clenched at the thought of him putting his hands on her... Alexa swallowed. This was wrong. Why was she reacting to him this way?

Like a bitch in heat.

He cocked his head, the lights of his eyes so bright they washed out everything else. Curiosity lit them, and she swallowed again.

Slowly, his hands came up on either side of her and locked her in.

He leaned in until their faces were level, and all she saw was him. Him, and blue, and nothing else. No death, no evil villain, just him.

"Your heart is pounding, Dear. I wonder why."

She licked her lips. His eyes snapped to them.

"Do it," she whispered.

"Do what?"

"What it is you're thinking right now, before I come to my senses." *Test me.*

His face moved closer.

"You have no idea what I'm thinking, and if you did, you wouldn't like it."

She blushed.

He continued, "What is it you want me to do? To you, that is?"

Her lips parted, the soft breath that escaped barely easing the pressure in her lungs. She couldn't breathe, not with him so close. She should run screaming, better yet, she should have a dagger in her hands to stab him in the back, but they were the last things on her mind. Right now, she didn't want him to die. She wanted him to pull down his mask and...

"I'm waiting for instruction," he said, his voice lowering, his face a gasp away.

"Captain..."

"Alexa."

Kiss me. She didn't even say the words aloud; she only formed them with her mouth.

He jerked back. A look of horror flashed across his eyes.

Her hands came up to fold over her chest in surprise.

Hysterian eyed her and took several steps back, like... like he was mortified.

Alexa pulled away from the glass, feeling her soul drop from her body from embarrassment, feeling the heat from him finally suffocating her.

"Get yourself cleaned up, "Hysterian growled, turning away. "I can't have someone on my crew fucking up today. You're dismissed."

He stormed through the lab and out the door, barking a command at Raul.

Inhaling, she twisted away and sagged to the floor, glad she was shielded from the rest of the room. She pressed her brow to the cool glass of the habitat.

What just happened?

She closed her eyes.

She just invited Hysterian, her enemy, to touch her —*kiss* her. What was she thinking? What was wrong with her? He was her enemy. She was here to find a way to destroy him. Not take him to bed. Not fuck him. Not offer up a challenge.

The thought of doing so should've disgusted her.

Instead, there were butterflies taking flight within her. A whisper of lust coiled between her legs, and she didn't know what to do about it.

Because it was there now. It was there, and no matter how badly she didn't want it to be, it remained.

Alexa buried her face into her hands. Hysterian was burned into her head, and she couldn't get him out.

She was never going to get him out.

And the worst part of it all, he had no idea how much he ruled her life. Every terrible minute of it for the past decade.

SEVEN

DIRT AND ROCKS crushed under his boots as Hysterian strode through the mines. He didn't try to hide the sound.

He was already fucked, that's what he was. Let Titan's bugs come after him.

Some giant man-eating bugs weren't going to change his status. So why bother playing it safe? Hysterian scanned the mine's winding tunnels, creating a mental map as he followed the blueprints that the taskmaster had given him.

All the while, images of a certain female haunted him.

It was idiotic of him to try to avoid Alexa. He'd managed to do it for a while—her scent, her presence was all around him. The *Questor* wasn't that big of a ship; avoiding someone on it took a lot of work. And the more work it took, the more Alexa stayed in his head.

The more he found himself wherever she was, having to fabricate excuses for it.

Her smell followed him everywhere. No amount of air filters could erase her dye. When he wiped her from his mind, he still smelled it, even if the scent wasn't actually in the air.

Dirt crunched as he barreled headfirst deeper into the shafts. Now and then, he'd pass an android working, but most were powered off.

The deeper he went, the less there was. Old blood and soil tickled his nose, but even then, he still smelled Alexa.

He cursed himself for making her show him the habitats.

I touched her hair. His fingers curled. He'd been wearing gloves, but the fact that he'd still touched her shook him. Hair hadn't reacted to his touch, but that hadn't stopped the glands hidden in his skin from opening up and secreting.

And he'd had Alexa there, trapped against the glass, his body so close to hers, his lips so close to hers... The nanosuit under his uniform kept his secretions in, but it had happened. Just one drop of it could have killed her if it had gotten on her skin.

He cursed his body.

If he'd been a normal man—hell, a normal Cyborg—he would've shoved his mask down and kissed her. He would have licked her face, run his tongue over her cheeks and down her neck. He would have tasted her.

She wasn't nearly as cold as she looked.

He could make her hot.

Hysterian was either too far gone to care if she was, or he actually, really wanted her. Either way, he was desperate, and the *Questor* was too small for the both of them avoiding one another.

I'm going to have to fire her.

The last thing he wanted was to fire her, but it was the only way to keep her safe. Maybe with space, he'd find clarity again—maybe some goddamned patience and calm.

God knows there wasn't enough boiling water to keep him from going insane.

He sensed movement up ahead in the shadows.

A sour smell filled the tunnel. Glancing above him, there was slick, wet-looking webbing in the cracks between the rocks and dirt.

Hysterian tugged off his gloves, shoving them into his back pocket. His eyes went straight to the hairband on his wrist.

His scowl deepened.

He tugged it off his wrist and dropped it on the ground. Next port, he was going to find an AI-operated sex bot and be done with it.

Hysterian only took two steps before he turned back and picked the hairband up again. He stretched the band out between his fingers, wiping the dirt off that had gotten on it.

He'd hoped being away, back on a planet and in the open air, would be enough to fix him, at least for a time, but he was coming to find out even Titan wasn't going to be enough distance. Once the job was done, he'd be back on his ship, and Alexa would only be several metal walls away from him, one floor down. And he'd be jacking off to the image of her pressed up against the glass enclosure of a habitat, blushing and inviting him to kiss her.

She invited me to touch her...

So that's why she was outside my quarters the first night.

Alexa Dear wanted him.

It wasn't unusual for a woman to want him so bluntly, but for one to risk her career and her job to approach her superior? That took courage. There were scores of women who had a Cyborg fetish, and his subordinate was apparently one of them. No one would want him any other way.

He had the looks to attract a woman, but everything else? He had nothing but problems to give. The moment he peeled off his suit and touched her, shit would go downhill from there. Whether his poison was lethal or not, he wasn't about fucking a body that was out of its mind on drugs—or lifeless.

He killed men for less.

That'll change.

Once Nightheart delivered on his promise, Hysterian would be able to pick his woman out from a crowd of them. A willing woman. He could have his fantasy—not someone like Alexa who wouldn't attract him on a normal day.

If she was still around when he was cured, maybe he'd take her to bed—just to get her out of his systems—but until then, he needed to keep his head.

Hysterian slipped the hairband back onto his wrist. At least he'd have it to keep him company until then.

His audio tech picked up skittering, stealing his attention. Shadows shifted, and a rancid aroma met his nose soon after. He pulled down his mask, tugged up his sleeves, and activated his poison. Whether it worked on these bugs or not was yet to be seen.

He just needed to find a male and a female, and as for the assessment... He didn't care about the assessment. Still, he took a sample of the wet webbing and shoved the capsule in his pocket.

Something emerged from the darkness up ahead, and Hysterian spread out his feet, loosening his limbs. He couldn't fully shift, but he was springy.

Enclosed spaces weren't preferred but were manageable.

A clacking, snapping echoed in the mines just as he lowered his head and shot down the passage.

He landed atop the creature and pummeled it before it even knew he was there. Segmented legs, too many to count, went wild. They clawed and lashed out, slicing the ground. They couldn't bend back to reach him. He bore the entirety of his weight onto it and wrapped his bare hands around its middle.

The bug had a chitinous exterior leaving the back and legs protected, but the underside, like many bugs, was significantly less armored.

Hands covered in poison, Hysterian held them onto the creature's underside, expanding his fingers out to touch as much of it as he could. The compound of his secretion shifted to the bug's organic makeup as his systems were fed knowledge about it.

Within seconds, the poison took effect.

What started as a clash ended in silence. The bug's many legs gave out first, and then its body fell. Hysterian kept his weight on it long after it stopped moving, making sure it wasn't a trick.

With a bored sigh, he got up and rolled the bug over. It was half his size, and not nearly as large as Titan's ambassador said it would be. But figuring out whether it was an adult, or a male or female was another matter. Every fucking alien species was different.

Hysterian unlocked his net and shot it over the creature. The webbing cinched around it, ensuring it was trapped.

When he was done, he stepped back and shook out his hands. He stared at his acquisition as his poison dismantled and evaporated from his skin.

He was almost done with the job. He itched to return to his ship, to check on his crew. He didn't know what they were doing or what they were up to, and that bothered him.

Was Raul jacking off to Alexa? Was Daniels cornering

her? They wouldn't be leaving for a drink at the local port bar since Titan didn't have an official one. It had a landing zone of bleak cement.

He needed to know what Alexa was up to. Was she in her room? Was *she* touching *herself?* Did she ever? Was she thinking of him? He wanted answers, and he wasn't going to get them down here.

He hoped Alexa snuck her hand between her legs and drove her fingers into her cunt fantasizing that it was his hand instead of her own. It would be a small conquest against his misery.

Was she avoiding the male locust? Even Hysterian had noticed the male's fascination with her. It was much like his own—including the fucking wall that stood between them.

His fingers twitched, wanting so very badly to be driving into her pussy and exploring it thoroughly, stretching it. Was her G-spot smooth and soft or bumpy? Would she gasp when he stroked it? She was small of stature, and his fingers were long. He could do a lot to her and more.

Hysterian's cock thickened.

I need to know if she squirts when she cums.

He fucking hoped so.

His mouth watered imagining it.

Not wanting to linger, Hysterian strode down the dark chamber. He snapped images of the slick webbing growing around him as he went. More critter noises reached him, but his passing was nothing but silent now.

Something skittered across his feet, and he paused, adjusting his visuals. A hatchling. The tiny bug climbed the wall next to him.

The ceiling shifted above him.

He looked up to find thousands of hatchlings. His lips twisted in disgust.

And worse, his stomach growled. It fucking growled.

For a Cyborg who stole most of his replenishments from the air and molecules around him, the small bugs made him ravenous.

He snatched one from the nest. The bug fought his grip but a tiny dose of his secretion quickly took care of that. He pulled out another capsule from his belt and put the hatchling within.

He snatched another and stuffed it in his mouth. It fought as his teeth crushed it and his poison simultaneously killed it. Swallowing, Hysterian closed his eyes.

Strangely sweet, slightly bitter, the bug settled his stomach. He grabbed another.

It gave him information, more than any scientist could discern in a day.

The bugs didn't have venom—anything for his systems to replicate. But they did have blood. The hatchling's chitin was not developed yet either, making them easy prey. They only had two segments, making them part of the arachnid family... If they'd been discovered on Earth.

Though they had more than eight legs.

Something crunched the rocks around the bend of the passage ahead. Thousands of more hatchlings were gathered on the ceiling before him. He continued anyway, eating as he went, his systems usurping everything useful and destroying the rest.

The crunching grew louder as he neared the bend.

He quieted his approach. A breeze gently slipped across his cheek, and his brow furrowed. The air grew chillier with each step.

He turned the corner.

A giant cavern lay before him, one crawling with alien spiders. Throughout lay other passage openings similar to the one he stood in, pocketed amongst the thousands of creatures. There were so many they climbed atop each other.

They swarmed.

There were so many his systems could only give him a rough estimate. And as he recorded the cavern, he noted the bugs came in many sizes. Some, far below, were the size of a small house. The biggest ones had antennas that were three times their body length. They dug at the walls with their many legs while dust and rocks fell from the cave ceiling high above.

It's a hive.

One that had been here long before any human ever knew Titan existed.

Fuck this.

Titan's ambassador lied. How hadn't Hysterian caught it? *Because I was thinking about fucking black-haired little human females who are way too serious.*

They had to have known what was down here. Hell, I bet the tunnels weren't even made by machines. Looking back, the tunnels didn't have the clean finesse of perfection. He'd thought perhaps Titan's miners cut costs by using old tech.

They're sending men and AI—sentient shells—down here to die. And they want me to help them eradicate this?

He couldn't eat all these bugs in a day.

Nor was he planning to die today. Not here, and not on Titan of all planets. It was a drummed-up mining planet similar to Earth, but worse. In every possible way.

Hysterian slid to the wall and calibrated his suit to shift in color and texture. Releasing a minuscule drone from his pocket, he sent it flying into the cavern. It was programmed to send the feed to his databases.

He made sure the spiders didn't attack his drone before he did a final once-over. The cavern was miles deep... Not only was Titan a shit planet, but it was also infested.

Cursing, he turned to leave before he was spotted.

Hysterian stopped, startled.

The hatchlings are gone.

Hysterian paused. His scans showed the entire passage as being empty.

How?

He glanced behind him to make sure the hive was still there. They were. He rubbed his mouth.

There was nothing to tell him where the hatchlings had gone, and they had to be somewhere. There were far too many for them to vanish entirely. But they had, and they had done so within the minute he had his back turned.

The only ones that remained were being digested and dissected in his stomach.

Something moved up ahead, catching his eye. His tongue shot out catching it, bringing it back. A hatchling. He swallowed it as he moved forward.

It had been heading back the way he came. His brow furrowed.

Leaving his drone behind to collect data, he made his way for the surface, watching for the hatchlings as he went.

He came across them a short time later.

A wave of them, to be exact, filling the entirety of the passage and blocking him in. Chittering and screeching pierced the damp air, echoing low. Stunned, he watched as the hatchlings swarmed the larger bug he'd caught earlier, devouring it whole. It had woken up just in time to be eaten alive. And they were fast, so much faster eating than they were moving about.

Yeah, Titan has a problem.

A real big one.

And he suspected they already knew that. Hysterian's nostrils flared.

He waited until the hatchlings finished their meal—when they noticed him—before he pulled out his laser gun. They charged at him right as he twirled the weapon, melting them where they skittered. He continued until there was nothing but guts and sizzling remains. Even still, hundreds remained.

He grabbed some of the stragglers and placed them in his remaining capsules, kicking out and swiping the ones that got on his boots and suit.

On his way out of the mines, he blasted one of the lower passages, closing off the hive to the surface. At least from this access point.

When he stood in front of Titan's ambassador two hours later, Hysterian tossed him the hatchlings, sent him the video access from the drone he deployed, and told him to get his people evacuated out of the area and to leave these mines alone. To go far, far away and hope they never encounter the billions of aggressively hungry insects beneath them.

Life was too short, after all, for a human.

Even a sick one like him.

Then Hysterian told him to go fuck himself.

EIGHT

"Leave," Hysterian ordered.

Horace and Daniels stopped what they were doing and stood. They walked out of the bridge when Hysterian changed his mind.

"Daniels," he barked. "Stay." Hysterian triggered the door to shut once Horace was on the other side.

Hysterian had just returned from his meeting with Titan's ambassador. He had yet to wash the dirt and guts from his suit. The ambassador had been furious Hysterian hadn't offered a solution to their problem. Having a bloated man yell at him did nothing for Hysterian's mood.

Titan's ambassador reminded him of Raphael, and not in a good way. *At least Raphael came up with his own solutions.* He massaged his brow.

"Do you need something from me, Captain?" Daniels asked.

He pivoted to face his bridge officer. "Why were you in my quarters?"

"Your quarters? I don't know what you mean, I wasn't in them."

He always knew a lie when he heard one.

Daniels is good at lying.

Or I'm losing my mind. Hysterian's mood soured further.

"Don't bullshit me. I have you on video. I have everything that goes on in this ship on video. It all streams back to the source: me. I knew you were in my quarters the moment you walked in. I won't ask again."

Daniels crossed his arms, straightening. Hysterian had to give it to the man; Daniels wasn't as intimidated as he should be being confronted by battletech like Hysterian. Daniels was either confident or dumb. Hysterian hadn't paid his officer enough attention the past few weeks to know which it was.

He just hadn't fucking cared.

"I was in your quarters, Captain, several weeks ago," Daniels said. "I was looking for my stash. I thought you may have found it, confiscated it, and I wanted to prove to you I can still use and do my job well."

"Your...stash?"

"Simple boosters, just enough to tweak my energy, nothing more."

"And you thought they were in my room?"

"I didn't know where else they could be, sir."

"I didn't take your fucking stash. I don't care if my workers use drugs. Get off my ship."

Daniels finally flinched. "Get off the ship? Are we boarding on Titan?"

"No, the *Questor* is disembarking tonight. You are not."

"It was a mistake. I've done nothing wrong."

"You're a fucking liar, that's what's wrong. And you threatened another crew member while you were at it. The only reason you're still employed is because I couldn't get rid of you sooner. Now, get out. I'll have Mia transfer you your final paycheck and help you find boarding on the next commercial transport off this planet."

Daniels's chest swelled. *He's going to fight.* Hysterian wiped the grime from his sleeve, ready for it.

At least a fight would stop him from searching for Alexa and stupidly finding out how tight her cunt was with Hysterian's *still*-twitching fingers. That was, of course, if her quiet invitation was to be read correctly. He could stretch her; he just had to wear a damned glove on his hand first.

"So I get sacked and stranded in space, while you, a messed-up Cyborg with more issues than a wingless fly, gets off the hook? You don't fucking deserve to be a captain," Daniels spat.

"You're playing with poison," Hysterian growled.

"I know you bounced with Raphael in Elyria, a fucking drug dealer. Do those hiring you for these important 'jobs' know? I sure as hell wonder what the media would say if they knew what kind Cyborg you really are, especially since so many already want you dead."

Hysterian cracked his jaw. "So you know about Dimes?"

"I was a regular there between jobs. I know everything," Daniels sneered.

"And you applied for this job because?"

Daniels's nostrils flared.

"If you know so much, you have nothing to lose in telling me. Go ahead." Hysterian waved his hand. "Though my inclination to kill you is increasing. And just so you know, I *wasn't* going to kill you to start. Remember that."

"Do it. I dare you. The rest of the crew will find out. You said it yourself, there's footage in the security feeds. I'm sure those above you will have access to it. They are Cyborgs as well, aren't they?"

"Why, Daniels, did you take this job?"

He turned to leave. "Fuck you. I don't need this shit."

Hysterian stopped the doors from opening. Daniels slammed his fist into them when they didn't open for him. He slowly turned around. "I'm leaving, isn't that what you want? Or have you changed your mind?"

Hysterian uncrossed his arms, took a step toward his former bridge officer, and removed his glove. Daniels's eyes snapped to it.

Hysterian held it out between them. "Go ahead."

"Fuck you, you fucking cyshit." But Daniels's gaze didn't move from Hysterian's hand.

"You obviously know about me. You know what I can do. Not many outside Raphael's inner circle know, so you must have connections on Elyria. Go ahead, take my hand, unless you're scared?" Hysterian flipped his hand over. "Isn't this what you came here for? Isn't this what you want? People pay thousands of dollars to touch me, they pay hundreds of thousands the second time. You couldn't afford it, could you? "

Daniels hesitated.

"You were looking for me, weren't you, in my quarters? At least a part of me, the part that intrigues you," Hysterian continued.

"I told you, I was looking for my fucking stash," Daniels muttered.

"I'm better than whatever your stash is. Far better. I'm the best thing you'll ever experience. One touch is all it takes, and you'll be dancing in the heavens. The universe will finally right itself, any pain you might have will vanish, and a sublime delirium will take you over. That's what you've heard, wasn't it? A druggie looking for a higher high?"

Hysterian's palm glistened as millions of microscopic glands opened up. Invisible to the eye, they produced an opioid that was, to a druggie's dream, a high to die for.

"But if you take too much, you'll miss that bliss and fall asleep instead. You'll fall asleep and never wake up. And even if you survive, you'll never find another drug that can do for you like I can. You'll go mad with desperation for more. Do you dare?"

Once people had a taste of his opioids, they were ruined.

Daniels stared at Hysterian's hand with want. A hungering want that Hysterian had seen so many times in his past. So. Many. Times. He'd refused to count. He hadn't only been a bouncer and bodyguard to Raphael; he'd made the man a lot of money.

Daniels swallowed, reaching out his hand.

"How long—" Hysterian began.

"Ms. Dear is requesting permission to enter the bridge, Captain," Questor's AI said.

Daniels startled, freed from his trance, and Hysterian drew his hand back.

Daniels grabbed his head and turned away. "Fuuck!"

Hysterian slipped his glove back on. "I suppose she saved you once again," he said with disgust. He wasn't a saint. He hoped Daniels would touch him and take on the consequences of his actions. "Let Dear in," he announced to the ship.

The bridge doors opened, and there she was. The bane of Hysterian's recent thoughts. Stiff and cold, straight spine and all, arms crossed behind her, Alexa glanced between him and Daniels.

"Dear," Hysterian said, "what do you want?"

"Am I interrupting something? I can come back later."

"No, you've arrived at the perfect time," Daniels answered with a growl. "Like always." Daniels clenched his hands and, without another look at Hysterian, stormed through the doors. He rammed his shoulder into Alexa on his way out.

Alexa stumbled and righted herself.

"Are you okay?" Hysterian asked, rushing to her and clasping her elbow.

"Yes." Her soft brown eyes met his. "I, uh, can really come back another time, Captain."

"No. You will stay. I'll be right back."

He released her and stalked after Daniels. The fucker chose death, and so death he shall have. Hysterian had been inclined to let the man live, even if he'd taken what Hysterian had offered. But he'd touched Alexa, disrespected her in front of her superior, and thought that he was going to get away with it?

No one touched what belonged to Hysterian.

He caught up to Daniels just as he passed the menagerie's storage.

"Daniels," Hysterian called out.

The man swerved. Hysterian pounced forward and grabbed him by the neck, crushing Daniels's larynx with one swift pinch, and dragged him into the storage room. Daniels screeched, coughing and clawing at his neck. Hysterian shoved him to the floor.

Daniels jerked away and crawled to the other side of the room, gasping for breath. Hysterian followed him.

He hadn't planned on killing Daniels today, but whatever.

He hadn't planned on his fascination for Alexa Dear either.

When Daniels sagged, shaking with his last twinges of life, Hysterian flipped him over onto his back. Hysterian pulled down his mouth covering and planted a soft kiss upon Daniels's brow. A gift.

The fear left Daniels first, then his eyes dilated as he slumped to the ground.

Hysterian gently laid the human flat. "You shouldn't have touched her. You'd be walking away from this ship right now if you hadn't."

Daniels didn't look at him. He no longer registered Hysterian's presence at all. A smile crept onto Daniels's face, and then he was gone.

Hysterian gazed at his former officer for a moment, never liking this part. That moment when a human succumbed to the reaping. He always thought if they fought it hard enough, death wouldn't come.

Daniels hadn't put up a fight at all.

With a sigh, Hysterian picked up Daniels's corpse and carried him to medical. He had no fear of being caught; he already knew the path was clear. He placed the corpse into one of the cryo units and sealed him in.

No one would look for Daniels there. And at the end of the day, when the *Questor* returned to Earth, he'd make sure the man would at least have a marked grave.

Hysterian straightened, pulled up his mask, and made his way to the bridge.

The last twenty-four hours had been hell. He questioned his decision to hire a crew. Because, apparently, death and drugs followed him wherever he went.

Maybe his brethren had it right all along: surrounding themselves with machines instead. Or just the one or two crew hands when things got out of hand... If Hysterian had machines working for him, he'd never have to worry about them doing the work—though they did lack the added touch of a human. But they always listened, and weren't killable, weren't poisonable. He would just have to keep their software updated and code them to his liking.

He tried to be like Cypher, but it wasn't working. Having spent two months on the bear's ship, witnessing Cypher's affection for his woman, Hysterian wanted that for himself. *Hah.* His boots thudded as he approached the bridge. He'd seen Vee in her little red dress, he'd seen the way Cypher fucked her mercilessly like he would *die* if he didn't.

Hysterian had been fucking envious.

He wasn't a good enough being to win the heart of someone like Vee. She was far too young and innocent for him. She kept Cypher's bed warm every night, but there was no past haunting her eyes, nothing that made her *real* to someone like him. No, Hysterian needed someone who didn't care about his flaws, someone like a psychotic sycophant groupie. Either way, he was going after a woman that he could call his once he was cured.

For now, he'd enjoy Alexa.

Her back was turned to him when he entered the bridge.

She gazed at his seat and the controls of the ship, turning her head only to glance at the main station controls Horace and Daniels used. She was completely unaware of his return.

He leaned his shoulder on the door frame and watched her.

NINE

Alexa couldn't believe her luck. She rubbed her shoulder as she glanced about.

She was in the bridge. She was in the bridge and Hysterian had left her there, knowing she would be alone.

The word *perfection* fluttered through her head.

She'd been surprised to find Horace making his dinner and having a beer in the lounge, and even more surprised to find Daniels and Hysterian in the middle of what seemed like an argument, but none of that mattered anymore, because now she had the freedom to find what she was looking for.

It also gave her another moment to collect her wits. Yesterday, when she'd invited Hysterian to kiss her, she'd been deranged and frustrated.

Waiting for Hysterian's return from Titan had wrung her dry. Her thoughts were all over the place, and all she felt was guilt. The dried tears on her pillow were evidence enough of that.

How could she betray her dad?

What kind of person was she, wanting her dad's killer to kiss her? Even if it was a test.

There was her loneliness too. Pigeon had asked her if something was wrong, and even Raul had started talking to her again, but she couldn't confide in them. Alexa hated to admit it, but she was beginning to care for some of them despite her best effort not to. She couldn't stop hearing about their lives, their jobs, their woes, and their happiness when they conversed around her.

She imagined what it would be like to be one of Pigeon's daughters, living without this burden of loss and hate. She even considered accepting Raul's invitation to become something more with him.

Lovers. It'd be easy. They already slept in the same room. And maybe having Raul beside her would distract her from whatever was happening with her regarding Hysterian.

I'm going to kill him. That's what's happening.

Raul could be easy and fun...

Alexa cleared her throat.

Today was a new day, a new evening. She'd come to find Hysterian to apologize for breaking protocol and to reset boundaries between them, to figure out where the bugs for Titan's ambassador were, to finally get into the bridge, and most of all, remember why she was here in the first place.

Alexa inhaled and looked around her some more. She didn't know how much time she had.

She moved away from the door after waiting another few seconds, just in case Hysterian watched the security feed later. He could be heading back at any moment if his business with Daniels was done.

She closed in on Daniels's station first, slowly making her way to her target: the captain's logs. If she knew she wouldn't be caught, she'd have followed Hysterian to over-hear his and Daniels's conversation. Maybe she'd find out what Daniels was looking for in Hysterian's quarters...

She shook her head. *I'm not here for Daniels.*

The screens ran continuous feeds at Daniels's station. Numbers and alerts popped up in the air directly above the hardware. There were calibrations and readings of the *Questor's* systems, their usages, and maintenance specs. It was strange information for someone on the bridge to be viewing but not wholly unusual.

The ship's water supply and recycling were at their max. The *Questor's* AI suggested water replacement imme-diately due to an unusual number of unknown substances in it. Strange.

Alexa pretended to stretch and swiped her finger across the specs, pushing them away. New information came up. Navigational specs, random coordinates, and more popped up. A correspondence from Elyria? Her eyes widened at the planet's name coming out of nowhere, and when she stretched again, she was dismayed but not surprised the correspondence was locked.

She moved away from Daniels's station, cutting her gaze to the ship's windows in the front.

Titan was a beautiful planet, but the tarmac was not. Condensation evaporated off the cement, making the view foggy.

She made her way to Horace's station next.

His station was a complete disaster, and she wondered where the cleaning bots were, but she had also interrupted the officers in the middle of something, so maybe they hadn't had time to clean up and organize their stations before the next shift cycle.

Horace eluded her. She'd barely spoken to him in the

weeks they'd been traveling. He was a quiet man with a testy demeanor. Neither she nor Horace made the effort to get to know one another.

But his screens were filled with correspondences, and her curiosity piqued. It made sense. Horace was the communications officer, their expert on the various sects of humans across the universe. Snooping on his mail would be satisfying, but she wasn't here to get distracted. She back-tracked to stand beside Hysterian's chair.

The captain's seat was front and center, and above the others—even the empty stations across the bridge. Power, it screamed. Authority. Leadership. She didn't belong anywhere near it.

Alexa would never be a captain of anything. She was lucky enough to have the position she trained for. She'd been poor growing up and only had her dad. He taught her how to survive up until his own death. He never taught her how to survive without him though.

He would've made a great captain.

Dad never left Elyria. He never so much as stepped onto a spaceship. He'd been a Trentian half-breed. Part-human, part-alien. Alexa reached out and ran her fingers over the back of Hysterian's chair, soothed by the soft, rich leather she felt.

Dad never had a chance to be anything more than what he was. He could work for neither government nor any organization affiliated with both. Humans didn't trust him; Trentians tolerated him. And since Elyria had more humans than either Trentians or half-breeds combined, life had been hard for him.

He found work wherever he could, using whatever resources were available. There were half-breed communities that helped, but when every half-breed had the same problem, some just got shuffled to the end of the list. Dad spent his free time giving help in return.

He cared. So much. *He wanted a better life for me. For us. For all half-breeds.*

Women like her didn't have it nearly as hard as a man with the same predicament. They had it hard, but in an entirely different way.

Purebred Trentians overlooked the human part in the women of her community. They didn't care. They needed women to replace the countless they lost in the war, and so half-breed Trentian females were a desired commodity. Knights from Xanteaus, the Trentian homeworld, would come to the slums once a year to gather willing women of age, and offer them a chance at matehood, and a way off Elyria—a better life.

Many took the opportunity, while some, like herself, hid.

Dad made her fully aware of her predicament. Alexa's heart fell. He protected her with every ounce of power he held, which wasn't much.

Then a Cyborg killed him. Her eyes narrowed. *The same Cyborg I tempted to kiss me.* Alexa snatched her hand back, rubbing the feel of the leather from her fingers.

And if anyone found out she was a half-breed...she was doomed.

Or as good as dead. She'd been on Earth, in the presence of her species' greatest enemy. An enemy who would either kill her on the spot because of it, or turn her over to the authorities.

She'd paid a lot of money for her fake medical records and for the glamour surgery to change her eye color. She tried to blend in.

Her eyes snapped to the screens in front of the captain's

chair. Screens with dozens of different windows to search through.

"You've been staring at that seat. Is there something wrong with it?"

Alexa stilled, the blood draining from her face. She slowly turned around.

Hysterian stood in the bridge's doorway. He was leaning against the side. He had the look and demeanor of a man in charge, but none of the virtue. He was strikingly handsome, exotically so, with his lean frame, tight armored suit, and blindingly white hair.

But he was also a complete mess.

Dirt covered him from head-to-boot, gross dried green splatter stained his uniform and gloves, and even his hair fell in an unkempt, windswept mess. If she hadn't known where he'd been, she would have assumed that he'd just returned from war. There was a wild spark in his eyes.

They twitched, bulged slightly but when she blinked, they were back to normal. Again.

If she cared, she would ask how he got that way. If she cared, she would show concern for him. Her lips flattened.

Arched brows and amused eyes met hers, and she braced. The wildness in them remained despite his obvious amusement.

Her heart hammered.

She'd lost her chance—again—to find something that would help her, but she found something much greater, her need for vengeance renewed.

"Nothing is wrong with it, Captain," she said. "I was just imagining what it would be like to sit in such a seat."

Hysterian pushed off the wall, and she swallowed. How long had he been there? Had he been watching her? He came to stand in front of her, and Alexa straightened even more—to the point her spine threatened to lock her in place forever.

"It's just a seat. Here, sit." He moved past her, unlocked the chair, and swiveled it in her direction.

"I can't break protocol, sir."

"Haven't we already? It's just a seat, Dear. It won't eat you. I promise."

Her eyes dropped to the leather chair and the enormous amount of power it held. She hesitated.

"Go on."

Alexa took a step back. "I'm sorry, Captain, but this is part of the reason why I'm here. I wanted to apologize for my actions in the menagerie yesterday—"

"No need," he snapped. "I should be the one apologizing. I led you to believe I want something more with you, and that was wrong of me. You are my subordinate, and I'm your captain. I have no intention of taking advantage of the position I'm in beyond what incurs for a job...that is."

His words burned. Why did his words burn?

"Good," she mustered. "Thank you...for understanding."

"You're welcome."

They stared at each other.

Alexa couldn't break eye contact with him to save her life. He was a mess, and she had a feeling that if he hadn't been a Cyborg, he may have died today.

Good.

A niggling, annoying spark of concern churned her stomach.

If he had died, then she wouldn't get the satisfaction of killing him. That's what she told herself.

"Is this why you're here, Dear?" he asked. "Or was there something else?"

Alexa internally shook her concern away. "Where are the creatures?"

Hysterian lifted his hand and looked at his fingers. "Still on Titan."

"Were you not able to procure them?"

His gaze shot back to hers. "Are you questioning my abilities?"

"I'm only trying to do my job, sir." But she wanted to kick herself for caring at all. Who cares if he procured them or not?

"Your job is to answer me when I ask you a question, to make certain any acquisition we bring aboard this ship remains healthy and intact. It does not include questioning me."

"But I am questioning you," she snapped.

Teal flashed in his eyes, and she managed to catch it.

"I chose not to procure them," he said, dropping his hand.

"Why?"

"Those who gave me this job left out some key elements to the reason why it needed to be done. I don't like being lied to, not when that lie can lead to the eradication of a species, human or otherwise. Not when that lie puts me in a position to decide such fates when I should have no authority to do so. Titan's officials need a solution to their problem because they are bleeding money and resources, and their solution was us. They paid a lot of money to shift the blame on another. What they didn't realize is that they're already fucked from here across the galaxy. They invaded a hive in the mountains, rich with iron. An active hive of a species that predates them by many millennia, I assume. A species that clearly rules the bowels of this planet. I closed off what I could of the hive to the surface and did what I thought best. It's not my job to decide what comes next."

"But isn't that what we do? Make these decisions, and help others make similarly tough decisions that may be out of their scope? You're sent because you offer a unique perspective—"

Hysterian held up his hand. "Let me stop you right there. That's what the other retrievers might do, but not us. We procure, we transport, and we provide. That is the job we've been hired to do and the job we will do. We're not experts, not seers. We are living, breathing beings like anyone else. Even if one of us has metal for bones."

"So you closed off the hive and left?"

"I did what I thought best. I told them to find a new prospector and move their mining equipment elsewhere. Whether they listen or not is not our concern."

"Will these creatures... Are these creatures that dangerous?"

His gaze sharpened. "Only if you invade their domain and provoke them."

"Am I provoking you?" Alexa was feeling brave—or reckless. She had no idea. But he was answering her, and she...she was listening.

"If you were, you would know."

"I only want to do a good job," she lied. He was bothered, it was obvious. Was it because of whatever happened with Daniels before she arrived, or was it because of Titan?

What could bother a Cyborg like Hysterian? She needed to know, she had to know. A weakness meant everything. But it was more than that...

She was also genuinely curious.

"You've said that already."

"Is there something wrong with that?"

"No."

"Good." Alexa adjusted her jacket. "Wh—"

He interrupted her, "You're done asking questions."

She knew when to back down. "Yes, Captain."

Hysterian's gaze trailed over her, and she tensed. "If there's nothing else, you're dismissed, Dear."

"Thank you, Captain."

Alexa felt a rush of tension leave her at his order. *I made it. I made it through a conversation with him without making a fool of myself.* And she learned he could be bothered, could be manipulated. Since she'd first encountered Hysterian, he'd been cold and calculating, but now she knew he could feel more, that he wasn't just a machine under his man suit.

That was something, wasn't it? It had to be.

Perhaps I need to find Daniels, try and find out what happened...

She turned to leave.

"Wait," Hysterian ordered.

Alexa inhaled sharply, tearing her eyes away from the passageway of beautiful freedom, and faced him. Suddenly, he was right there, pinning her with his number-laced eyes. Loose, messy strands of his hair fell forward, making him look mad. The heat coming off him enveloped her.

She stilled, fully aware of how very close they were. She closed her fingers into her palms and stopped them from pushing those loose strands of hair out of Hysterian's eyes.

"Captain?"

He didn't respond, didn't say anything at all. He just stared at her.

Alexa waited for him to speak, but with each passing second that he didn't, her chest constricted a little more.

"Captain?" she inquired again, barely breathing the word in question.

The next thing she knew, she was lifted off the ground and being carried. She yelped, straining in fear, but then she was set down in his seat. Her hands came to the armrests and gripped them as Hysterian stepped back. She tried to rise.

"Don't," he shot. "Stay there." He leaned back on the control console behind him.

Alexa pressed back into the seat, closing her legs tight. He'd picked her up like she'd weighed nothing, moved her with a speed she couldn't defend against. Her pulse raced.

"I told you I didn't want to break protocol again," she breathed, pressing her feet into the ground, not sure whether to be afraid or furious. "You have no right to touch me!"

"And you have no right to question me. We're even."

"This does not make us even! You had a choice to not answer me. I would've been satisfied." She pushed up from the chair. "It's time for me to leave."

He snapped forward, making her drop back down. "I ordered you to stay."

She was trapped. He blocked her in, and if she wanted to leave now, she'd have to shove against him or climb over the chair. Both actions made her uncomfortable.

"You are taking advantage of your position," she said, unable to meet his eyes suddenly.

Something inside her heated, danced, and begged. Begged for this, more of this, more of him, and try as she might, it only grew.

"Are you going to tell on me, Dear?" Hysterian taunted her. "It's only right to go back on my word when you so immediately went back on yours. Protocol? Hah."

"I didn't?"

"You did."

Her cheeks heated. Alexa felt his gaze on them, and she turned her face away.

"You look good when you blush," he said.

"Don't," she bit out.

"Don't what?"

"Don't do this—whatever this is." She couldn't handle this, this thing between them that shouldn't be there. It was wrong. So, so wrong.

Alexa faced him, and he tilted his head to the side like she was something to be studied. She hugged herself.

"Yet you're the one who propositioned me to kiss you, touch you even."

"It was a mistake."

"Oh, yes. It was a mistake."

Silence filled the air between them as they watched each other. His words filled her head, taking over everything else. They often did these days.

Alexa waited for him to make a move, any move, so she wouldn't have to.

He leaned forward and she pushed back into the seat.

His eyes searched hers, and she wetted her lips.

He moved closer and there was nowhere left for her to go. All she could see was his eyes, his brow, his partial mask. *He can't kiss me with his suit up over his mouth. Can he?*

Will he?

Did she even want him to kiss her?

Would she get to see his face?

More of his heat closed in, making her brow slicken. Hundreds of tiny numbers ran up and down his irises, mesmerizing her. She could get lost in his gaze...if he weren't so evil.

"Do you know what happens when you're wanted by one of my kind?" he asked.

She shook her head, lamely.

"You lose your choices, your freedom. It's subtle at first, but we take them away, slowly if you're not amenable. You lose privacy, in all things. Because we can't stand secrets, we can't stand not knowing every singular movement and thought of something we crave. You find yourself consumed, because we demand it. You'll find yourself claimed, because we need complete control. And you may resist, you may fight, we might even fight it as well, but there's no escape, not for someone like me, and certainly not for someone like you, who has offered."

"What are you saying?" she whispered.

In her periphery, his hands tightened around the armrests.

"I'm saying, Alexa, that it's too late for us. Protocol or not. Whether we like it or not."

"It's never too late."

"We'll fuck, you and I. It'll be hard and merciless, but it'll be satisfying. I'll have you stretched and spread and screaming, and you'll have bliss. I've decided to take you up on your generous offer because that's the only way..."

She could barely breathe. His threats went past her head and straight to the pinnacle between her legs. "Only way for what?"

He swayed his finger between the two of them. "To rid ourselves of this tension. For you to keep your job, because you're good at it and I don't want to fire you, and for me to stay sane and not be in such misery."

Misery. Misery? The word sent a bolt of ice straight to her heart.

"Misery?" Her anger surged, barely breaking through

the haze. "You have no clue what misery is," she hissed. She pushed against his chest and fought her way out of his trap. He leaned back. "Don't speak to me about misery." She spat. "You know nothing about it."

Hardness and mischief etched themselves into his gaze. Her fury grew.

Alexa put several feet of space between them. "We won't fuck, and we won't so much as touch, let alone kiss each other. It's not too late for us. It's never too late. I came here to set boundaries, not break them, Captain. I think it's time for me to go."

She strode toward the exit.

"Alexa," he called after her.

She stilled at the threshold but refused to look at him. "What?"

"Your roots are showing."

She gritted her teeth and stormed away.

TEN

Raul looked up at her as Alexa stalked by him. "What's wrong? Did you find out about the bugs?"

"Yes," she quipped, not stopping to talk. She didn't want to see anyone, let alone speak to anyone. She was furious and felt wrung out like a damp towel. The day shift wasn't over yet, but she was done. She'd done enough today.

And to make it worse, the male locust was pounding on the glass enclosure. The last thing she needed right now was another male—of any species—wanting to fuck her because she was the only woman around.

It was nauseating. Men were the worst.

She'd just made it to her quarters when Hysterian's voice came through the intercom.

"Be ready to depart Titan. We take off at twenty hundred hours."

Her nostrils flared. "Fuck you," she said under her breath.

"Hey, what happened?" Raul came up behind her.

"Nothing." She walked into the room, hoping Raul wouldn't follow her.

Her hope died the next moment.

"Something happened. You're pissed as hell."

Alexa swerved. "Am I? Pissed, that is? I'm furious, but most of all, I want to be alone!"

"Whoa, calm down. I'm not the bad guy here. Tell me what happened."

"I've got nothing to say."

"He's a real fucker isn't he."

Alexa's eyes narrowed, and she pursed her lips.

Raul cupped the back of his neck, his gaze softening. "He...he didn't hurt you, did he?" he asked in a low voice. Then fury hot enough to match her own crossed his face. "I'll fucking kill him. If he so much as touched you, I'll kill him."

They both knew who Raul spoke of.

"He didn't hurt me," Alexa said. "It's not like that at all. It's nothing like that."

Raul stepped forward. "I'll fucking kill him, Alexa. You just say the word, and I'll take care of this."

"Stop. Stop," she said before Raul worked himself up any further. "He'd swat you like a fly if you even tried. It's not worth your life. And he didn't hurt me, like I said." She was trying to calm down for Raul's sake more than her own. "It's not like that. We argued that's all. Nothing more."

Raul remained rigid, ready to go to battle despite her words.

"Raul, please, calm down." She groaned. "I don't need you sticking up for me. I don't need anyone going into battle for me! I take care of myself."

"I know you can take care of yourself. That's obvious. But I don't like him, Alexa. At all. I should have gone with you."

She didn't know that Raul didn't like Hysterian. Had

something happened between them that she wasn't aware of? Raul was a good guy. Though she tried not to care about him or any of the others, she'd grown fond of Raul regardless. He may go into quiet spells, but he was kind to her, and thoughtful. He gave her her space even when there was very little to be had.

She reached out and took his hand, squeezing it in reassurance. Seeing Raul worked up like this somehow made her feel better, less alone. He settled down and squeezed her hand back.

Alexa studied him for a moment. Raul really was classically handsome.

"We argued. That's all that happened," she told him. "I asked him what happened on Titan today, and he didn't like me questioning him. That's all. I overstepped, and he put me back in my place."

"I've never worked for a captain who couldn't just fucking talk with his crew like a normal fucking person," Raul spat. "I've always heard how heroic and great Cyborgs were. If they are, Hysterian certainly isn't one of them."

"He was right to check me," she said, defending Hysterian. "He's the captain, our leader, and nothing like you or me. Can you imagine how lonely that is?" She let go of Raul and rubbed her brow.

"Don't pity him, Dear."

"I'm not pitying him! I'd never pity him. I'm just trying to understand. Anyway," Alexa said, wanting to change the subject, "we need to wipe the specs of the habitats and see if the resources we used can be salvaged."

Raul waved his hand. "I'll take care of that. Did he say what happened?"

"Only that Titan's officials weren't forthcoming with all the details of their request. That the problem was about money, and the solution they wanted would result in death. He doesn't want us to be a part of their schemes or to take the fall. He was already in a mood before I approached him."

"Hmm." Raul's eyes hooded in thought. "So that's why we're leaving so soon."

"Yeah."

He breathed deep and let it out slowly.

Alexa relaxed. She didn't have to worry about him running off to her rescue when her back was turned. She didn't think she could live with another innocent death on her hands. Especially since the real reason she was upset wasn't because of Hysterian, but herself.

Part of her had wanted the Cyborg to grab her again when she had walked away. Part of her wished she'd pulled down Hysterian's face covering and kissed him.

She was curious what it would feel like, curious what would have happened if she had. The tightness between her legs hadn't eased, and she was beginning to realize what it meant.

She wanted Hysterian. She wanted everything he threatened and more. She wanted him to take her hard that there'd be pain, so much pain that it would erase everything else. She deserved it. And to be hurt by the very being that turned her this way? It felt like a sick sort of justice for her failings.

Maybe if she was consumed with physical suffering, it would take all the pain in her thoughts away.

Alexa swallowed. *I should've stayed. I should've agreed. He could be breaking me right now on the floor of the bridge if I hadn't run.*

God, she needed to be broken. Maybe then she could pick up the pieces and rebuild herself the way she wanted this time. Without the guilt, without the loneliness. Without fear.

Without alien DNA coursing through her veins.

Alexa closed her eyes and exhaled. *If only it could be that easy.*

"You sure you're okay, Dear?" Raul asked. She opened her eyes as he took another step forward.

He studied her. She studied him back.

Maybe it didn't have to be Hysterian who broke her. Maybe she should embrace Raul's flirtation, open herself up to it. If she let him in, maybe this fixation on her enemy would go away.

I've been thinking of Hysterian and only Hysterian for far too long.

Raul was handsome, and kept fit. *Maybe with him, I won't need to be broken. Maybe I can fix everything more easily.* She slid her eyes to Raul's chest, his arms. He could easily dominate her if she needed him to, like her mind wanted. He was nothing like Hysterian, though, and not intimidating in the least. That was a good thing.

She closed the distance between them.

Raul's eyes widened, but he didn't pull away.

"I'm okay," she said. "But I could be better..."

"Alexa? Are you—"

"Yes."

He slowly nodded.

This is good, she thought. *This will work.* Raul could help her. She reached up and clasped his neck. His arms came around her and jerked her into his chest.

It was warm, hard, but not so hot that it threatened to suffocate her. Raul smelled like shaving cream, not like burning metal. His cock hardened against her hip. He pressed it against her.

Take Hysterian out of my head.

Raul's hands glided up her back until they reached her hair. He hooked his fingers into her bun and pulled out her band.

Her hair tumbled down her back.

Fuck Hysterian, fuck him.

"I've wanted to see you with your hair down since I first saw you," Raul murmured.

"Oh..."

"You're beautiful, far more so than a man like me should ever have the honor of holding."

Beautiful? *Hah.* She'd never been called beautiful in her life. She tried to meet Raul's eyes but couldn't, looking at the collar of his suit instead. "Thank you, I think." He was complimenting her, wooing her, and being nothing like Hysterian.

He chuckled. "You're welcome." He tilted her chin, forcing her head back up. "I'll make this good for you. I'll make you scream my name."

Scream? She startled. Hysterian had said the same thing. Her nails bit into Raul's neck. Hysterian said he would have her screaming and more.

"Kiss me," she demanded. "Kiss me or leave me alone. But do it now—"

Raul's mouth slammed against hers.

He pulled her close, grabbed her head, and threaded his fingers into her hair. His lips moved on hers. Alexa pushed against him, forcing her lips to move with his. His mouth was so hard, though, that all she could do was let him maul her. Her nails bit harder into his skin.

When his tongue probed her mouth, she opened it, letting him in. He filled her up, licking her everywhere, pushing his tongue against hers. He was a force all his own, one without any finesse.

She may be a virgin, and may not have kissed a man before, but she had seen her share of lovers on the network, and all that being a lover entails from there. This wasn't a good kiss. She'd had better back in grade school with boys.

Would Hysterian's kiss be this forceful?

Alexa moaned with annoyance. Raul laughed into her, pressing his advantage, obviously taking her moan the wrong way. His hands dropped down her back and grabbed her ass, tugging her against him.

He jerked his hips, rubbing his hard cock against her. "You have no idea how badly I want you. This will be good, so good between us, baby."

She wanted to agree but couldn't.

Raul groped her ass before grabbing the lapel of her suit jacket, tugging it open and down her arms.

"You'll see, Dear. You'll never want another man between your legs after me." He pulled her shirt over her head. His hands, slightly cold, came up and cupped her breasts over her bra. "I knew you had a rack to die for hiding under all these layers."

Raul squeezed her breasts again, and Alexa let him, waiting for that spark to hit her. The spark that would make her want to tear into his clothes as well.

"Let's get these tits out to be kissed, shall we? They'll feel better lavished in kisses." He tugged down the cups of her bra.

If Hysterian saw us this way, would he care?

Cold air breezed her nipples.

Alexa grabbed Raul's hands and stopped him. "Wait!"

She was cold as a fish on the dark side of the moon.

"What's wrong, baby?" Raul asked.

When he cupped the sides of her breasts, pushing them together, Alexa yanked his hands off her. "I can't. I'm sorry —I can't."

His face fell. "Was it something I said?"

Alexa turned away and rubbed her face. She quickly picked her jacket off the floor and covered herself. "No. I'm..." What to tell him? "I'm not ready. Tonight's been rough, the last few days too." She needed to let him down gently enough so they could continue working together in peace.

But he'd felt her up, kissed her now. Was that even going to be possible?

Exhaustion overcame her. She'd fucked up, again. What had she been thinking? Sleeping with a man just to get another man out of her head? Even if she let Raul try and wipe Hysterian from her thoughts for a few hours, he'd only return.

He'd taken up residence long ago. Hysterian wasn't going anywhere until she finished what she started.

Raul cupped her shoulders and pressed his fingers into her muscles. "I can still make it better without sex." His fingers rolled and rubbed. "It's been a shitstorm of days. At least have a drink with me in the lounge tonight?"

A drink did sound good.

"I promise it won't be anything more than a drink," Raul continued.

Alexa just wanted to be alone. *But a drink may fix things...*

She faced him. "A drink then."

He smiled. "Good. It's a date."

"Okay," she whispered.

Raul backed up and adjusted his cock so it wasn't tenting his pants. "Great! I'll go finish up work and get everything stabilized before takeoff. You take some time. I'll pick you up after shift. The room is yours."

She mustered a smile. "Okay." *Please go now.*

Raul swiped his wristcon to unlock their quarters. The door zipped open. "Until this evening, Dear."

Alexa rushed to the door and locked it behind her, exhaling. She looked down at herself. Topless, with her hair down and a mess around her shoulders.

Your roots are showing.

She grabbed at her hair anyway and stormed to the bathroom. In a matter of seconds, she stripped off her clothes. She glanced at the mirror but quickly looked away.

She didn't like looking at herself. There were scars, scars she never had the time to get cosmetically removed from her flesh that she didn't want to acknowledge. They were a tribute to those first years alone, working to get off of Elyria. They were another reason, an easier reason for her never to get attached to a lover. She could blame the scars and not her DNA.

Alexa tugged open her locker to grab her dye and hesitated when a simple, silver canister sat in the front of her belongings. Marked on its side were the words *Better Dye.*

She threw it across the room at full force, clanging as it rattled the metal walls.

"Fuck you!" she screamed at the top of her lungs.

She twisted to the shower unit and turned it on, setting the water at lukewarm. *Fuck him. Fuck Hysterian.* The canister rolled to her foot, and she kicked it away.

Stepping into the stall, she cursed him over and over, pummeling the unit around her. When her exhaustion returned, she was panting, sliding down the wall. The water drenched her from above.

"Fuck you," she whispered, pushing her hand between

her legs. Her fingers found her clit, and she dropped her head. She rubbed hard and fast, needing release like it was her next breath. Nerves sparked down her legs, making them shake with each hard stroke of her clit. And when it wasn't enough, she pressed her thighs closed and writhed into her hand, mimicking sex.

Imagining what Hysterian would do to her...

"Fuck you," Alexa moaned. She tossed her head from side to side. She pinched and rolled and rocked, growing desperate. The orgasm eluded her, though, and the longer it took, the more she lost her mind.

She screamed, pretending it was the scream Hysterian threatened to coax from her.

Alexa pinched her clit, begging for the tension to end, but it only grew worse. She imagined what he would be doing to her right now if she had stayed.

'I'll have you stretched and spread and screaming...'

She tried to picture Raul in Hysterian's place, but couldn't. She didn't want Raul.

But I can stretch myself, I can spread myself, and I can scream without him.

Alexa pushed open the shower unit and reached for the canister, bringing it into the stall with her. She put it between her legs and rubbed against it. Thick and blunt, steely, it was Hysterian, and she slumped forward with a moan.

She wanted it inside her, eradicating this pressure. Alexa lined it up to her sex and pushed. She could do this. She could do anything to herself that Hysterian could do to her.

It was solid, without any give, and there wasn't any tapering to work herself with. She wiggled and bit down on her lower lip, giving it her best effort. She couldn't make it fit.

Alexa slumped, defeated.

The water sluiced down her skin as she pulled her hands from between her legs, giving up. Disappointment filled her. She wasn't going to get herself off, no matter how hard she tried. She wasn't going to make herself scream in release with all the effort of her fingers. All she could do was spread her legs, and even then, the stall was too small for much of that.

The water cooled. It soothed.

After a time, she pulled herself upright and into a sitting position. She pushed her hair out of her face. The water had long ago gone icy. Lifting her head, she let it cleanse her, calm her, and take everything else away.

Getting to her feet a short time later, noticing the wrinkles on the pads of her fingers, she grabbed the canister and sprayed the contents into her hair. Citrus and flowers invaded her nose. No chemicals, no cheap burn. It slickened her hair like silk.

Resignation was all she felt anymore. But with it came a little bit of peace.

She dressed and tugged her wet hair back into a bun.

"Takeoff is commencing in five minutes." Hysterian's voice filled her ears.

She smiled, left her quarters, and sat down at her desk. Raul saluted her. She buckled herself in, ready to leave Titan. To leave, have a stiff drink, and...

Never come back.

ELEVEN

"Contact Libra station. Let them know we're coming and that we'll need to restore the *Questor's* resources and supplies," Hysterian ordered, tapping his finger against the cloth covering his mouth.

Horace swiveled in his chair. "We're heading back to Gliese then? Should I contact them as well?"

"No. We're only laying over at Libra. There'll be no other stops in the sector."

"Yes, Captain."

Horace swiped several of his correspondences away and brought up new ones. For the past few days, it had only been Horace working the bridge with him, and Hysterian preferred it that way. Daniels had done an okay job, but Hysterian preferred not keeping an eye on the bastard.

Overall, there was only minor curiosity in regards to Daniels's abrupt departure. Hysterian hadn't needed to provide his other bridge officer anything but the simplest explanation.

That Daniels left.

Horace had shrugged. He even grumped when

Hysterian asked him to collect Daniels's belongings from their shared quarters so they could be dropped off on Earth the next time they landed on the homeworld. Apparently, Daniels hadn't been liked, and morale had...gone up since his disappearance. It seemed that way. It might also have had something to do with the fact that Hysterian promoted Horace to second-in-command, and with that came a steep pay increase.

Horace was good at his job. He never questioned any decisions made, and promptly got his work done. All a captain could ask for in a subordinate.

Unlike some others in his crew.

Alexa was avoiding him.

It pissed him off, but he couldn't do much about it. She needed time to come to terms with what he'd told her. What he planned to do to her.

What he wished to do to her... It was better that she accepted it on her own terms, in her own time. He had time.

He was going to have Alexa. Especially if she chose to remain in his employment after what he'd said. Hysterian couldn't live with her otherwise, being tempted, because someday it would get the better of him. A mistake would be made. His mistakes often resulted in dire consequences. His job was dangerous, and if he planned to stay for the entirety of his contract with Nightheart, Hysterian needed to keep his head on straight.

Alexa made that hard as fuck with their current situation.

It may be a while before he found his perfect woman. Having Alexa around to enjoy in the meantime would make the wait immensely more tolerable. She would get whatever it is she wanted from him—if it was a pay raise or a promotion she's after—and he would get his practice on her.

Hysterian rubbed his brow.

He wouldn't be here either if it weren't for his...problem.

His future meant nothing if Nightheart couldn't deliver. If Hysterian couldn't touch living flesh without killing it, or making a person addicted to him, there would be no true relief. Alexa or not, he'd be doomed to suffer.

There would be no escape.

It wasn't only his secretion production that kept him away from others, from Alexa; he also had no reason to approach her. He'd come up with dozens of great ones but they were all lamely crafted excuses in his head.

I shouldn't need a fucking excuse to talk to one of my crew. Hysterian's jaw ticked.

He understood now why so many ships hired a live-in prostitute or invested in a state-of-the-art sexbot. He'd only ever fucked sexbots in the past, and although they were good—really good—at giving the illusion of a real woman, it wasn't the same. They were too perfect. Too...plastic. It was the imperfections that made something real. Something warm.

He couldn't have Alexa the way he needed yet, but he could fuck a sexbot and much more, plastic or not. *One hard night with one will ease me.*

It was decided. He was going to hire one on Libra.

"Captain?" Horace called to him, interrupting his thoughts.

"What?"

"Besides the problem with our water supply—which I assume we will have looked at while we're on Libra and get the necessary items to fix it—are there any other supplies you would like to request?"

Hysterian thought it over. "Ask them if they have any

suppliers or incoming transports of nanocloth." Anyone could get nanocloth and manually configure it the way they wanted, but a Cyborg could control it on a cybernetic level. It was why they all wore a suit of nanocloth under their uniforms.

"Yes, sir."

"We'll be warping tomorrow once we get to Juda. First thing. I want to get there quickly." Hysterian scanned through his navigational specs. "Let the others know so they can prepare. Shift ends in five. Enjoy your evening."

Horace raised his hand in acknowledgment.

Hysterian pulled up an information packet of everything on Libra station, familiarizing himself with the giant space port and what it had to offer. It was one of the biggest waystations in human territory, central to many of the planets humans now colonized. His crew would want to disembark for a reprieve as well.

Horace rose from his station. "Goodnight, Captain," he said, making his way out of the bridge.

Hysterian nodded, continuing to download whatever he could about Libra for future use.

"Captain," Horace said from behind him.

Hysterian broke his connection to the network. "What?"

"The crew's been gathering in the lounge for drinks in the evenings. You should join us."

Hysterian lifted his head and stared at Horace.

Is...is he inviting me? Odd. The crew had recently started to gather in the lounge, but he hadn't paid it any thought. He only knew of it because Alexa joined them, and because of that, he couldn't get her alone elsewhere. He didn't give a fuck what the others did as long as they stayed in line and did their jobs.

"I'll consider it," he said.

Horace grumped and left. When his new second-in-command's footsteps receded, Hysterian leaned back, commanding the bridge doors to close.

An empty quietness settled in once he was alone. The subtle buzz of tech hummed in his ears. He focused on it, letting his mind clear within the white noise. These few minutes after the end of the day shift were his favorite. He savored it, knowing what was in store for him for the rest of the night.

Water, pain, secretion, replenishment, and more secretion. More pain. The nights were getting worse. He was naturally diurnal, and the constant darkness of space shimmering at him through the port windows was fucking with his mind.

He couldn't sleep. Couldn't power down.

He could only secrete, empty his body, and start all over again, hoping, for once, he'd tire out and deplete his systems long enough to get through the next day.

When was the last time I slept? Weeks. It was weeks ago. Hysterian leaned his elbows on his knees and ran his hands over his head. His systems urged him to rest. He ignored them. But for how much longer?

He eyed the timing it would take for them to get to Libra. Three days if the port had a spot for his ship. Three days until he could have a better outlet than his hand. He stared at the tent in his uniform. Hysterian reached down and squeezed the growing bulge.

He knew why he suffered.

It hadn't always been like this.

Once, he'd been head interrogator. During the war, he was known as the Tormentor because of his special ability. He could ingest any poison—toxin or otherwise—and his systems could replicate it within seconds. With a small touch, he could make men scream, go mad, or spill their guts and come clean.

He just couldn't make his secretion benign...

Traitors, deserters, murderers, and spies were delivered to him, and it'd been his job to get them to confess, and during the war for which he'd been made for, his superiors brought him droves of prisoners. He could make anyone confess. If not with torture...with getting them ravenously addicted to him.

He smirked, remembering the good times.

Hysterian had more control then. He had an endless outlet that kept him satisfied.

He'd come to realize he'd been built wrong as the years went by, as the bodies piled up. He may have not spent much time on the front lines of the war, bringing down battleships, but he'd killed more than his fair share. And unlike his brethren, he was tasked to kill and torture humans.

Stepping into Dimes and becoming Raphael's glorified pet had been an easy transition after Hysterian left the service.

Almost too easy.

He rubbed his shaft through his pants.

He always envied human men who could commit atrocities and not be bothered by it. He didn't know how they did it, being entirely made of organic matter. If he didn't have his systems to check him, to manually lessen his emotions, he wouldn't know what would become of him.

I've spent my whole existence perverting life. And sex... He squeezed his cock again. Sex creates life. At least it could...

It wouldn't fix him but he hoped it would help. And he

didn't want to create life as much as lose himself in the act of it.

Somewhere, in the back of his royally screwed up DNA, his animal demanded he fertilize. Fertilize what? Who the fuck knew? Humans didn't fucking lay eggs. And there was no pleasure in the thought. But he was certain, until his animal was wholly satisfied, he was never going to stop overproducing secretion at the merest touch. A primitive need demanded he spill until his animal was appeased.

He was built wrong because his fucking doctors and engineers didn't account for a frog's mating habits.

If he'd known then what he knew now, he would have killed them all for their sins.

Hysterian's mood soured. The silence became too much, and the incessant buzzing! His tongue begged him to be released and snap at everything that hummed. He shot to his feet and stormed out of the bridge. Nothing would help until he got into the shower.

Laughter sounded down the hallway. It came from the lounge at the end of the hall.

Clenching his hands, his frustration built.

More laughter reached his ears, and he immediately recognized Alexa's. She was laughing? Her? Of all the people he'd ever encountered, he never imagined his by-the-book cold crew hand laughing. Had he ever seen her happy, or even pleased, in the month they'd traveled together?

Her blushes, her anger came to mind, but for the life of him, he could not bring an image to his head of Alexa with a smile on her face. He didn't have one stored. He didn't even have a fake one created for his amusement.

Hysterian stopped and stood outside the lounge.

"It's not like you have a better choice. It's either this shit or liquid brown."

"Liquid brown?"

"The crap you guys call coffee," Raul said.

"Even calling the sludge on this ship liquid brown is too much. It's acid scum," Horace grunted.

"Or Locust piss!"

There was more laughter.

"More like our captain's piss." Raul again. "Here, hand me the vodka. If I'm going to suffer, I'm going to suffer wasted."

Liquid pouring, chuckles, and clinking glasses sounded as his crew's camaraderie continued. Maybe he wasn't the only miserable one.

"What about you, Alexa? You want another drink?" Raul asked.

"It's on the house," Pigeon added with a chuckle.

"I think one a night is enough for me," she answered with a laugh.

Hysterian crossed his arms and leaned against the wall. *Good choice.* His crew could say whatever shit they wanted to about him, but he cared about what Alexa said and did. She was new to life out in space. It was so obvious, it was sad. A little cute, but also sad.

He found himself intrigued.

"Aww, come on. You always only have one drink, and it's never stiff enough for you to let the load off. Relax for once," Raul whined. "We'll make sure you get tucked in safe and alone in your bunk tonight, I promise."

"Don't listen to him. He's slurring his words." Pigeon laughed. "We'll need your help getting him into his bunk —alone."

"We might find him curled up with one of those female aliens you got caged if we don't," Horace rasped. "Or you,

Pigeon. We know you're in need of something to hold onto at night that isn't a teddy bear."

"Hey! It was a gift from one of my grandkids!"

Alexa let out another laugh.

Hysterian wished he could see her face.

"Fuck you guys. I'm not slurring my words," Raul said. "Alexa, hand me that bottle."

"Don't! We'll find him with that big horny male locust instead," Pigeon warned.

"Shut your trap. Drinking is the only way to get to sleep on this ship. For being brand new, it sure has loud fucking pipes! And who cares if I end up with the animals? I don't."

You deserve the animals. Hysterian sneered.

"Here," Alexa said. "You can make your own choices."

"Thank you, Dear. You're a princess."

She coughed then guffawed. Hysterian lips twitched up.

"I'm not a princess," she stated, sounding offended.

"You're my princess," Raul cooed.

"Then what does that make you, Raul?" Pigeon asked. "You can't just give up her secrets without repercussions. She may have wanted to keep her princess status on the down low, you fool!"

"I'm just a lowly frog that wants her to kiss me!"

Hysterian tensed. A cacophony of laughter filled his audio. The wires seized inside him, pulling his body taut. Raul's words were too close to the mark, and a strange needling of dread wormed its way through Hysterian's systems.

But it was the picture of Alexa kissing Raul that rocked him. Waves of red washed over his vision.

"She'll never kiss you, Raul, so get those thoughts out of your inebriated head," Horace taunted. "But a fucking frog you are. Maybe you can get one of the cleaning bots to kiss you, 'cause that's the only thing on this ship that will."

"Let's change the subje—" Alexa started to say.

"Oh, I don't know," Raul quipped. "I think I'm more enticing than that. This is our third date, is it not? And a third time's a charm. But I can wait!" Raul quickly added. "Twelve time's a charm too or even the twentieth."

Red burst in Hysterian's eyes like wildfire. He pushed off the wall and stepped into the lounge.

But no one was looking in his direction. His crew was gathered around a table in the back corner in various positions. They all stared at Alexa. Was that a blush on her cheeks?

A heated blush that made Hysterian's skin run cold with need.

"You don't say?" Horace muttered.

"You guys dating?" Pigeon asked when Alexa didn't answer, deciding to bury her face into her hands instead.

"Well..." she started but trailed off.

"Alexa wants to take it slow, and so slow we shall go."

Muscles straining, fingers twitching to break bone, Hysterian growled. "What's going on here?"

The easy camaraderie of the group dissipated. They turned to look at him as one. Raul got to his feet, Alexa dropped her hands and went white, and even Pigeon's smile fell.

"Captain," they said, and the last of the easy laughter vanished into the ship's buzzing.

"We're enjoying a drink, Captain. Why don't you join us?" Pigeon pushed a bottle in Hysterian's direction.

He didn't want a drink; he wanted relief. He wanted Alexa to meet his eyes instead of staring hard at the cup between her hands. Was what Raul said true?

Dating? Who the fuck dates? And three of them?

How had he missed that?

His ship wasn't that goddamn big, for fuck's sake.

What else had he missed?

"Captain? Can we do something for you?" Pigeon asked, a little uneasily.

Hysterian stared at Alexa, waiting for her to answer. She sat beside Pigeon, and not Raul. Hysterian was pretty sure if she had been, Raul's blood would be dripping down the walls already. Raul was still close, too close, and Hysterian couldn't remove him without someone else getting hurt.

This was why he fucking hated ships.

Without destroying everything Hysterian strived for, he couldn't break Raul's neck in front of everyone. He wanted to, but the risk was too great.

There was no way he was going to have Alexa if he traumatized her.

His crew shuffled uneasily when he didn't answer. They glanced at each other.

"Yes," Hysterian said after a minute. "You can leave."

Horace gulped down the rest of his drink and strode out of the lounge. Pigeon offered his hand to Alexa to help her rise, but she shook her head. Pigeon sighed as he walked out.

Hysterian turned to Raul. "I said leave." *Leave or die.* Right now, Hysterian couldn't decide which choice he wanted Raul to make more.

Raul glared at him, unmoving. "I'm waiting for Alexa...sir."

Hysterian stepped forward. "When your captain gives you an order, you follow it. Anyone teach you that in basic training?"

"I plan to, sir." The disgust on Raul's face couldn't be more evident. "When she's ready."

"Raul, go. I'll be right behind you," Alexa said, and with good timing too, as Hysterian was about to snap Raul's neck.

"I'm not leaving without you."

"I'm not giving you a choice," she said. "Go."

Raul turned to Alexa. "He's telling us all to leave. We'll leave together."

"Raul," Hysterian said, his voice lowering with menace. He did not like the familiar way Raul was addressing Alexa. Or the gleam in his eye when he looked at her. "She's not your fucking princess, and she's never going to fucking kiss you, you drunken piece of shit. The bruises on your neck are gone, and I'm finding I'd like to replace them."

Raul straightened and scowled. He reached up and rubbed his neck, but he backed away from Alexa and, with a final show of defiance, downed his drink and slammed the cup on the table.

"You're right, Captain. You always are, aren't you?" He strode toward the exit. "Except she has kissed me, but of course, you're right. She's a woman, not a damsel in distress." Raul glanced at Alexa. "I'll wait up for you. I hope you know what you're doing."

Before Hysterian could drag him back and drink his blood, Raul was out the door and gone.

TWELVE

He planned to take care of Raul. Later. Where there were no witnesses.

In a flash, Hysterian was on Alexa, pulling her from her seat.

She gasped and grabbed him as he sat her down on the table, blocking her in and pushing his body between her legs. To his surprise, her hands went to his face as she pummeled him.

"No!" she cried.

Hysterian jerked back before her fingers made contact with his brow.

"Stop!" he ordered.

She continued to squirm and fight him, though didn't make another sound.

He caught her wrists before she reached for his face again. "I said stop! You'll hurt yourself!"

Then he noticed the fear in her eyes.

She kicked him hard and twisted away with a terrified shriek. He held her, confused. No matter how fiercely she tried to get away from him, it would never be enough. Never. No human could match the strength of a Cyborg.

She's fighting like she's about to die.

His brows furrowed. "Do you think I'm about to kill you?" Hysterian released her, horrified. "Stop it!"

Stop it or I might. On accident.

Alexa hit him several more times before stopping. Panting, she went as still as stone, staring wide-eyed at his chest. He forgot about the kiss between her and Raul as Hysterian took her in.

She was already near transparent, but now any sign of color was gone. Had he done this to her? He waited until she calmed, until he could hear her beating heart tone down before he demanded answers.

He opened his mouth to speak and promptly shut it. Alexa pressed her forehead against his chest.

His chest. For comfort, no doubt.

Words left him.

What the hell is happening?

No one had ever sought comfort from him before, or used him for comfort. Hysterian didn't know what to do. His hands twitched. He wanted to touch her, but knew if he did, she might lash out again. He didn't want her to get hurt.

He stared, unable to look away.

She was so small against him. Had he ever noticed that? How small, weak, and soft she was? The woman perplexed him. He could crush her like a bug, tear her to pieces on a whim, and she was still using him as comfort.

Something this small, this delicate, needs to be taken care of. How had she survived so far without protection? Maybe that's why he noticed her.

I could protect her.

Once the thought hit him, his systems vibrated. He swallowed, trying to clear the tightness in his throat.

"You dyed your hair," he said softly.

And cursed himself for choosing those words over others. Shit words.

She didn't respond. She still trembled.

He needed a response, demanded one. "Why were you fighting like I was about to kill you?"

Had he really frightened her that much?

She slowly leaned back, and he missed her against him but relaxed knowing he didn't have to offer comfort anymore. He didn't know how. His immediate response was to offer her his touch his flesh, and that was the last thing he wanted to do. Ever. Especially to her.

He could make her feel good, real good if he did that. He could blow her mind and fuck it sideways, but he'd end up losing her in the process. She'd eventually come back for more, again and again. He couldn't do that to her. Even the good stuff was still poison in the end.

She leaned back even more but still wouldn't look up at him.

He knew he should give her space but he didn't fucking want to. If she ran from him and went to Raul, Hysterian would lose his mind.

"I was startled," she said, quiet as a mouse.

"That was more than being startled. You were fighting for your life," he corrected.

"I want to go. Please move, Captain."

Irritation surged. She was acting like nothing strange had just happened. "You're not going anywhere until you explain to me exactly why you reacted like that."

"I..." She turned her head to the side, exhaustion etched into her face.

"You?" he prompted.

"I was scared."

His fingers curled into his palms. Of course she was scared. He'd grabbed her, and for what reason, he had no idea. It wasn't like he could touch her, strip her, kiss her. He'd grabbed her so she would be in *his* arms, not Raul's. Hysterian's jaw ticked.

The only solution, he decided, was to get Raul out of the picture and off his ship. Hysterian couldn't have her running to someone else, especially another man.

"I'm scared of you," she whispered.

His gaze narrowed. "Have I done something to frighten you enough that you would think I would kill you?"

She shuddered, and his brow creased.

Did I?

"It doesn't matter." She pushed at his chest; he didn't budge. "I just reacted, and now I'm tired. Please let me leave."

"No."

Her eyes finally found his. "No?"

"If you won't tell me what's wrong—and I will find out, Alexa—you can't leave. I don't plan on hurting you, nor can I recall a time where you might think that I might."

"And telling me we're going to fuck and that there's nothing I can do about it isn't frightening?"

"Is that why you're scared? Of the goddamned inevitable?"

Her lips pressed together tight.

Hysterian placed his hands on the table on either side of her. "You're afraid that I'm going to lay you low, strip off your clothes, and push my body upon you? Is that it? That I'm going to nudge your legs open like I'm doing now, and stick my fingers deep into you so I can feel you from the inside? That when I'm done, and you're squirting into my hand, I'm going to press my cock into that tight space and ride out the rest of your orgasm?" His voice lowered. "That scares you?"

"It scares me because I don't want you!"

Fuck what she said; he was happy enough to hear anger in her voice again and not the gasping fear from minutes ago.

"That's a lie if I've ever heard one," he said.

She pushed at him again. "I could never want you. I don't want you. I don't even want to..."

"To what?"

"Look at you!"

"Would you rather look at Raul?" he snarled.

"Yes!"

He cupped the back of her neck. "Then why didn't you fucking leave with him? Why did you stay?"

Her nostrils flared. "Would you have let me?"

Hysterian narrowed his eyes. "Why haven't you fucked him?" he asked, low and menacingly.

"How do you know I haven't? We sleep in the same room, don't we?"

"Because I don't fucking smell him on you!" he shouted. She startled, really startled this time, and his hold on the back of her neck tightened, keeping her where he wanted her. "But I smell your arousal."

Her lips parted, and he slammed his covered mouth on them. His tongue shot out, licking at the cloth between them, moving his lips on hers, taking whatever he could from the kiss. He didn't care if her lips moved back. This was for him and his need. His sanity. Hysterian pushed into her until she was forced to lean back against the table.

Cups and bottles fell aside as he released her neck with one of his hands and cupped her sex.

Alexa moaned and jerked, and he groped her sex hard, pressing the pads of his fingers where her entrance would be, cursing the layers of cloth between them. Cursing because he couldn't remove them. Her sex was so warm, so welcoming, that he groaned, dying for more. Instead, his palm slickened with secretion under the confines of his glove.

He tore his mouth off hers and enjoyed her breathy gasp. He rammed his fingers as hard as he could against her. His thumb searched for the spot where her little clit would be.

Alexa's hands came up and gripped his shoulders. Her hips jerked with a moan.

"You should be glad I don't smell him," Hysterian hissed, rubbing her sex. "You wouldn't like it if I did."

She whimpered. "Why are you doing this to me?"

His thumb pressed hard into her clit, and she jumped. "Because you do worse to me."

Another moan filled his ears, and her face shuttered. Her tongue came out to moisten pretty, raw lips.

I did that. Hysterian slid his hand from her neck and rubbed them. *I made them raw.*

"Then take me and be done with it," Alexa cried, pushing her body up against his. "Do it now!"

He cupped her hard as her hips bounced. "You're not ready." *I'm not ready...*

"Fuck you—I am! Just do it already. I can't stand this anymore! I need you out of my head." She started tearing at his suit. "I need you out of my head," she said again with more desperation.

Hysterian surged back and caught her hands.

"No," she whimpered. "Keep touching me. I need more." She writhed, trying to pull her hands out of his grasp but unable to.

He licked his lips. "You need more, is it?"

"Yes!"

"You need me to stick my cock in you?"

"Yes," she cried again. "Please."

"Say it."

Her gaze implored him.

"That was a fucking order, Dear, say it."

"I need..."

"Go on."

"I need you inside me."

"Who?"

"You."

"Glad to hear it." He moved her hands above her head and held them there. "I'm really fucking glad to hear that, Alexa," he groaned. "Because when it happens, it's going to hurt."

"Thank you," she whispered.

Desire surged through him, erupting power through his systems. He looked into her eyes and saw pain and desperation within them. He saw what he often caught on his own face when he was alone: misery. Misery for wanting something you can't or shouldn't have, shame for being unable to be a better person, and the acceptance that you're a little fucked up in the head.

Alexa had secrets. He knew that now.

He wanted to know them... He wanted to fuck them out of her.

Hysterian reached up and pulled at her half-fallen bun.

Rich black hair, silken and slightly wavy, fell over her shoulders and down her back. No longer was it stiff and unnatural. He'd added sweet-smelling scents to the dye, scents that he enjoyed.

Beautiful. He slid his gloved fingers through a strand at her shoulder. Alexa Dear had beautiful hair. Long, soft, and easy to grab.

To yank.

"Please fuck me. I don't know how much longer I can take this." There was pain in her voice. A lot of pain.

His eyes found hers. He would love to do just that. But couldn't. If she just looked at him hard enough, she'd see that his entire body was growing damp and that his undersuit was sticking to him.

"I don't want you going near Raul again," he said.

Her brow creased. "I work with him—we share a room."

"Not anymore."

Hysterian straightened, and Alexa rose on her elbows. She reached between her legs when his hand left, pulling at the clothes bunched up there. He'd tried hard to pierce her cunt...

"Where am I going to sleep then? My things?" she asked.

"You can stay in my quarters." The words left his mouth before he could stop them. Hysterian backed up another step, putting space between them. He continued to watch her hand between her legs as she adjusted herself. "It's clean. I don't use the bed."

"Your...quarters?"

Her hand finally fell away. She closed her legs with a sad moan.

"Yes," he snapped. "My quarters." He pivoted away before he attacked her again. Because all he wanted to do was give in and take what he craved, regardless of the damage that would cause.

"You're leaving?" she asked, when he rubbed his face and made his way for the exit.

"It's late, Dear, and we have a warp to prepare for. Get some rest."

"Wait!"

He turned to see her standing, hugging herself, the very picture of haunted confusion. It didn't make sense. Her reaction tonight made no sense at all. She was combative, desperate, even scared, and he had no idea why. He needed to get away, for his sake, but for hers more.

She should be fucking scared. I'm not well…

Hysterian deleted the thought before he could finish it.

"Can I see your face?" she asked, curling into herself further.

My face?

He tugged down the part of his suit covering his nose and mouth. Secretion was all over his skin, but it wouldn't look any different from sweat. He faced her fully and she stared at him, hard, harder than any normal person should be. Like she was trying to figure him out…

"Well?" he prompted when she just continued to look. It was time for him to escape and lock himself in the bridge tonight. If he didn't soon, he was certainly going to risk her life and touch her.

He needed a shower more than ever, but he'd just given his room away.

"You look exactly like I thought you would."

His jaw ticked. "Then you have a good imagination—"

"Hysterian…" she interrupted. "Why are you doing this to me?" Her voice was so low he barely heard her.

"Because I want you, Alexa, and there is nothing in this

universe or the next that will change that." He turned and made his way to the door. "Goodnight."

He walked out, not waiting for her response. What he didn't tell her was that he would go to the worst lengths possible to get what he wanted. That he'd only begun to feel emotions like guilt and remorse recently, and he still shut them out most of the time. That he was beyond fucked, and easily jealous.

That she should quit and run, far, far away and never look back.

He needed the *Questor* to get to Libra Station quickly. For both their sakes.

Hysterian shook, forcing his steps to the bridge. Because if he turned back again...

He was either going to kill Raul, Alexa, or both.

ALEXA DIDN'T MOVE for a long time. Even when her desire died down, she couldn't make herself move. If she did, she was afraid her soul would fall right out of her and no one would be there to catch it, not even her dad.

Hysterian hadn't fucked her like he said he would, instead he fucked with her head. He always fucked with her head.

She didn't notice Raul had come back for her until he was standing in front of her.

"Alexa, are you okay?" he asked.

She shuddered. "Yeah. I'm okay."

It would be so much easier if she liked Raul. So much easier. She wished it was Raul who she wanted.

But she didn't and the more she tried, the worse it got. Any harder and she might start hating him instead.

Raul glanced at the table behind her. "What happened?"

Raul wasn't the one who'd taken up residence in her head. It wasn't his hand she wanted between her legs; it wasn't his smile she wanted to see. She only wanted the coldness that Hysterian brought.

"Nothing." She was so tired and desperate for her bed. "Let's go." She made her way out of the lounge before Raul could question her further. She heard him catch up behind her.

"I shouldn't have left you. I'm sorry."

"Please, I don't want to talk about it. I just want to sleep."

"All right. That I can do."

She didn't go to Hysterian's quarters. She couldn't go to his quarters, knowing what awaited her there. Even if he wasn't there, even if she could use his bed and explore his room, she just couldn't do it.

I begged him to fuck me. Begged him.

And he hadn't.

I begged him!

She'd never be able to sleep in his room after that.

And he hadn't even touched her. *I begged, and he made a fool out of me.*

Raul followed her into their shared quarters, and without even going into the bathroom to change, Alexa slipped into her bunk.

"Alexa," Raul said before she closed the privacy screen. "I'm here if you need anything."

She didn't respond, only closed her privacy screen. The darkness and quiet helped little. Hysterian was the only thing now, and she realized he was only ever going to be the only thing in her head. Raul had been a stupid distraction.

And now, she had Hysterian's terribly beautiful angelic face to curse her.

She stared into the darkness and only saw him.

She slid her hand down her body and under the lip of her pants.

THIRTEEN

Alexa feigned sickness and avoided Raul and the rest of the crew. Pretending to have a headache and her monthly made it easy enough to stop Pigeon from demanding that she go to medical and get checked out.

As for Hysterian, he was everywhere.

Everywhere. Like a waking nightmare. He'd always been in her dreams, but now he was there when she was awake as well.

She could've sworn that the moment she closed her eyes at night, he was sliding her screen open and staring at her. Even he tried to haul her into medical, saying he didn't smell her monthly, and she'd locked herself in her quarters since.

He knew she was lying.

Of course he knew she was lying.

Still, he was outside her quarters every time she left them. He was in the lounge at night after shift's end, keeping everyone but Pigeon away. He was leaving things for her to find whenever she least expected them.

First the dye, and then hair ties. She found high-quality coffee beans next to the brewer in the lounge, and a rare penny coin lying on her bedding. She knew it had to be him... There was no one else.

It was like he knew what he was doing to her and he wanted it to continue. He wanted her to think of him and nothing else. He was angry she hadn't moved into his room. When he brought it up, she changed the subject. Alexa shook her head. She hated him, but found he wasn't cruel or evil, but something she couldn't put her finger on. She wished he'd just *be* cruel and evil. There was no way he could know how much he messed with her head.

Could he?

She'd never told a soul about what happened to her father. And unless Hysterian dug deep, there was no evidence on the network to link her to her father. All Hysterian would find is her credentials, her credit, her lack of a current address, and maybe—just maybe—her link to Elyria.

Daniels had been from Elyria too, so it couldn't be an issue if she was, right?

As for Raul... It was easy for her to avoid him. She barely saw him anymore. Hysterian kept him busy. Raul tried to take care of her too, bringing her food and coffee, but it went untouched.

Raul now had double the workload, and it was because of her. But she didn't mind the space. She could live with the guilt. It would only be a couple of days. Hysterian wouldn't hurt him.

She hoped.

In the time she'd spent with Hysterian, he managed to be a decent captain, and rather level-headed when it came to everything but the two of them. It couldn't all be a lie.

It would be easier if it was.

Alexa straightened her uniform jacket. *I can't hide forever.*

She prepared to leave her quarters. It was the end of the night shift cycle, and she'd managed to dress without waking Raul. His snores filled her ears. Getting a start on the day and catching up on her work would make the transition back into normalcy easier. She wasn't one to slack off, and the last few days had taken their toll on her in multiple ways.

Alexa prayed Hysterian wouldn't be on the other side of the door.

She straightened and walked out of the room. Cold and dark, the large menagerie greeted her with blissful silence. She released a sigh of relief and headed for her desk. The lights brightened around her.

She glanced once at the door leading to the rest of the ship, but it remained closed. Comforted by that fact, she rubbed her face and fingerprinted into her station.

A thumping noise pierced the silence.

The male locust was standing on its back legs, staring at her. Its two lower hands banged the glass. But it was its ribbed purplish penis that caught her attention. The tip hit the glass and left a smear of something behind. It wasn't the only creature on the *Questor* hungry for something it shouldn't want.

The male held no intelligence in its gaze. It wanted one thing and one thing only: to breed and only breed. The female locusts, on the other hand, slept peacefully.

I'll make sure they'll get time together to play. They're probably thrilled to be kept away from a male like that.

If the male locust was intent on making her uncomfortable, she was going to make sure he felt the same. She and

Raul never let him with the females—they couldn't risk it. Alexa had read everything released on the network about the locusts of Atrexia. Most of the information came from the research labs that the *Questor* was currently picking up from and delivering to.

They were the closest related alien species discovered to the long-dead baboons of Earth, even resembling them in small ways. Why anyone cared about this was beyond her, but Raul, who was from Earth, told her Earth peoples had an ongoing initiative to restore the world to its former glory. That very few wild animals still existed on the planet. The rich living on Earth, along with activists, wanted the forests and animals back, if not for their own pleasure, then for bragging rights.

Thump. Thump thump thump thump!

She shivered and looked back at her screens. Related to baboons or not, she didn't know why anyone would want something like a locust running wild in their backyard.

The male terrified her. In a way that not even Hysterian did. Crazed and wild, she only saw monstrous intent in the locust's frenzied eyes.

The thumping continued.

"It won't be here much longer."

Alexa jumped and swiveled in her chair. Hysterian was standing directly behind her.

She shot to her feet. "Captain," she gasped.

His piercing gaze, so different than the locust's—but no less scary—scanned her from head to toe.

"You look like you're doing better," he said.

"I am." She spun her chair around and gripped the back of it, happy it was between them.

Silence clung to the air like molasses.

"I want to apologize," he said.

He wants to apologize? Now? She pursed her lips, holding back an absurd giggle.

"We land on Libra today," he continued like he had no idea what kind of turmoil she'd been experiencing the last few days. "Getting off the ship will be good for us, all of us." Hysterian's eyes slid to the closed door of her quarters.

Raul?

But he went on, his voice low. "I would have preferred you to have taken over my quarters, *Dear*."

"Would you have left them?"

"Be thankful he hasn't touched you again."

His words made her stiffen. "How could he? You keep him busy. He can't do anything more than work and sleep."

Hysterian cocked his head, twinkles of teal sparked like tiny stars in his irises. His hands reached out and grabbed the back of the chair besides hers. She pulled her hands away before his gloved fingers touched her.

"Then...I've successfully saved his life."

A laugh tore from her throat. "So you are a murderer."

Hysterian's eyes flashed, and he dropped his hands from the chair. "I never said I wasn't."

Somehow hearing him say it, hearing him confess, righted her head. She knew he was—she'd lived with his evilness—and now, she no longer had to doubt it.

Because she had. In the past month, she had begun to doubt it a lot.

"Join me," he stated, turning around and walking out of the menagerie.

She watched him go, twitching to deny him, but her curiosity won out. He was still her captain, after all. And she was intrigued.

She also just accused him of murder, and he hadn't denied it...

He was standing in the armory across the passageway from the lab, his back to her as he stared at a metal case along the back wall. She stepped to the threshold and glanced around. She'd only glimpsed the inside of this room several times during requisitions but had never been inside it. The room was much bigger than she expected with rows upon rows of locked metal and glass cases and drawers. The *Questor's* weapons stash had more space than all the crew combined.

Excitement filled her.

There had to be something in here that could help her. Alexa walked up to a random case.

It was locked by body scan technology and fingerprint analysis. She heard Hysterian approach from behind her—his abrupt heat clouded her mind. The case scanned him and the drawer opened for her.

Inside were more scanners, not guns.

Hysterian lifted one and tested it in his grip. "This is a Glamour. It distorts your appearance for a short time if you're wearing the corresponding suit. And this"—he picked up another, putting the first back down—"is a Stopper. It surrounds the user in a shell that blocks out external electromagnetic interference. A must-have for any Cyborg dealing with the underground."

"Underground?"

"The world that lies under the one we live in. Ruled by traffickers, mob bosses, and the like. They fight differently. They're better at it."

He handed it to her and she turned the Stopper in her palm. It wouldn't help her.

"Why are you telling me this?" she asked.

He shook his head. "No reason. And this," Hysterian said, keeping her attention moving, "is for you."

He took back the Stopper and handed her a gun.

Alexa stared at the firearm before taking it. "For me?"

"I don't want you leaving the ship without protection, and I will be too busy to do that myself."

Another absurd giggle escaped. "Are you sure it's not to protect me from you?" She turned the gun in her hand, liking the weight and feel of it.

"This, *Dear*, wouldn't be able to dent in my frame, but it will stop anyone else in their path."

"So what could make a dent in your frame?" she asked, meeting his gaze.

Mischief reached his eyes, and she knew he was smirking under his suit.

"Are you planning on shooting me?" he asked.

"Maybe?"

He cocked his head, rubbing his finger over the cloth covering his mouth. "Follow me."

Alexa sucked in a breath as he strode to the back corner of the room and stopped before a glass case. She followed him to see what he was going to reveal.

There was a weapon that could hurt a Cyborg? Perhaps easily?

And he was going to show her it?

The darkness of the glass vanished, revealing a myriad of guns in different sizes hooked to a rack within. In the middle lay something she'd never seen before. The silver metal of the weapon nearly glowed, and there was an extra glass case around it that the other guns didn't have.

"That, right there, is a Brickbuster," he told her, indicating the gun. "There are maybe several dozen in existence. I helped design it."

"What does it do?"

"It busts a Cyborg's shell open."

"Really? How?"

He laughed. It wasn't a warm laugh. "Should I be worried?"

"Yes."

"Very well. The buster uses pyrizian ammo simultaneously with laser tech. The same rare metal most Cyborgs are made of. It holds nanoparticles like organic matter holds bacteria. With the combination and force of the fire, it can break through our interior shell and straight into the organs protected beneath. The nanoparticles infect us, flooding our systems like a virus, ultimately skewing those same systems and corrupting them. When our systems shut down, death soon follows if we're not stabilized quickly. But a shot to the leg is nowhere near as deadly as a shot to the head."

"And you have one on the *Questor*? Why?"

"Every retriever for the EPED is issued a weapon like this in some capacity. Many of us already have something like it in our personal caches. We're prepared for any circumstance."

"Even going against your own?"

"We all know what happened to Zeph," he muttered. "You'd be surprised to know there are others out there like me who are not built like me, Alexa—neoborgs, cybots, and mechas. Who knows what kind of technology the Trentians are developing? Preparation is key."

She stared at the gun, at the power such a small thing held, and clenched her hand to stop herself from reaching for it through the glass. "Right," she whispered. This was it. This was what she needed to finish the job.

This, and Hysterian facing away from her so she could get a clear shot to the back of his head.

The glass dimmed and the weapons vanished. Hysterian motioned to the other gun she still held.

"That won't hurt me, or others like me, but it will startle me for a moment—perhaps a moment is all you'll need—and allow you to get away. It will stop a human or alien in its tracks, as long as you're a good shot. Are you?"

"I trained."

"Good. Keep it with you on Libra."

Alexa glanced at her new weapon once more and made sure the safety was on before sliding it into the lip of her pants. This wasn't a gift she wasn't going to take from him.

If the captain of the ship you're working on gives you a gun, you keep it. She licked her lips.

Hysterian's gaze dropped to her mouth before quickly leaving her. He moved to another case, pulling a weapon from it and sliding it into his own pants. And for a sliver of a second, she glimpsed something underneath his uniform. He wore another mesh covering she'd never seen the likes of. One of the suits needed for the scanners maybe?

Her eyes trailed back to that particular case.

It occurred to her that they were alone as she stared at it, and he was between her and the exit again.

Her heart thundered. He turned and looked at her, heated yet cold, and wrong in every single way.

Will he trap me to the wall? Her toes curled. *Will he...*

He turned and went to the door.

Her brow furrowed. The blush on her cheeks drained. Hysterian stopped and waited for her, standing at the open panel, as cool and unavailable as ever. She approached and slid past him, out of the armory. The door shut and locked behind her.

"I'm glad you're feeling better," he said.

"Thank you."

His hand came up, and she flinched. He cupped her cheek anyway. It was gentle, almost affectionate. Her heart stuttered. It was nothing like any of the other times he touched her. She wanted to move away, but didn't.

"If you ignore an order again, you'll spend the rest of your time here in the brig." Fury filled his eyes.

She jerked back, and his hand fell. He walked away, leaving her in the passageway alone.

Alexa collected herself before making her way back to her station. Just as she sat, Raul popped out of their quarters.

"Your stuff is gone," he announced with a broken yawn.

"What?"

"In the room, everything is gone. Did you clean up while I was sleeping? You going somewhere?"

Alexa shot to her feet and rushed into the room. Inside, it was the same, Raul's mess was everywhere, and her bunk —she shot open the privacy screen—was completely devoid of everything. She rushed to the bathroom to find all her toiletries gone as well.

"I didn't..."

He took it.

"You're not leaving us, are you?" Raul asked.

She shook her head.

Hysterian had taken everything she owned, and she knew exactly where he'd put it all.

Alexa stormed out of the room and ran to the second floor, Raul calling out behind her. At the end of the hall, she saw one of the ship's androids enter the captain's quarters. The bridge's doors were closed.

"Morning, Dear," Pigeon greeted as she rushed past him.

She pushed past the android as she entered the room.

And there her stuff was, upon the bed. Two other androids were taking her extra clothes and placing them neatly in a dresser. Another carried her toiletries into the attached bathroom.

"How dare he," she hissed, going to the bed and snatching her razor up. The android she'd pushed past took it from her hand and headed for the bathroom. Her lips parted.

"What the hell?" She rarely cursed. She grabbed the remaining stuff on the bed and made her way toward the exit. One of the androids stopped her. "Let me leave," she demanded.

"We are ordered to move your belongings into this room, Ms. Dear," it responded dryly, mechanically. "We must follow orders." It reached for her.

She held her items to her chest but the android pulled them from her grip. After a few minutes of struggling, she gave up. And when she turned, Pigeon and Raul were watching her from outside the room.

"You and the captain?" Raul said with disgust.

Alexa gritted her teeth. "I'm not with the captain."

Raul looked like he didn't believe her. Pigeon appeared shamed, curious. She stormed out of the room and fled to the menagerie, cursing under her breath.

He couldn't do this to her, he couldn't force her to stay with him. She refused. There was no way she was sleeping in Hysterian's room—ever. Just because she wanted him didn't mean she wanted to get any closer to him, especially in that way. She would never put herself in such a vulnerable position.

She wouldn't be alive today if she had in the past.

He's gone too far.

"Prepare for docking," Hysterian's voice invaded her ears from the intercom, "at seven hundred hours."

Alexa tugged the gun from her pants and threw it in the trash.

I can protect myself.

It may have had a tracker on it anyway.

FOURTEEN

Hysterian waited until the entirety of his crew had vacated the ship before he left. He wanted them to think he'd stayed behind so they wouldn't, so they'd find other arrangements and maybe not come back at all.

He'd been keeping tabs on Alexa for days, and knew she would probably kill him right now if given the chance, and he deserved it. He had given her a gun for that very reason. He deserved to be shot, quartered, and hanged. He deserved that tenfold and more.

He lifted her underwear to his nose and breathed in her scent.

Unfortunately, it was clean underwear, but he could imagine her arousal clinging to the cotton. He wanted them dirty. He wanted them covered with her slick and his semen. He'd been bucking for days, half-mad.

She refused an order.

He glared at the bed in his quarters. *Not for much longer.*

After today, he was determined to keep her close, when he knew he wouldn't harm her in his lust. Today, he was visiting a brothel knowing it would slake him. If he was lucky, it would do more than that and rid him of his obsession for Alexa entirely. A Cyborg could fucking hope.

Hysterian stuffed Alexa's underwear into his pants and around his cock. The cloth was damp within seconds, clinging to him.

He made his way off the ship and into the bustling port, barely acknowledging the androids restocking his ship. He trusted Horace's capacity to do his job.

No, he wasn't going to linger any longer. He had an appointment to make.

And he had Raul to take care of.

Libra Station was one of the rare, fully colonized stations around the known universe. It was originally established hundreds of years ago as a giant broken freighter ship, and over the years had expanded into a state. Ship after ship had been added to it until they were ships no longer, but instead an interconnected system of docks and floors where people lived and worked.

There were at least a hundred thousand or so inhabitants at any given time. Whether they lived on Libra or not, its docks were always bustling. Many crew workers would rent a room on a port like Libra—something no bigger than a hole with a bunk and a desk—and use that as their address. Those same crew workers only went home when their jobs happened to bring them there.

He'd checked if Alexa had a room on Libra. She didn't. She didn't have a room anywhere as far as his searches went.

It wasn't uncommon for people in her field to not have an address either, if they chose not to invest in a hole in the wall. It saved money in the long run. Sometimes, they were forced to put their earnings elsewhere.

Paying back fines, paying off bail, or perhaps they had a sick family member that needed help with medical bills.

He could've gleamed a lot about Alexa if she had a room. Though he still learned something because she *didn't*.

She was paid well. Above average for her position. His whole crew was paid well. If she wasn't keeping up a home, where was her money going? He'd have to request special privileges to see her bank account. He wasn't an expert hacker like many other Cyborgs.

People dashed past him as he made his way off the docks. Some stared when they realized there was a Cyborg, but most had other things on their mind. The further Hysterian got from Earth, the less people cared about Cyborgs.

He kept an eye out for his crew, mainly Alexa.

Deeper in the station were shops, hundreds of them, enticing those who were traveling to spend all their money and credits on items that they might not be able to get elsewhere. Stations like Libra were ruled by the government but since they were not rooted on a landmass of any kind, the laws were murky. Something that may be illegal on Earth or Gliese, might not be illegal on Libra. No one cared if you had stolen shells from Tau-Ceti here or bought a Coke with coke in it. As long as the systems ran and taxes were paid, those in charge paid no attention.

Though, if you did break one of Libra's precious laws and were caught, you'd spend the rest of your sentence regretting it. The jails on ports like this were some of the seediest. It was easy to forget about people in a place like Libra.

Which was why Hysterian averted his trip to Atrexia a little while longer. He could get his relief, and then expunge the security systems of his passing entirely. Systems, electricity, and power surged everywhere, ready to be manipulated and digitally fucked.

Hysterian made his way deeper into the hollowed-out halls of the port, lit up by neon signs, smoke, and the occasional exhaust outlet. Hecklers for wares called out to him while exotic scents, mixed with chemicals, invaded his nose.

Ahead, he saw the first strip of pink lights indicating the district change. The crowd wasn't nearly as big here as it was near the main shops.

He came to a stop in front of a giant, pink neon heart. A partially naked dancer swayed within it. She wore braids of shimmery white lingerie, that reflected the pink glow of the lights.

When she realized Hysterian was watching her, she bent forward and blew him a kiss. Her nipple slipped out.

This was the type of woman he needed. Someone without shame. Someone who wasn't easily offended, and knew the lascivious dance between a man and a woman. He wasn't interested in an inexperienced woman. Damsels in white gowns, the kind who needed saving, were better off being saved by a man who wasn't him. His patience was limited. His ability to be gentle almost didn't exist at all.

Hysterian rubbed his chest where Alexa had rested her brow. She was better off seeking comfort elsewhere, even with Raul.

His jaw ticked. Anyone but Raul.

It was bad enough knowing that Alexa had kissed him, really kissed him, when Hysterian was desperate for the brush of her lips and fingers on him. He hated Raul, was jealous of Raul, and he wanted Raul's blood in a jar for that reason alone.

Hysterian was created by some of the best minds, the

best tech in the universe, and he couldn't even have someone like Alexa? He twisted the wristcon on his arm and swiped some credits toward the dancer.

Pink hearts filled the smoky air above her head to shower down upon her. She danced amongst them. He smirked.

"Thank you," she purred, lifting her arms above her head. "Would you like to meet me inside?"

Hysterian powered off his wristcon. "I have an appointment."

The dancer pouted. "Too bad."

"Too bad."

He couldn't take her up on the meeting even if he wanted to. She was a human. He couldn't touch her.

If he could...he'd be fucking Alexa right now, and wouldn't be here at all.

Hysterian turned toward the entrance as a group of men took his spot. Pink hearts flashed around him as he shoved the drapes of cloth aside to head in. Thick incense enveloped him. The bustle of the port disappeared as the cloth settled back into place behind him. The brothel was dimly lit, with pink, red, and purple cloth draped over every wall and every table. Pillows were scattered across the floor, surrounding little tables where some patrons sat and drank and fondled the females entertaining them.

He went straight for the headmistress, an Amazon of a woman smoking a hookah with several others behind the entryway counter. Hooded eyes met his when she looked at him. Smoke trickled from the sides of her mouth.

She rose and sauntered to him. There was a deep scar on her chin, sectioning off part of her face. It didn't distract from her appeal, though, instead enhancing it. Hysterian would bet a hefty amount the headmistress accepted clientele—if they were willing to pay enough for her attention. Her enormous breasts alone were a young man's wet dream.

"How can I help you today, honey?" she asked.

"I have an appointment."

"Of course you do." Her eyes slid down his body. "Who's it with?"

"Your most expensive bot."

She smiled. "Ah, so you're the Cyborg. I thought you might be. Right this way." She turned and swayed her way down a passageway off to the left, past the tables and pillows, and into a dimly lit corridor hidden behind even more drapes of cloth. She lifted them and waited for him to pass through and join her.

Behind him, the sounds of the port rose in volume for a split second, indicating the arrival of another. Hysterian glanced behind him and stopped.

It was Raul.

"You coming sweetheart? She's waiting for you," the headmistress said, and hummed. "Just about in a frenzy for you."

Raul let out an appreciative whistle as he looked around the brothel. When he was about to turn toward Hysterian, Hysterian stepped into the corridor only to shift the cloth aside to watch his subordinate.

Of course Raul would be here. There were other places like this brothel on Libra, but not as well known or discreet. Hysterian had seen the man jerk his dick right out in the open, yards away from where Alexa was sleeping, where she could've seen him if she'd left her quarters.

Hysterian's hands clenched.

A scantily clad sexbot wearing a golden slave costume approached Raul. She placed the flat of her palms on his chest and leaned up. She whispered something in his ear.

"There something else I could get you, sweet pea? Someone catch your eye? Me, perhaps?" the headmistress asked when she realized Hysterian wasn't going to follow her deeper into the establishment.

"That man," he nodded toward Raul, moving the drapes aside enough for the headmistress to see.

She sidled up next to him. "What about him?"

"Change of plans. I want you to give him my appointment."

"You do? Are you sure?" The Amazon pouted.

"Yes, but I'll need to pay extra for discretion."

"What are you thinking?"

"I want to watch."

She eyed him. "You're a kinky one, aren't you, love?" She hummed some more, tapping her finger on her lips. "I'd have to charge you triple what you already owe."

"Quadruple it if you ignore the screams."

"Oh, honey. We always ignore the screams. We use safe words."

"These will be different screams."

The sexbot leaned away from Raul and jutted out her chest. Raul smiled and pulled down the strips of cloth hiding her breasts, cupping them in his hands when they were out on display.

Hysterian gritted his teeth.

Raul squeezed the sexbot's breasts, flicked her nipples, testing them and her response like she was a non-sentient piece of meat he was inspecting to potentially purchase. The sexbot moaned just as another approached from the side. He turned to her just as she pulled down her top.

Hysterian let the drapes fall back into place. The head-mistress straightened from where she was watching beside him.

"I'll need the money upfront," she said.

Hysterian flicked open his wristcon.

"I'll also need reassurance that whatever happens, my establishment, and all those who work within it, will be safe."

"They won't come to any harm. In fact, give them the night off. I'll pay for the house," he told her as he swiped an exorbitant amount of money her way.

Dollar signs instead of hearts materialized in the air between them. The headmistress beamed while the green glow illumed her face.

"Oh, you're just a doll. The room is at the end of the hall, last door on your left." She flounced past him and back through the drapery. The headmistress clapped her hands and went straight for Raul and the sexbots gathered around him.

Hysterian watched as the headmistress talked Raul up. When one of the sexbots started kissing Raul's neck, disgust filled Hysterian and he made his way to the room.

Alexa could do better. What she saw in Raul, Hysterian had no idea, but he loathed that she'd been sharing a room with the sex-crazed cretin for over a month now.

Not anymore.

He made fucking sure of that. Alexa was going to be in his bed tonight, whether she liked it or not. She'd be safe there.

Hysterian scanned the room, finding a place to wait. Like the rest of the brothel, the walls were littered with drapes. The sexbot—his sexbot—was perched on the bed, wearing nothing but a scrap of red panties.

She watched him curiously but didn't say a word, eventually turning back toward the door.

He didn't have to wait long.

The door opened, and Raul stepped into the room, whistling out a breath when he saw what awaited him.

A state-of-the-art partially sentient female bot, perfect in every way. A man's dream. It didn't matter whether you liked redheads or blondes; the sexbot was able to shift her appearance based on the arousal level of her purchaser.

"*Holy God*," Raul muttered as he approached the bed.

She went from being perched to turning over and spreading her legs on all fours. Her long blond hair shifted to black, and her flesh paled as she pushed her ass out for Raul.

His hands came out to frame it.

The sexbot took on the appearance of Alexa. In every way but her frigid primness. Raul rubbed his hand across his mouth as the bot looked back at him.

"I need you," she whimpered. "Daddy."

Oh fucking hell. Hysterian had enough. He surged forward and threw Raul up against the wall. The sexbot ran out of the room behind him.

"What the fuck!?" Raul yelled, thrashing. "Captain?" His surprise soon gave way to fear.

Hysterian threw Raul onto the bed by his neck.

He twisted and fled to the other end. Hysterian grabbed Raul's boot and dragged him back.

Raul kicked like a child, raising his hands to his face. "Fucking hell! What the fucking hell!?"

Hysterian leaned over him, clasping Raul's neck. "Hello, Raul."

His eyes widened, then he sneered. "Do it," Raul spat. "Do it! You piece of shit! You want to. I can tell."

Hysterian gripped harder, pressing into Raul's trachea.

Raul coughed, croaked. "Kill me, you Cyborg mother-fucker! She'll never fucking forgive you."

Hysterian's systems seized. His fingers bit into Raul's neck, breaking skin. All he could see was Raul jacking off, Raul laughing, Raul teasing Alexa. "You should have never kissed her." He saw that.

He saw everything.

He found it on the *Questor*'s security footage.

Raul's face went from white to red. "Fucking worth it."

Hysterian's nostrils flared. His fingers twisted.

"She'll never be yours," Raul rasped. "You don't know her like I do."

"You think you know her?"

"I know she isn't what you think she is."

Hysterian scowled. After one last brutal squeeze, he tore his hand from Raul's neck and yanked off his glove.

Raul's hands shot up and wrapped around his neck. Curling onto his side, he sputtered and coughed. Hysterian folded his glove, setting it on the table next to the bed. Raul met his eyes when Hysterian turned back to him.

"You have no idea what you're doing," Raul wheezed.

"Stop. Fucking. Talking."

Raul shunted and rolled off the bed. Hysterian grabbed the back of Raul's uniform and yanked him to his chest. He wrapped one arm around Raul as his crewmate cursed and yelled, forcing him to still. He placed his bare hand before Raul's face, his long fingers outstretched.

"What are you doing?"

Hysterian covered Raul's face with his hand and closed his eyes.

Raul thrashed and tore at Hysterian's hand. "What the fuck are you doing!?"

"'*You'll see, Dear. You'll never want another man between your legs after me. I knew you had a rack to die for hiding under all these layers,*'" Hysterian whispered Raul's words back to him as Hysterian's glands opened. A danger-ously high dose of batrachotoxin, mixed with nanobots to pierce the skin layer, released from his glands.

It was the first toxin Hysterian ever had in his arsenal. The one he was created with. The one his body naturally made, implanted within his systems by the very doctors who built him, enhanced to meet Hysterian's worst needs.

Raul screamed, kicked, rammed his elbow into Hyster-ian, but ultimately succumbed. Everyone always succumbed. Within moments, Raul had enough toxin in his system to send him straight into paralysis. His body went limp, and Hysterian dropped his hand from Raul's face. He hauled Raul's body onto the bed and laid him out.

Hysterian pulled out a needle from his inside pocket and injected Raul with tetrodotoxin, a counter to his poison. Just enough to keep Raul alive, alive and in misery until he recovered.

Hysterian dropped the needle and crushed it under his boot. He stared at Raul for a time. The ion blocker would be in Raul's system even with the counter for weeks to come. Hysterian made sure of it.

"You will suffer a day for every second you were touching her," he whispered into Raul's ear.

When Raul finally did rise and have full use of his body again, the *Questor*, Alexa, and the rest of the crew would be on the other side of the universe.

Hysterian exhaled, tugged his glove back on, and turned for the door. He stepped out to find the headmistress and the sexbot he ordered waiting for him on the other side.

"Is it done?" the headmistress pushed off the wall where she had been leaning, smoking a cig.

"I'm satisfied." His eyes slid to the sexbot, who retained Alexa's features. Her black hair, her pale skin. But the eyes were wrong, and the shape of the sexbot's face. Everything was off. Her scent, her straight nose, even her height. He flicked his eyes back to the brothel's owner.

"Very good. We like it when our patrons achieve satisfaction, especially well-paying patrons such as yourself." She ran her hand down his arm.

He grabbed her hand. "Don't."

The headmistress smiled. "You still have your appointment." She stepped back to indicate the sexbot, tugging her hand free. "If you're in the mood."

All he was in the mood for now was to get off of fucking Libra and back into space, far, far away from the trouble lying in the room behind him. Killing Raul would make his life easier, but Raul had done nothing personally to Hysterian besides touching what was his. He'd killed Daniels already. His quota for this trip was done. And he still had the body to dispose of. Killing Raul would start a precedent Hysterian wanted to avoid.

He'd left Raphael and Elyria to start a new life, a better one, one he could be proud of having. He wasn't going to have that life with a wake of corpses floating behind him.

Nightheart could deny him the cure if that happened. If Hysterian fucked up as badly as some other Cyborgs working for his new boss had in the past, Nightheart would lose his shit. It wasn't worth the risk.

"I'm not," he told the woman. "But the man in the room behind me will need a place to recover. He'll need to be taken care of. Do that for me, will you?"

"I think we can manage that." The headmistress smiled again. She turned to the sexbot. "He's yours, love. Make him happy, okay?"

"Yes, ma'am."

The sexbot moved to enter the room.

Hysterian grabbed her wrist, stopping her. "Turn back into a blond and stay that way. Are we clear?"

The sexbot nodded, changing the color of her hair and skin back to the way they were earlier. He released her, and she fled into the room. Hysterian nodded at the head-mistress and exited the brothel, far more satisfied than he ever planned on being, leaving it.

He stretched his fingers before curling them into his palms. The noise of the port flooded his audio.

He hadn't felt this good in months.

His head was clear. He may not have fucked, but Raul was gone and Alexa was all his now. Hysterian didn't have to worry about what was happening when he was busy. Raul was going to pay for touching what Hysterian wanted most.

He had no qualms with the rest of his crew. They were good workers who stayed in line, obeyed orders, and didn't ask probing questions. They were all a captain could ask for.

Hysterian cracked his neck and made his way through the seedier parts of the port, back toward the shops.

A weight lifted off his chest as his distance from Raul increased.

Hysterian scanned the rusty, piped ceiling, wondering how high it was—*at least two stories*—and how much force he'd need to be able to jump and reach it. The frog in him was eager, excited. Sprightly. Moments like these, when he didn't hate the universe and everything in it, were rare.

Hysterian cleared his throat and continued.

A textile shop caught his attention. He'd asked Horace to find out if there were any shipments of nanocloth on or coming to Libra while they were docked, and Horace hadn't gotten back to him yet. Hysterian shifted course and made his way to the store.

He had extra time on his hands.

He wasn't needed back on the *Questor* anytime soon.

And if the shop had what he was looking for...

His lips twitched under his suit. The day would end on an even better night.

FIFTEEN

Alexa fingered the soft material of the dress. It slipped across her hand like flowing water. She didn't have anything like it in her wardrobe—she'd never owned *anything* so nice, let alone own a dress at all. She had no need for one growing up, and so never had a reason to own one.

She didn't need one now either. Maybe later, maybe someday.

Alexa dropped her hand and she moved onto the next store where activewear and standard-issue space uniforms were being sold. She needed new clothes, but not a dress, and especially not the silky green one in the last shop.

Making her way toward the discounted stuff, she checked the time on her wristcon.

Eighteen hundred standard shift hours. She had thirty more minutes to waste before she had to meet up with Pigeon and Raul at Termite, a bar Pigeon insisted they all go to for a drink. She didn't want to go and had no intention of getting a drink, but anywhere was better than being on the ship.

She grabbed a couple of packs of medium shirts, pants,

and a sweater for something to wear when she needed to pretend to be cold. And socks. She couldn't forget socks. Alexa paid for her clothes and ducked out.

For the past two hours, she'd been in and out of stores. She thought—when everyone disembarked to leave the *Questor*—that she'd just follow one of the other crewmates and join them on their errands. Raul at least would be free, right? But when her boots hit the terminal, they'd all vanished into the crowd, leaving her without a place to go.

That's fine. Alexa chewed on the inside of her cheek. *I shouldn't have expected company anyway.* She was used to it.

It was her fault for getting attached.

Libra wasn't anything new. The port didn't have the tri-suns of Elyria, the history of Earth, or the vastness of Titan. It was just a hunk of metal floating through space. Though she was swept away by the noise and Libra's buzzing crowds. Humans from all over the universe swarmed around her. Watching them was surprisingly interesting.

She gave them backstories and wished she was among them, that she was a captain of one of the many ships docked. It would never be, but she liked to pretend.

Alexa glanced at her wristcon again.

She had fifteen minutes until she needed to be at Termite. The bar was at the end of the dock and up the rafters, where people could drink and watch the bustle below at the same time.

She stopped at the last store on her list. The one Alexa had avoided. A lingerie shop. Stringy, lacy garments hung off androids in the front in colors of red, black, and gold. Some had chains, others were made of leather, and still, there was an entire corner where there wasn't any color at all—only bridal white.

Like anyone's coming here to buy wedding night under-garments.

Alexa shifted on her feet. *Maybe people here are into roleplay.* She glanced around uneasily.

She pretended to look at the store beside this one, selling textiles and bolts of cloth. But her eyes kept shifting back to the lingerie.

Damn it, just walk in.

She gritted her teeth and entered the shop. Glitter, sweet-scented perfume, and soft music met her upon the first step through the archway. She swept her gaze over the room. There, in the center of the store, clearly in view of the entrance, was a table with piles of underwear upon it in every material and color. Her fingers stretched out for the cotton underwear but stopped midway.

They fell upon silky black panties instead.

They would barely cover her, and there was a slit in them down the middle. *So you can wear them while having sex?* She rubbed the material between her finger and thumb. Alexa flushed, imagining what that would be like.

What Hysterian would do if he saw her in them...

Her callouses snagged in the material.

"Those are a favorite with the men here," a woman said from behind her.

Alexa pivoted, clutching the underwear to her chest. "I'm only looking."

It was an android. A beautiful, older-looking one. She wore a silky red robe, open in the front, to reveal perfect breasts wrapped up in ruby satin. Auburn hair fell over her shoulders in thick waves, ending on a curl down her back.

Alexa gripped the panties harder.

The lady smiled. "They'd look good on you."

"What would?"

The android's eyes twinkled. "Those panties, of course."

Alexa dropped her eyes. "Oh, right."

"I know just the thing to wear them with," the shopkeeper said, turning on her heel and stepping toward a rack exploding with black lingerie and lace. She yanked something out, and then another thing, and returned before Alexa could tell her not to. "This. This would match those panties and make you a goddess. Men will fall on their knees to worship you."

A black robe fell between them like a waterfall, and with it, a lacy garter belt with a matching bra. The back of the bra had a large, black bow.

A *gift*.

More than anything, Alexa wanted to touch the fabric. "You think so?" she whispered.

She imagined what Hysterian would do if he saw her in something like...*that*. A rush of excitement flooded her, and though she was thrilled in it, she hated it at the same time.

"A goddess." The android nodded. "Whoever the lucky guy is won't know what hit him."

Alexa inhaled.

The shopkeeper folded the lingerie in her arms, turned, and went toward a table where another android was helping a man.

Alexa had no choice but to follow.

"I don't know if I should..." she started to say.

The android wrapped and bagged the lingerie. "Nonsense. You have the assets. Now use them."

Alexa turned her wristcon on and swiped the funds toward the shopkeeper. Alexa looked down at her body and her lack of curves. "I don't think so."

The man beside her stepped away and checked her out.

Alexa stiffened.

He hummed, grabbing his bag from the android helping him. "She's right. You'll be fine." He inclined his head at Alexa and left the shop, leaving her an embarrassed mess as one of the shopkeepers nodded with him in agreement.

Alexa snatched her bag and peeked into it. What had she just bought? She closed it up tight and stuffed the bag in with her purchase from earlier. She turned to the android helping her.

"Make him beg," the android said.

Alexa shivered but nodded, her excitement wavering somewhere between dread and longing. Hysterian would never beg. Never.

But she really liked the idea of it.

She started to leave but pivoted right back, remembering why she was here at all in the first place.

Fifteen minutes later, she was rushing through the port toward Termite, having spent much longer in the lingerie shop than she had planned on. The shopkeeper convinced her that she could do her job wearing silk, satin, and thongs instead of cotton and linen. Now Alexa had more panties and bras than she would ever, ever need and in materials she never thought she'd ever own.

She pushed through the crowd gathering out in front of Termite, searching for Pigeon and Raul. The smell of liquor was strong here, and so was the laughter. Pushing through a group of men, she found Pigeon at the bar, holding a beer.

He waved when he saw her approach.

"Sorry I'm late," Alexa said. "Where's Raul?"

Pigeon shrugged. "Not here yet. And no worries, I was just enjoying a beer in the meantime. The Terraform Championship is on." He flicked a finger toward a screen behind the bar.

Alexa saw the two empty glass bottles next to Pigeon's elbow. "Or three."

"Hey. I'm on break, and it's not like there's anything for me to do anyway," he teased.

It was a running joke with the others. Pigeon was an engineer for a brand new ship that did not need an engineer...yet. He was often found reading a book in the lounge or playing word games on his wristcon in the middle of the day shift.

"And the Captain's hired help didn't like me sticking around to check out the *Questor's* water system with them," Pigeon continued. "Apparently, it's working just fine. It was fine the twelve times I checked it, but why listen to the expert?"

"Really? They found nothing wrong?" The water was almost always cold on the *Questor*, at least during the night shifts when most of the crew showered. "Odd." She liked cold water, so she didn't mind if the water system got fixed or not.

"It is what it is. They don't want us peons getting too comfortable now." Pigeon smiled.

Alexa leaned her elbows on the bar. "I think you're right."

Pigeon cocked a brow. "You go shopping?"

She started to shake her head but stopped, recalling what she'd bought, what was hiding in the bag hanging over her shoulder. "For some new clothes," she muttered. What would Pigeon or Raul say if they saw what she splurged on?

What would they think? She had no intention of wearing it, ever, especially not for Hysterian. If she wore the lingerie, it would be for herself.

What if Hysterian finds it?

Hell... Alexa secured her bag to her side. *I need to return it.* What if someone found it, even if it wasn't Hysterian? No one would look at her the same way. A month ago, she wouldn't have cared what Pigeon, Horace, or Raul thought about her. She did now. She cared a lot.

She liked having their respect. She wanted to keep it.

The man sitting on the stool beside Pigeon strode off. Alexa slid into his seat. "Can I...ask you a question, Pigeon?"

Pigeon lowered his beer. "Depends."

She swallowed. "Have you ever really wanted something? And I mean really wanted something, something you knew you shouldn't have, whether it was because it would be bad for you, or it was out of your reach?"

She wanted Hysterian. She shouldn't want Hysterian.

"Yeaah... Why?"

"What did you do?"

Pigeon swiveled to face her. "Well, that's not the kind of question I was expecting from you. Want to tell me what's wrong?"

"No."

Pigeon rubbed his chin. "Okay. It's private. Is this about you and the captain?"

Alexa stiffened. "What?" *How did he...?*

"You and the captain? That's what this is about, isn't it? Please, don't tell me it's about Raul... You can do better than that."

"I—" What was she supposed to say? "How did you know?"

Pigeon laughed. "I've been around a long time, been around a lot of women too for a great deal of it. I know when a man's messing up the peace. As a dad, I hated it. The captain has eyes for you. Is that the problem?"

"No, that's not it."

"Are you worried we're going to care if you start something up with him? Because I can tell you right now, I don't give a damn. I only want you to be careful."

Alexa threaded her fingers together on the bar. "I don't know what to do."

"Well, you need to break things off with Raul."

She sighed. "I know."

"He's not going to be happy about it."

Boy did she know that. She suspected sharing a room with Raul wasn't going to work long-term. "I don't want to want the...captain," she admitted.

"We don't always get to choose what the heart wants, kiddo. Sometimes it chooses for you."

She placed her hands in her lap. "What should I do?"

"I don't know what to tell you. Except that...if it's only chemistry, then I'd think long and hard about taking the leap with someone like Hysterian. He'd treat you well. I've never heard of a Cyborg treating a woman wrong—even with all the stuff on the network lately," Pigeon waved his hand. "But he's also your boss. If things went poorly—"

"I know."

"—you could find yourself out of a job."

Or dead. Alexa wanted to say. She could wind up dead. "Being a Cyborg doesn't make him a good person."

"No, but neither does being human, and what's a person that isn't human?"

Alexa rubbed her face. God, how she wished she could tell Pigeon everything. Spill her guts and have some of the weight of her secrets given away.

She couldn't, especially not to him. She'd be putting him in danger if she did something so selfish. *He has daughters.*

"An alien?" she teased, answering him.

Pigeon laughed. "Yeah, an alien. But we both know our captain isn't that."

She joined Pigeon in his laughter, almost comforted by the absurdity of her situation. It was funny if she thought about it. The absurdity. She was a half-breed pretending to be a human, working for a Cyborg—a being who would kill her without a thought if he knew what she was—and she wanted him, even though he killed her father.

And he had no idea about any of it.

Alexa laughed a little harder.

"That'a girl," Pigeon said, patting her back. "Whether you take up with the captain or not is no one's choice but your own, Dear. No one can take that freedom from you. And if you do take up with him, he'll be one lucky man. But be careful, whatever your choice ends up being. Our jobs don't allow us to settle down, or have meaningful relationships. We're constantly moving, traveling across the universe, visiting dangerous places. Sometimes it's years before we find ourselves back home, and our families? They may not be waiting around for you when you do."

Alexa nodded. It wasn't really the situation she was in. She'd never put any thought into her future. She had no family as it stood anyway. But it was something to consider...if she managed to survive.

"Thank you, Pigeon," she said. "You've given me a lot to think about."

"Good. There isn't any harm when it comes to thinking." His head snapped up. "Where the fuck is Raul? He's an hour late."

Alexa straightened and looked around with Pigeon, having forgotten about Raul. She looked at her wristcon, but there were no messages from him. *I'll break things off with him tonight. Before anything else happens...* She decided, even if she stayed away from Hysterian, she still needed to break things off with Raul. There just wasn't a spark for her when it came to him.

"Maybe he forgot?" she said.

Pigeon snorted. "Wouldn't put it past him. Are you going to order a drink?"

Alexa closed her hand around her bag, catching Pigeon's gaze. "No. I think I'm going to see if he's looking for us outside. I'll be back."

He seemed to know what she was saying. "Be careful. Let him down gently. I don't want to have to carry him back to the ship in the morning. He's a fat fuck."

Alexa laughed.

"I'll try," she said, slipping off the stool with a smile. She left Pigeon with his beer and made her way out. She hadn't seen Raul inside. If she could catch him alone, it would be easier, and she wanted to do it while they weren't on the ship.

There wasn't enough space on the ship for a breakup.

The crowd thinned once she left the bar. Looking down into the port below, she saw that fewer people were gathered, and most of the shops were closed or were in the process of closing. As she glimpsed the lingerie shop, the shopfront lights blinked off.

Damn. She wasn't getting her money back.

Still, she didn't see Raul. *Maybe he went back to the ship?* Alexa sighed, wondering if she should return to Pigeon and wait with him inside. Spying a trash receptacle below, she yanked the lingerie out of her bag, heading for it.

A large wall of chest slid into her path.

"Where the hell have you been? Do you know how fucking late it is?"

Her gaze shot to Hysterian's face. Her lips parted.

A brief flash of teal sparked within his eyes.

"Captain," Alexa gasped.

"Where have you been?" He grabbed her arm and turned for the docking bay, dragging her with him. "I've been searching everywhere for you."

Her feet fell over each other as she caught up. He tugged her into his side.

Alexa stilled as cloying heat closed in around her. Hard, heavy, metal heat. The scent of it eclipsed everything, and it was mixed with a spicy, leathery musk.

"I asked you a question," he snapped.

She jerked out from his side and tugged her arm from his grip. He grabbed it again without missing a step.

She gritted her teeth. "None of your business. Let go of me!"

Hysterian swiveled on her, his eyes fully teal. Alexa stopped, the intensity of the color stunned her.

"I'm your captain. Your business is my business when we're on the job. I found the gun in the ship's recycling, Dear. The *Questor* alerted me of the find. Did you think that was smart? Being given a weapon, by your captain no less, only to toss it out on his own ship? You're lucky I don't fucking fire you. Wandering a scummy port like Libra alone, without a weapon? I thought you were smarter than that." Long fingers threaded through his hair.

Her cheeks burned. "I didn't want you to track me."

Hysterian's eyes flicked over her face, the fury evident. "With the gun? It didn't have one on it. But it fucking should've." His eyes shot away to look around them before returning to her. "Do you know how easy it is to be hurt in a place like this? Even with security around? One wrong turn, one opportunistic shop clerk, and you're dead, with a body being broken down for fertilizer in the pits below."

He ran his hand down his face, briefly dislodging his mask. He tugged it back up but not before she glimpsed his face.

It wasn't fair. How handsome he was.

"I know all about wrong turns and opportunistic shop clerks. I grew up in the Elyrian slums," she said tightly. "I don't need a gun from you to protect myself. I don't need *this* either!" She waved between them and his hold on her and the few people hanging around, watching them. "Everyone's watching us." In the corner of her eye, Alexa saw the beautiful android shopkeeper.

"Then we'd better get out of sight." He started dragging her toward his ship again.

"Let me go!"

"No."

"I'm not some fucking child! I'm your coworker." They passed through Libra's security and started down the ramp toward the *Questor*. "You're being an asshole!"

She didn't want to be alone with him. She didn't want to be on *his* ship, alone with him. He could lock her inside, and she'd have no way to escape. He could keep everyone else out. She knew what a Cyborg was capable of. How powerful they were. How they could manipulate technology and so much more.

But above all, she didn't trust herself to be alone with him.

They passed through the *Questor's* hatch, and she heard the thud of it shutting behind her, followed by the pressurized blast. She tore out of Hysterian's grip as he turned to face her.

Alexa held her hand to her chest so he wouldn't grab it again. "You didn't have to drag me," she quipped. "If you weren't such an asshole, I would have just followed you."

She hoped it was a lie.

"Right," he said.

She pursed her lips.

His eyes hardened. "Where have you been?"

"On Libra, shopping, of course." She held up her bag.

He snatched it from her before she could pull it back. He tugged it open and looked inside.

She grabbed it back and fled with it toward the lab. She heard him follow.

"You have no right," she hissed, storming to her quarters and tossing the bag in her sleeping bunk. She shut the privacy screen and turned to face him where he stood at the threshold of her quarters. "You're not my keeper, my husband, or even my friend. What I do with my free time is my choice, same with who I spend it with, and what I do during it."

"The night shift is half over," he said, leaning his shoulder on the frame.

"So? I was with Pigeon and Raul at Termite, having a drink. You and I have no plans."

Hysterian cocked his head. "Raul?"

"I was looking for him when I found you."

"You mean when I found you. Alone, where you could have easily been abducted, or worse."

She threw up her hands. "I can take care of myself!" Her face was flushed, and frustration weeded through her. Why did she want this man? This Cyborg? He was insane. "I don't need you or a gun. I don't need you checking up on me or giving me gifts. I need nothing from you!" Alexa exhaled. The sexy things in the bag behind her? She was never going to wear them for Hysterian. "Get out."

He stepped into her room. "You forget, Dear, you're on

my ship. This is my room I'm letting you stay in. If you want to continue being on this ship, you have to follow the rules."

She guffawed. "Have I ever stopped following your rules? Tell me. I don't see you dragging Pigeon or Horace to the ship—and in public!"

He stalked forward, trapping her against the bed screens. "Address me as captain," he ordered.

Alexa ducked under his arm, but he lowered it, stopping her. "I think we're past that."

"Until you hand me your resignation and walk off this ship, I am your captain. I'm in charge of you. As for Pigeon and Horace, they don't fight me tooth and nail."

She stopped trying to escape and faced him again. "That's not how things work."

He leaned in. Her heart shot into overdrive as his presence closed in on every side.

His hands settled on the screen behind her, and his face slid close to hers.

She licked her lips. If his mouth was free from his suit, only a hairsbreadth of space would be between them. Every fiber of her body paid attention now, waiting for the moment when Hysterian touched her again.

"Get out of my room," she whispered. *Please.*

"Not without you," he whispered right back.

Her lips flattened, and she threw herself against him, pushing him away, hitting him with her fists.

Hysterian straightened as Alexa attacked him with everything she had.

"Why do I want you?" she screamed, beating her fists against him, trying to make him back up. "Why do I want you? You're a monster. A fucking monster!" Alexa pushed him as hard as she could, shoving her body against him, but he didn't budge, not an inch. She let out a cry as she pushed and shoved and railed against the wall of his chest, trying her hardest to move him.

She needed to hurt him like he had hurt her.

She needed *something*.

"I hate you," she cried. "I hate you!" Everything she'd been feeling exploded out from her, all the thoughts, emotions, the confusion.

She fought until she tired. Still, he didn't stop her. He just stood there, letting her try and hurt him, letting her use him as a punching bag. Alexa sobbed, shaking, falling into his chest. She was never going to be able to hurt him how she wanted.

Because she loved him.

She fucking loved Hysterian in a twisted, dependent way. She'd been consumed by him her whole life, and at some point, it stopped being all about vengeance. It became an obsession. A dangerous one. One she couldn't shake, no matter how hard she tried. An obsession she loved.

She wanted to deny it. For years she had.

Alexa coiled her fingers into his suit and cried. "I shouldn't want a monster like you."

His arms gently embraced her, holding her like she was some delicate egg, and a torrent of tears burst forth. *Why does he have to be gentle?* Why had he killed her dad?

She pressed into him, knowing she'd lost the battle. She'd lost long before she stepped aboard the *Questor*. Long before Hysterian knew she existed. There was never going to be a good ending for her.

He lifted her into his arms and carried her out of her quarters, through his ship, and into his room. She didn't fight it.

It's what she had wanted all along.

SIXTEEN

HYSTERIAN PLACED Alexa on the edge of his bed. She sat upright to rub the last of her tears from her face. He watched as she composed herself. He kneeled in front of her.

She met his gaze when her courage returned. His eyes hadn't stopped glowing. She shivered, knowing she was at his mercy now. Whatever happened, there was nowhere she could go where he wouldn't follow.

The realization made her shiver.

I'm just as much his enemy as he is mine.

Part of her wanted to do to Hysterian what she'd almost done with Pigeon. She wanted to tell him everything. To spill all of her secrets so they wouldn't be hers alone anymore, so the burden wouldn't be so heavy... To tell him she was a half-breed—that she had alien blood coursing through her veins. The same aliens Hysterian and his Cyborg brothers had once killed by the thousands. Hundreds of thousands.

Would he kill her right now if he knew? If she told him?

What would he do if she mentioned her father?

Would he remember...?

What if she told him she had spent the last decade stalking him, watching him, studying him and his kind from afar, hoping to one day kill him? Possibly the rest someday too.

Should she pull out the faded picture she had of him from the liner of her duffle bag? A picture she had stared at for years? The one of him staring off at something out of frame? Where he was handsomely decked in his military uniform?

She'd always wondered what it was he had been staring at.

Alexa grabbed hold of the bedding, wrenching it in her hands. His eyes dropped to them before flicking back to her face.

She waited for him to do something, anything, so she wouldn't sign her death warrant and tell him all her secrets. *Let the chips fall where they may...*

Because despite all her choices so far, she didn't want to die.

"Hysterian," she started when he continued to stare at her, like he was trying to figure her out. "I—"

"Stop talking."

She shut her mouth and released the bedding bunched up in her hands. He reached out, and she flinched. His eyes exploded with light.

"Why did you flinch?" he demanded.

She shook her head.

"Do you think I'm going to fucking hurt you? I'm not going to hurt you," he growled.

"I can't help it..."

Some of the light faded from his eyes. "Whatever shit happened to you, Dear, I'm going to want to know all about it someday, because I'm not going to fucking hurt you—no one is—if I have my way about it. It's clear there's something you're dealing with and I hate secrets. But tonight, we're not going there, you got it?"

Hysterian kept his hand poised between them, waiting for her to respond. Alexa calmed, knowing he wasn't going to demand an answer out of her. At least not right now.

She nodded.

"I want to hear you say it."

"I got it."

He pulled down his mask, settling the excess material around his neck. "Good."

Alexa's breath hitched. He'd removed the mask without her asking.

Perfectly shaped, masculine lips—with the barest hint of deviance—revealed themselves, along with a sharp chin and jawline. Hysterian wasn't just an angel, she realized, but a fallen one. Because despite the attractive deity kneeling before her, she could still see the marks of a long and traumatic life etched into him.

She didn't think Cyborgs had the capacity to suffer like humans.

"Give me your feet," he said.

"What?"

"Your. Feet. Lift them. Now."

Alexa furrowed her brow when she realized her legs were clamped together between their bodies. Did he want her to lift them—?

"Now, Alexa," he ordered.

She popped her feet off the ground. Hysterian cupped the back of one of her ankles and tugged off her boot. He did the same for the other. He cupped her sock-covered feet and pressed his thumbs into her arches, kneading them.

She held herself stiffly. "What are you doing?"

"What does it look like I'm doing?"

"Massaging my feet?"

"Proving to you that you have nothing to fear from me."

"By massaging my feet?"

But his words made her toes curl. Oh, how she wanted to give in. A breath whizzed out from her parted lips. Hysterian pinned her with his dazzling eyes. She wanted to believe him. So much it hurt.

"Lie back," he said, lowering his voice.

There was a hint of something else in it, a challenge, like he wanted to see if she would do it. If she was willing to take the risk. She stared at him hard, searching for a hint of evil that would send her running—maybe her sanity—but all she found was *him*.

Just him.

Alexa slowly leaned back. With one final look at Hysterian, she lay down on his bed. The lights dimmed. His hands closed around her feet and shifted them so she lay straight. He stood, looked down at her, and ran a hand over his mouth.

She remained tense, uncertain of what he was planning.

Gone was the light in his eyes, and the golden hue from the room's lights. His face was cast in shadows, his body a dark silhouette. Some of her tension melted away. The darkness shielded her, made things easier.

Hysterian unbuttoned his jacket. He shrugged out of it, folded it over his arm, and placed it on the small table next to the bed. Returning, sat on the edge of the bed and removed his boots.

It was such a simple act, done by such a strange man. A Cyborg, no less. Alexa curled onto her side to watch him more comfortably.

Excitement filled her, wondering if Hysterian was going to take off all his clothes, if he was going to be so vulnerable with her. Would he be just as stunning under his uniform?

Would there be scars?

He stopped after his boots.

Alexa rolled her tongue before she offered comfort or encouragement. He needed neither, especially from her. She had scars she didn't want him to see either.

Hysterian turned toward her, placing his hand on the bed on the other side of her body, leaning above. She rolled onto her back.

"You never need to fear me, Alexa," he said. "I would have you come to me, not run from me. Whatever happened in your past, whatever's been done to you, I will fucking fix it." His words were spoken with conviction and without anger. He was being sincere.

It broke her heart. "You can't."

"Let me try?"

She shuddered, unable to tell him what he wanted to hear. He would know it was a lie. She nodded instead.

Some of the strain left him.

He turned away and rested his elbows on his knees, inhaling deeply. She stared at his back and wished she knew what he was thinking.

He didn't stay there long, grabbing something off the nightstand next to the bed instead. In quick movements, he pulled off his gloves and slid on another pair. A thinner pair. She couldn't get a good look, but she assumed it had something to do with his skin. When he was done and his other gloves were folded neatly atop his jacket, he faced her.

This wasn't the Cyborg she'd come to know. Gone was his craze, the anger at the brink, ready to be unleashed, and instead was a man. A man who...was nervous?

"Hysterian," she whispered, reaching out and taking his hand, squeezing it. He tensed but didn't pull away. "Convince me?" She had no idea what else to say, what she could say to a being like him.

But saying nothing seemed wrong.

Hysterian took her hands and pushed her back onto the bed, climbing atop her. "Whatever you do, Alexa," his voice turned rough, "do not touch my skin, okay?"

One touch: bliss or death.

"Okay." Easy enough. She pressed her fingers against his and he gripped hers back.

"Good. Keep your hands above your head. You drop them? This ends."

What was she supposed to say to that?

Was it that easy to get him to go away?

"Okay," she agreed.

He released her, and she kept her hands where he placed them. Heart thrumming, he slid down her body and took hold of her feet again. He peeled off her socks and kneaded her soles. The sensation of his new gloves was strange, but not unwelcome. They felt like skin, but without the natural satiny feel of it and only a hint of heat.

He rubbed her soles, her arches, and tickled and traced her ankles. Laziness coursed through her veins as she succumbed to his ministrations. His hands slid from her feet and under the hems of her pants, exploring, reaching up. He slipped them out and kneaded her arches again, like he was reassuring her he would go slow.

Slow was not like him.

"I need…" she started to say before she stopped herself.

His hands paused. "Need what?"

Warmth flooded her cheeks. "More. I need more." He was going to make her say it anyway.

He withdrew his hands from her. She held her breath, waiting to see what he would do next. She wanted him to kiss her, fully kiss her, without there being a cloth between them.

Her fingers danced where they lay on the bedding, jittery with anticipation.

Hysterian stood.

"Don't fucking move," he ordered, his voice returning to normal. He strode into the lavatory, shutting the door behind him.

Her brow furrowed.

She rose onto her elbows, but he had already returned and was headed straight for her. Her lips parted.

He was decked in a full skin-tight black latex bodysuit. The light from the bathroom haloed his imposing body for a split second before it turned off, revealing everything. Alexa gasped, straightening.

He pushed her back onto the bed. "I told you not to move."

Alexa's gaze dipped to his body, and she reached for him.

He caught her hands and growled. "What did I say?"

"Don't touch you?"

He placed her hands back above her head. "Don't touch me."

Alexa settled back but was still confused. "You're in a... You're not naked."

The suit covered everything; his white hair, his beautiful face, his severe lips. "I'm not. If I were, you would already be dead," he said.

"What?"

He didn't answer her, instead, he released her hands to capture the button on her pants. He hooked his fingers under the lip and yanked them down her hips. She lifted to help him, kicking her pants off. He folded them as well, placing them beside his clothes. He dove in for her shirt next.

Alexa gasped when he untangled it from her arms, taking it away, leaving her in nothing but her underwear. She clasped her hands when he pulled back. She wished she had changed out of the plain, cotton undergarments and discarded earlier when she had the chance.

"Fuuuuck," Hysterian hissed, making Alexa squeeze her legs together. "You're just fucking perfect, aren't you?"

Her eyes trailed his shadowy outline. Was he wearing the same material over his body that he wore on his hands? Were his gloves latex, too, and she hadn't realized it? It was easier thinking about him than it was receiving a compliment. A fake one, obviously. "So are you," she said. Whatever he'd put on was demonic, but so was he.

Hysterian let out a raspy laugh. "Not in any way that matters."

The bed dipped as Hysterian moved over her, straddling his knees on either side of her. She didn't know what he was talking about. He was the most attractive man she'd ever laid eyes on. There was no one in the entire universe she'd spent more time studying. How could he think less of himself? It wasn't fair. She'd wanted him for years, hating herself for it the entire time. She knew that now, having buried her desire so deep that she was still wrecked with the truth of it.

Hysterian was a dark and powerful Cyborg, and if she couldn't take away his power, she wanted him to punish her for her failure.

She cupped his neck and rose, planting her lips to his before he could stop her.

He jerked, pushed her back onto the bed, falling over her.

"Is that what you want?" he demanded. "To die?" He grabbed her hands and thrust them back above her head, forcing her legs open with his knee. "Obey me!" he roared.

She wiggled her legs out from between his and curled them around his waist, clamping them. With him draped in black, he was Hysterian, her enemy, but more. He was a bruise in her fantasies. One she wanted healed. Right now. She writhed.

He reached down and pinned her hip with his hand while still keeping her hands trapped with one of his. His fingers bit into her flesh.

Alexa sucked in a sharp breath.

Hysterian shot upright with a heave and stared down at her.

She clamped her thighs harder. "Please," she whimpered.

His eyes flickered in the darkness. "Hell, Alexa."

"I need you. Please. No more teasing."

Another growl tore from his mouth, and she trembled. He shifted, and the bulge of his cock pressed into her pelvis, spurring her on.

"You don't want me to fuck you gently, do you, Dear?" he rasped, releasing her hands and grabbing the cups of her bra and snapping the thin strap between her breasts. "You don't need me to prove anything to you, do you?"

"No," she gasped.

"You don't want to be pampered with foreplay, or prepared? Fingered and splayed for when I thrust into you the first time?"

Why did he want to embarrass her?

Hysterian cupped her breasts and rolled her nipples

with his thumbs. "Fine. Have it your way," he purred. He lifted up and grabbed the side of her panties with both hands, shredding them. The cloth fell away, leaving her sex bare.

She pressed up, rubbing herself against the smooth latex of his body suit. It slipped over her skin like silk, there was no rubbery hitch. His cock rested between them, where the heat coming off it threatened to brand her. The suit had give. Her belly knotted. The bedding snagged in her fingers. Hysterian exhaled loudly, grabbing her hips and squeezing. His palms ran down her body, finding her backside, and he squeezed her again, a groan leaving him.

His imposing form filled her vision. "You have no idea how long I've waited for this." His hands groped her once more before spanning out, pressing into her everywhere.

Not nearly as long as me. Alexa clamped her mouth, refusing to beg anymore.

Large hands moved up her body, feeling every inch of her. Curiously, probing fingers whispered over her curves and hidden places, leaving no spot unexplored. His palms were warm, almost too warm for a cold-blooded creature, but she endured. He explored her like he'd never touched a woman before, like this experience was just as new to him as it was for Alexa.

Bundles of nerves that have been tangled in her soul for years began to uncoil.

"You're cold. Why are you cold?" he whispered, grabbing her hair, letting it go, only to clasp his hands around her neck.

She shook her head. She was on fire.

He groaned and pressed his thumbs into the dip of her throat. "So delicate," he said, rubbing her neck.

"It's not. I'm not."

He squeezed her throat gently. "To me, everything about you is delicate. But I'm going to fuck this someday, Alexa, and it won't be delicate." He tapped his finger on her throat before letting go of her neck. "Someday."

She shivered, knowing it for the threat it was. It excited her. His hands covered her breasts again. Her toes curled.

"And these," he groaned.

Alexa really didn't want to beg, she tried to bite down on her tongue to keep the words in, but when Hysterian started worshipping her body like he had her neck, he made it so much harder for her.

She couldn't wait any longer. She needed him inside her. Madness wormed its way into her head, clawing at her mind. How much longer was he going to make her wait?

Another decade?

"Captain, please," she whimpered, knowing what would happen.

Hysterian stiffened. The room blazed bright with light, streaking out from his eyes. The large shadow of a man feeling her up vanished, and she was shot with the image of a frighteningly, dangerous machine. His tongue shot out of his mouth, plastering itself into the suit, stretching it. The light glistened off it before it and the light vanished too, plunging the room into darkness.

Alexa stilled, uncertain of what she'd just seen.

Hysterian rolled her onto her front before she could make sense of it. Her legs were thrust apart as his body rose above her. "Captain, is it?" He pinched her cheeks, spreading them.

"Captain," she repeated, breathless.

"I tried to be gentle. Remember that." He shunted against her, his metalized cock spearing her flesh between the dip of her ass. "Oh, I tried to be gentle," he growled.

She felt him grab his cock. He tapped it on her backside. His fingers fluttered over her feminine area, feeling her everywhere, pinching, spreading her arousal, and groaning all the while. He pushed one finger into her, then another, invading her in the one place no one had before.

Alexa squeezed from the intrusion, shocked despite how desperate she needed it. The invasion hurt and she wrenched her eyes closed, but not before she slumped forward on the bed, sticking her butt out as far as she could, opening herself up for more.

Hysterian thrust another finger into her. "This what you want, Dear? Is this it?" He pumped the digits in and out of her, forcing her to take a fourth. "You want to be fingered by me?"

She whimpered when his fingers vibrated, and bit down on the bedding when they frenzied.

"I'm your fucking master," he rasped. "Fucking hell, you're tight."

Pain spiked up her spine, but also pleasure each time his fingers pushed into that sweet spot inside her, making her lift and lower for him repeatedly. Alexa jerked away and pressed back, unable to decide if it was too much. Or not enough.

Should I tell him?

His other hand pet the length of her spine while continuing to thrust his soaked fingers in and out of her. When he twisted his hand and cupped her sex, pressing the pad of his thumb to her clit, she decided not to tell him.

He'd want to be gentle with her, and she couldn't handle that. She didn't deserve it.

His hand rubbed down her back again, coaxing her higher. His thumb rolled her clit. Heat blanketed her, and she panted like a cat in heat. She didn't care. Alexa pushed back with a whimper and gave Hysterian what he wanted.

His fingers pulled out of her, and she felt him line his cock up to her opening, his thumb tweaked her clit. He pressed his body down, his thighs behind hers, and she winced, already a little raw.

"Alexa," he said, his voice a rough whisper as he pushed into her.

A cry tore from her throat, and she fell forward onto the bed, her knees giving out. He stretched her to her limit, filling her completely. The breath *wooshed* out from her lips, her hands grabbing the bedding, her teeth biting down hard.

Hysterian didn't move, holding over her, inside her. His brow resting on the back of her head. She turned her face to the side to see his arm holding his body up. Despite the suit, his muscles strained and bulged. Veins popped from his biceps. *It couldn't be latex.* An ache bloomed inside where he was seated. She constricted, testing to see if she could handle more.

Hysterian groaned thickly. Her skin prickled.

She bit down on the bedding and clenched around him again. Little by little, the rawness morphed into something else, something warm. Exceedingly warm. His cock burned her from the inside, branding her in the one place she'd never shared with another. Alexa whimpered as heat burst between them, her alien DNA made her sweat profusely.

"Alexa," Hysterian rasped. "Why do I smell blood?"

His body went tensely still.

SEVENTEEN

Alexa shook her head, panting, refusing to release the bedding pinched between her teeth. She felt the bed shift, and Hysterian's fingers slipping into her hair, grabbing hold of it. She didn't want him to move... The pain was sweetening by the second, making her feverish.

She sagged, loving it.

Hysterian lifted off her, slipping out of her body, and she mewed in protest. He flipped her over.

Bright, furious eyes stared down at her. They were the only part of him that wasn't covered. He rose up on his knees, and straddled her again. He looked down at his cock, lit up by the blue of his eyes. Turgid and ebony sleek.

"You were a virgin?" he growled.

She stared at Hysterian's cock. It was massive and... bulky, too big for the material he was wearing. She could've sworn it contained more than his cock within, like he may have orgasmed already, but she couldn't be sure... Her gaze flicked over his chest, his arms, lit up by his eyes, and noticed the rest of him resembled his cock.

Was something happening to his suit? She decided it was a trick of the light.

Hysterian groaned, and her eyes snapped back to his hand where he held his cock. There was a trickle of dark red blood sliding down the side of it. They watched as it gathered and dripped onto her belly.

He shot upward. "Why didn't you fucking tell me!"

Alexa reached down, took hold of his cock, and squeezed it.

He strained away and groaned before snatching her hand off of him. "Alexa, why didn't you say anything?"

She raised her arms above her head.

Heat infused his eyes as they landed on her breasts.

She smiled lazily. "Because it doesn't matter."

"It does to me, Dear. I could've been gentler, approached you less like a fucking monster."

"It wouldn't have been you." If he had been gentle, she would've hated him even more. She shimmied her legs out from between his.

He grabbed her ankle as she opened her legs, holding it prone.

"I don't want gentle, Captain Hysterian," Alexa said.

The light from his eyes blazed, and her heart fluttered as his gaze dropped to her splayed sex. He gripped her foot harder and moved it outward.

"I'm not the type of man to give your virginity to," he rumbled. "Why does your blood smell sweet?"

A sliver of fear sliced through her. "You're not," she agreed quickly to his first sentiment, hoping he'd forget that her blood wasn't quite right.

"Then why?"

"I want you."

His eyes softened. Alexa was beyond denying it. What

was the point? He had already won. He'd won the first time they spoke.

Hysterian seemed like he wanted to say something. His lips were moving, shifting the suit, but nothing came out. She hoped he wasn't focused on her blood any longer, having never thought he'd be able to smell a difference from it. His sudden vulnerability reassured Alexa he wasn't thinking about that at all.

Her brow furrowed. She'd never seen her Cyborg as anything but a sociopath.

Her heart flipped. Her fingers shook, and she curled them into her palm, stopping them from trying to comfort him with a touch. His gaze shot to her sex, and he spread her thighs open. He released his grip on her ankle and touched her between her legs.

With a whisper of a caress, his finger circled her opening, as if apologizing to it. She rose on her elbows to watch him, nerves fluttering.

Hysterian's voice was barely a murmur when he finally spoke.

"I've waited for so long for this." Hysterian wiggled his finger into her. "For something real. I'm not..."

She clenched around his finger.

"I promised I wouldn't hurt you." He hooked his finger, pressing into her sweet spot. "But hell if I can make myself stop."

"Don't."

He slipped his finger out and cupped her thighs. "You'd have to kill me to stop me." He lowered his face between her legs, pushing his mouth over her sex. An animalistic sound came from him, she felt its vibrations over her sex. He rubbed his mouth over her like he couldn't get enough of it.

"I'd kill everyone on this port to taste you. Every last one of them."

He lifted up after one last pained groan.

Hysterian dragged his body up over hers, trapping her to the bed. Her legs wrapped around him as he pushed the tip of his cock to her opening.

"So you don't want to be a virgin anymore? Is that right?" he taunted, searching her eyes.

Alexa's lips parted. "I don't want to be a virgin."

"Good." He eased inside her slowly, pinning her with his gaze. Was he waiting for her to balk? To run screaming?

A moan escaped as he filled her, invading her bit by bit, forcing her to feel every inch of the stretch. The sharp ache of her broken virginity made her wince, but he stayed with her through it, pausing before he continued. Unlike the first thrust, his movements were slow and deliberate.

She exhaled as the heat of his body burned across her flesh.

When he was fully seated between her legs, she sagged onto the bed. She'd been holding her body so tensely, her muscles quivered.

He held still. "Are you okay?"

She nodded.

His eyes closed and the light vanished. Hysterian gathered her hands and placed them back above her head. He held them there as he began to move.

Slow at first, he rocked into her, each movement careful, like she was breakable. It was driving her mad. But then he'd push deep inside her again, bottoming out, giving her a dose of pain. She gasped when he pushed too far.

It would never be enough.

"More," she begged when he pulled out completely.

He paused and thrust back in, looking between their

bodies.

"More," she urged.

He drove into her harder, giving her what she wanted.

She strained from the impact. A raspy chuckle joined his next thrust, pushing her body up the bed. His fingers threaded hers on his next impale.

The bed shook, and her whimpers built. The ache of penetration vanished each time they came together. Body feverish, pleasure shot up Alexa's spine, and she held onto it, suddenly not wanting the pain to return.

She stared at Hysterian, awed by the pleasure. Pleasure he was giving *her*. Gone from desperation to bliss within moments, Alexa clenched.

Hysterian curled over her, bending to jerk his hips quicker, harder, faster. She wrenched her eyes closed.

He groaned her name again. *Alexa.* He knew who she was. Tears threatened to spring from her eyes. He ruined her mentally and physically. She knotted up, squeezing around him with each forceful thrust.

She gasped, trying to catch her breath. Sweat slickened her body, feverish from the heat. His warmth was making her light-headed.

"My little virgin no more," he purred, lifting off her again and hitting her sweet spot with his hard tip. His body trembled and he plunged forward. He stopped and jerked his hips in frenetic succession.

She screamed. Her body seized. She thrashed, unable to cope with the sensations taking over her. Her orgasm ripped, her joints simultaneously locking and giving way.

He rolled his hips.

Another scream burst forth; another ripple of pleasure surged through her.

The heat—Alexa gasped, losing her mind, fighting his

hold on her hands. The heat was too much.

"Hysterian!" she cried, tearing her hands from his, dropping her legs from around him mid-orgasm.

He released her, but instead of allowing her to leave, his arms came around her back, lifting her body to straddle him, forcing her to sink down on the entirety of his length. She squirmed and clenched. Her core pulsed with devastating pleasure, and she buckled. Alexa pushed at his chest, trying hard not to faint.

"Hysterian, please," she rasped.

His hands dropped away from her. "What's wrong?"

She tore off him, rushing to the bathroom. She shut the door and she sank to the ground. Her vision wavered.

"Alexa, what's wrong?" Hysterian demanded, his voice muffled but clear through the door.

The panel slid open.

She put her hands on it, keeping it from fully opening. "Nothing," she wheezed. "I just need," she gasped again, "to use the bathroom."

He released the door and she shoved it closed, her sex pulsing wildly the entire time. Her thighs slipped against each other as she moved.

"I know a lie when I fucking hear one, Dear," he warned. "You and I are going to have a nice long talk when you're done, Alexa."

Without responding, she crawled to the shower and turned the water on. She was focused on one thing, and one thing only: cooling down before she fainted.

She couldn't be taken to medical.

She didn't want to die.

With the last of her strength, Alexa entered the unit and curled up on the stall floor. The shock of cold water was heaven on her flesh. Growing accustomed to the light, she lapped at the water pooling on the floor, hydrating herself like an animal. When her head cleared, she ran her fingers over the flushed skin of her arms.

Even under freezing water, it took much longer than necessary for her to cool off, but she wasn't willing to leave until the redness from her skin was gone. She'd already risked enough.

Does he still smell my blood?

Alexa pushed to her feet. She brushed out her hair with her fingers. Glancing around the stall, she discovered it devoid of any toiletries. Not even soap.

She spread her legs and peered down, feeling her sex. The only burn that remained was the one between her thighs. The blood was gone. She rinsed her hand and pressed her palm to the stall door and opened it.

Finding the bathroom empty, Alexa released a relieved sigh. Hysterian hadn't snuck in while she was focused elsewhere.

"Alexa," his voice rumbled from outside the bathroom. "You're making me worry. Don't make me worry. I don't fucking like worrying."

She was nervous to face him, but she couldn't stay. She'd already been in his bathroom for much longer than she could easily explain away, shower included.

"I'm," she paused, "coming." Alexa flinched, knowing how that sounded.

She found a towel and dried herself, soon realizing she didn't have any clothes. Now that she had time to calm down, the last person she wanted to face was Hysterian—especially naked.

She scrubbed her face. Exhaustion hit her hard, and she wondered what time it was.

She padded to Hysterian's folded suit. A top of his suit

was a pair of her underwear. She paused, uncertain how they got there or why they were there at all. He'd moved her things into his room. Had he...left them in here for her?

She snatched the underwear, checked if they were clean, and tugged them once she confirmed they were. Of all the strange occurrences lately, she didn't question it. He could have stolen them. Even if he had, it wouldn't have changed anything.

She wrapped her towel around her body and headed for the door, pausing once more.

Why was she so nervous to face him? He'd just taken her virginity, he'd just touched her in her most private area, and she'd given herself to him knowing all that he'd done.

I let him see a side of me no one else ever has. That was significant, wasn't it? He hadn't commented on her scars. The one's hidden on her thighs where she used to cut.

He was the same man—Cyborg—as he was before. Just because they fucked didn't mean he would be different. He was still her captain and her enemy. Though killing him now seemed like it would be much easier and harder. Easier because he wanted her.

And harder for the same reason.

Alexa couldn't imagine her life without him in it. She used to fantasize about it all the time. If she killed him, she knew she'd miss him.

The bathroom door slid open. Hysterian was gripping the side paneling of the doorway on the other side, his gaze dark, his face and body once again hidden behind a fresh uniform. The black bodysuit was gone. He looked unhappy. His eyes trailed down her body and back up. She held the towel tighter to her, incredibly aware of him and how handsome and fiendish he looked.

"It's time for the truth." He pushed off the wall.

EIGHTEEN

Heaven.

The word streaked through his mind. That's what it felt like being inside Alexa. It was heaven.

Which was a fucking problem since he was destined for hell.

He forced himself to calm.

He hoped she was telling him the truth but he knew that even if she was, there was a problem. He knew something was wrong. Trauma from the past? Abuse? The way she reacted to him now and again suggested it. Like she was waiting for him to hurt her, hit her. He was sick of it, and he hated secrets.

Even if they had nothing to do with him.

Alexa wasn't allowed to have secrets anymore.

I took her fucking virginity.

Hysterian pushed off the door and stormed to his bed with its rumpled bedding. It was wetter than it should be. Wet from perspiration. He knew he ran hot—all Cyborgs did—because of the hardware and metal within him. It was why, even when he was in a cold environment, he never fully found relief from the poison in his veins.

He scanned the blankets.

The bedding wasn't just merely wet, it was soaked. He turned the lights on and searched for what might have poisoned her—if he even had. He cursed, rubbed his jaw.

He'd been so careful. The suit was the same quality other Cyborgs shifted in. It molded to his frame, expanded and contracted, and kept his skin temperate. He had many uniforms in nanocloth, but nothing that fully sealed him off. He was lucky the textile shop on Libra had any extra cloth at all.

There wasn't much time for him to help her, especially if she'd gotten some of his toxin on her skin.

If he'd been a normal fucking dart frog, a simple anti-dote would help, as it had for Raul. But he was a cybernetic war machine with intelligent toxins.

A little could kill many...if he configured his toxins to change in potency. Luckily, that didn't happen unless he concentrated. If he'd poisoned Alexa, it would be the same thing he'd given Raul.

It was the last toxin he had his systems create.

'I shouldn't want a monster like you.' He recalled her tears, the way her voice slipped when she had said it. The way she'd hit him, and he let her because he knew deep down, she'd needed to hit him. He'd thought she was struggling with unfounded guilt about what was between them...

He saw a spot of blood on the bedding, and his jaw tensed. Yanking down the suit from his head, he grabbed the blanket, brought it up to his mouth, and licked the blood. *No poison.* There was nothing but salt and sweat, and Alexa's arousal.

The taste bloomed.

She tasted better than she smelled. So sweet it was wrong. No man or Cyborg would be able to resist it. He'd never tasted something so delicious. He'd told her the truth when he had his face between her thighs—he'd kill everyone on Libra just for one fucking lick of her.

It never occurred to him that Alexa could be a virgin. He wasn't worthy to be the ground she walked upon, or the air she breathed. He'd never wanted anything to do with virgins, but now that he had been given the honor— Hysterian rubbed his mouth—his fantasies shifted.

I tried to be gentle...

He was a fucking monster, no doubt about that.

Hysterian licked the bedding once more, needing another taste of her. He wanted to remember it, even after tonight. He wanted the memory front and center in his hard drives so he could enjoy them whenever he wanted. His hand wrapped around his cock.

She didn't want gentle. He palmed himself, hating the covering gripping him, listening to Alexa move in his bathroom.

Even her blood smells sweet. He paused, tasting it once more. *Human blood isn't sweet.*

Is she sick?

Hysterian seeded into his ship and programmed the cleaning bots to come in and take care of the bed. He threw the sheets against the wall with his clothes. Within moments, bots entered his room and cleaned up the mess.

He strode to the bathroom when the shower turned on, intent to join her and demand answers. Because now that he thought about it, she had perspired a great deal, and she hadn't even been that warm... He had tried to warm her up when he had her naked beneath him.

She has to be sick.

Concern punched him in the gut. His hands fisted. He stormed out of his room and made his way to the gym's shower. He stripped out of the suit and tossed it aside, stepping into the water. It was freezing.

He washed quickly and was back inside his quarters a handful of minutes later.

Alexa was still in the shower.

He waited, his worry escalating.

He hadn't been gentle enough. Hysterian paced. Alexa wasn't some Elyrian whore who knew how to handle clientele and their unique needs. She was an average woman—for some devil's unknown reason—who wanted to work for a glorified delivery service. Their paths wouldn't have ever crossed otherwise.

He realized how little he actually knew about her. It wasn't like him to not know everything about a person he was fixated on. Though, it was their fears he usually looked for. Alexa's recruitment paperwork had all the basic information, but the rest?

The details were missing.

Why had she fought him so hard in the lounge? Her eyes had been glazed and she had dissociated. He recalled now how she seemed to relish the idea of taking a risk. How one moment she would be fighting him, only to suddenly give in and clutch him instead.

Who the fuck hurt her?

Hysterian scowled at the bathroom door.

He was going to fucking find out. *She's from Elyria.* Daniels had been from Elyria too, and Hysterian had thought nothing of it at first. It was odd, having three crew members out of the original five being from Elyria. It couldn't be a coincidence.

The odds were miniscule. The EPED was stationed on

Earth.

He needed to start on Elyria. Hysterian re-entered the *Questor's* systems, and connected to the network. Within moments, he double-checked Alexa's files and verified she was from Elyria.

But hacking into secure systems wasn't his forte, and Hysterian loathed the idea of asking Nightheart or even Cypher for anything.

Hysterian cursed again and shot Raphael an encrypted comm. His old boss would know where to dig up information on someone from his home planet. Raphael was one of the most powerful men on Elyria. Corrupt, murderous, and psychopathic, Hysterian understood Raphael better than other Cyborgs.

Raphael never hid his nature...from anyone.

He would get Hysterian the info. Hysterian was willing to pay Raphael's price. However steep it was.

I just need to be patient.

His fingers twitched.

The minutes bled into each other as he glared at the bathroom door. The water kept falling, and his audio blasted the noise through his head.

When the shower finally turned off, he was at the door and gripping the sides, keeping himself from barging in.

Be gentle.

His scowl deepened.

He heard Alexa approach on the other side of the door, but she stopped. The door remained closed.

Be gentle, he reminded himself again.

His tongue snapped out to lick the inside of his suit. The door remained closed and his body pressurized furiously. His glands threatened to open.

Right when he was on the brink of secreting, he shot electricity into the door and forced it open.

Alexa, wet, flushed, with dripping hair, was directly on the other side. Her eyes widened when she saw him, and he pushed off the frame before he lost his mind with frustration.

What he wouldn't give to have been a fly on the wall as she showered.

"Time for the truth," he growled, pivoting before he caught her up in his arms. He didn't trust his strength right now. She followed him into the room, and he shut and locked the bathroom door so she couldn't hide from him again. He sat on the bed and faced her, resting his elbows on his knees.

She stood in the middle of the room, hugging her body tightly. Naked under her towel.

Hysterian palmed his mouth. This was not how he saw this night going. He wanted to remain the scum he was, pull her to him, and tear off her towel so he could see her body again. Covet it because just having her here was incredibly precious.

But he couldn't be that man with her right now. Maybe ever.

He pinned her with his eyes.

"First off, you can get dressed if you like," he said, handing over her clothes.

She took them with one arm, while the other stayed over her chest. "Thank you."

She turned for the bathroom.

"Stop," he ordered. "You can dress right here."

She turned back toward him, the hesitation in her expression growing hard. "In front of you?"

"I don't want you hiding from me anymore."

She exhaled but didn't fight him. He wondered if it was because she knew she'd lose. Or maybe it's because it was fucking late and she had to be tired. And aching...

"Fuck," he snapped, rising to his feet and storming to the replicator in the corner of his room. He had it create acetaminophen tablets and pulled out a globule of water. By the time he came back, she had fastened her bra and was reaching for her shirt. "Take these." He handed her the pills and water. "It's a basic painkiller."

She took the tablets from him and shot them back, ignoring the water. He stared like a man obsessed as her throat bobbed. Hysterian cleared his throat.

"Thank you," she said again, agitating him further.

"Don't. It's the least I can do."

He walked down the short steps to the front of his quarters, needing to be away from the bed he'd just taken her virginity in. He wasn't a drinker but wished he'd tossed back vodka while he'd been waiting.

"What time is it?" she asked, following him.

"Late. Shift starts in three hours."

"Do you think—"

He spun to face her. "No."

"I'm tired."

"You can take the morning off, catch up on your sleep then."

"But the locusts..."

"Alexa..." His voice held warning. "I'll deal with them. Sit." He pointed to the sectional to his left.

She sighed, and he never wanted to put someone over his knee and spank them as much as he wanted to right now. If ever. Everything about Alexa plagued him, and he never fully understood why.

Was it sadness? Or was it something else? Whatever it

was, somehow being near her calmed him as much as it drove him crazy. He recognized something in her.

Now that he'd broken whatever innocence she had remaining, he was adamant not to break anything else.

She sat stiffly, tangling her fingers together.

"Are you sick?" he asked.

"What? No," she answered quickly.

"Why don't I believe you?"

"I'm not sick. I'm not. Is this about the blood?"

"It's about a lot more than that! You couldn't get away fast enough. The bedding was soaked with sweat. I need to know..." He hadn't found any trace of his poison, and she seemed fine, but he had to be certain. "Do you feel light-headed at all? Do you ache anywhere besides there?" He indicated her middle region. "It's important, Alexa. Do you feel strange, in any way?"

She looked down at her body, confusion flitting over her face. "I feel..."

He strode forward, closing the distance between them, and kneeled before her. "Tell me."

"I feel fine."

"I didn't hurt you?"

She shook her head. "Not in any way that I didn't want."

The air expelled from his lungs. He didn't know how much he needed her to tell him that. "Good."

"Why did you wear that...black suit?"

He knew she would be curious. He was surprised she hadn't brought it up sooner. His gaze roved over her. She looked fine. She was acting normal if a little weary. She wasn't sick.

"That first day, when I caught you and Raul in the storage talking? He told you I was defective." Fuck, he hated saying the word out loud. It was a fucking travesty that countless billions had been put into him, only to be unable to control his systems as well as he should. Hysterian waited for her to nod. "I have a skin issue."

It was more than that, but he didn't need to explain all the gritty details. She wouldn't understand anyway.

"You"—she licked her lips, checking him out—"have a skin issue? A Cyborg?"

Hysterian straightened. "Yes."

"Does it have something to do with your animal?"

He stilled. "My what?"

"Your animal? You're a shifter."

"How do you know that?" That information was private, like almost all information on his kind. Only the people closest to him knew his vendor number—and even then, they didn't know what he could and couldn't do.

"Raul told me," she said a little too quickly for his liking.

Of course, Raul told her. Somehow that guy knew more than he should about Hysterian. Raul had been a recommendation from Nightheart, and a previous crewmember of Cypher's before being transferred to Hysterian's ship. Raul might have had access to classified information at some point. They had been on Cypher's ship at the same time for a short period—though had not spoken more than a simple greeting while traveling together to Earth.

Hysterian was even happier now that he'd gotten rid of Raul. But he also didn't believe Alexa.

He didn't believe that she wasn't sick, either.

She's lying to me.

A lot.

He hated liars.

"Yes," he growled. "It has to do with the kind of animal I am. I'm dangerous."

"Dangerous?"

He rose to his feet. "It's nothing you need to concern yourself with. As long as there's a barrier between us, you're safe."

"So...you wore a body suit to be able to have sex with me? You...planned this?"

Her expression was curious, concerned, and he didn't like it. "I wore a suit so I could touch you. I bought a suit tonight so I could give myself a little damned hope that it would happen. Do you know how badly I want to touch you, Alexa? It's insanity. I'm mad with it, having you right here, right in front of me, not able to lay my hands on you and feel your skin. I licked our goddamned bedding so I could have a taste, just a taste of what I was missing. And you know what I found?"

Her eyes had gone wide. "You licked the—the bedding?"

"I want another taste, right fucking now. You're sweet. Too sweet, and nothing about you is sweet, why is that? Why the fuck are you so sweet?"

Annoyance flicked across her face. "How am I supposed to answer that?" she whispered.

"You're hiding something."

Alexa pushed off the sofa and stormed to the door.

"Oh no you don't!" Hysterian jumped in front of her. "You're not going anywhere until you tell me everything."

"Then we're going to be here forever because I have nothing to tell you!"

"Lies."

Her face hardened.

"I know a lie when I hear one, Dear. I'm a damned master at it."

"So threatening me to tell you what you want makes

you an expert? I'm tired. It's been a really long night, as you know." She tried to get past him, but he wouldn't let her.

He grabbed her arms. "I want to know who hurt you, Alexa."

She went rigid. Fear—no, *terror*—fell across her features, sending his systems into overdrive. His need to hurt whoever made her this way grew.

"Tell me who."

"I—"

"I'm going to fucking kill them."

Alexa startled, jerking out of his hold. His hands fell, and he fisted them.

She parted her lips and shook her head. He saw her eyes glaze over, going distant. Her flesh lost any remaining color it had.

He hadn't realized how easy it would be to break her. How delicate she was. Gone was the walled-off subordinate he knew—the one he wanted to shake and warm up. She'd been replaced with a girl. A lost girl.

Had he known Alexa Dear at all?

"I..." Her voice shook, enraging him further. "I can't tell you that."

"I'm going to find out. One way or another, I will find out who hurt you and I'm going to destroy them," he warned. "I'll make sure they never get a chance to hurt you again."

Her eyes shot from his to stare at the wall. She swayed. He was losing her.

"Tell me," he ordered.

He needed to know. He needed to know as if his life depended on it.

"Alexa, make this easier on both of us. I'm going to find out eventually," Hysterian urged.

Her face only grew whiter. When she finally spoke, it wasn't what he wanted to hear. It was his worst nightmare.

She wobbled on her feet, breathing suddenly labored. "Captain, I'm tired. Really tired, and raw. Maybe...I don't feel right." Her eyes hooded.

He waited for her to say more. She stared at the door.

"Alexa?"

Her eyes were filmy now.

"Alexa?" he said again, louder this time. His soul quaked. "What's wrong?"

She slowly brought her hand to her face. "I don't—"

He caught her against him as she fell. Her head rolled to the side, and she vomited all over his floor. He shifted her in his arms, grabbing her hair to keep it out of her face.

She fainted.

"Alexa?" he shouted, turning her over. "Wake up!" He hauled her into his arms. She was so much lighter than she should be, so small.

No...

He sprinted to medical. "Alexa, wake up. Wake up, damn it!" he ordered again as he laid her on the pallet, programming the ship's AI to scan her body.

Hysterian's systems blared, his eyes bright teal, lighting up the medical devices around him. His thoughts came to a halt as he stared at Alexa. *Wake up.*

"*Questor!*" he screamed. "Find Pigeon and get him here, now!"

Robotic arms shot from the wall to take Alexa's vitals. Her eyelids fluttered, lips turned blue.

She was overdosing.

She was overdosing, and it was because of *him*.

NINETEEN

HER BODY FELT HEAVY. Her heart, weak. She was weighed down, trapped by a blanket of molasses. Her thoughts spun. Sometimes they made sense, but most of the time they didn't. Not at first, at least.

But whether they did or not, she didn't care. She knew she was going to forget them anyway.

When she finally managed to open her eyes, it was to a room so bright that it made her head burst with pain. Beside her stood Pigeon and Hysterian, and she managed to smile before she lost consciousness. If Pigeon was here, she was safe.

The next time she opened her eyes, the room was dim, and it was Hysterian alone next to her. She tried to speak, and he shot over her, said her name, but that was all she heard before the pain in her head returned and she fell back under.

The only constant was the heaviness and the forgetfulness. Besides that, she didn't know what was happening, except that when her head wasn't throbbing, time was passing, and she was comfortable. Someone was keeping her that way.

Bit by bit, things returned. Thoughts stuck.

Her conversation with Hysterian returned.

His skin? He said it was dangerous...

Alexa stared at the ceiling of the lab. She knew someone was beside her bed, but she didn't turn her head to see who it was. She wasn't sure if she wanted to go back to sleep yet or not.

If she needed to pretend.

Because she had needles in her arms, and her medical charts—though unclear—were on the wall opposite of her.

If Hysterian and the crew hadn't known she wasn't fully human, they did now. They had to know now. She'd been to the doctor before in her youth, and with one vial of her blood, they knew she wasn't fully human.

So why am I not dead?

Hysterian was a Cyborg, and Cyborgs had been created for one thing only, and that was to destroy Trentians, the same thing she was...a little. She knew that 'little' was still a lot to a Cyborg, who'd been programmed since creation to kill her kind without mercy. Though they hadn't waged war in nearly seventy years now, there were still skirmishes that happened between Cyborgs and Trentians frequently enough to keep the animosity alive.

She always thought that maybe Hysterian killed her dad because he married a half-breed. But then she'd shoot it down, knowing that wouldn't make her father a target of a Cyborg. It wasn't humans they were programmed to destroy after all. Just aliens. Her dad had been human.

And try as she might, she couldn't figure out how she got into the medical lab at all. One minute she'd been in Hysterian's bathroom, and the next? It was all a blur.

We talked. She knew they talked.

Alexa closed her eyes and tried to focus, but the more she tried, the harder her head throbbed. She whimpered.

It hurts. It hurts so much.

She raised her arms so she could bring her hands to her face, but they were too heavy to lift, they remained at her sides. Her pulse raced from the effort, and before she could sink back into stasis and stop her anxiety from building, a beeping sounded in her ears.

"Alexa?"

Pigeon appeared above her. The beeping stopped.

"You're awake!" he exclaimed, glancing over his shoulder. "How are you feeling?"

"My head..." she croaked.

"Right," he said, shuffling away. Something happened with the pallet she was on, and the IVs were changed by the robotic arms attached to it. Pigeon returned. "That should help, I hope."

Pigeon glanced over his shoulder again. She tried to see what he was looking at, but there was only the closed door of the medical lab and some equipment.

He faced her. "I need to talk to you if you can manage it. It's important, and we don't have much time. Do you understand?"

She thought she did. She at least could tell Pigeon was worried about something, and since the pain in her skull kept her thoughts blurry, maybe whatever he had to say would jar them back into place.

"Yes," she wheezed.

"Good. Try to stay awake and listen. I know you're not human."

Her eyes closed. There it was. Her stomach churned.

The words had been uttered aloud.

It's over. If I'm not dead by the end of the day, I'll never see Hysterian again. He'll hate me as much as I should be hating him. She didn't know why that made her miserable.

"I don't know how much longer I can keep it from the captain." Pigeon kept talking.

"He doesn't know?"

"He probably suspects something isn't right, but I've been manipulating and destroying your data as it comes. I'm not running the tests you need to help you heal. It's why you're still here. He's been believing my excuses, but I don't know how long I can keep it up before he finds out. He's... not well. We need to get you off this ship. Now."

Alexa's heart raced. She couldn't leave. How would she manage that? She could barely think straight, let alone walk off this ship without Hysterian noticing.

"I have a guy outside waiting who will take you and hide you, at least long enough for you to get on your feet, but we have to leave now, if possible."

She tried to nod, but her head decided to split open instead.

Pigeon glanced at the door again. She wanted to tell him that Hysterian had access to security feeds, and just saying the words out loud was enough to fuck everything up, but it was too late.

Pigeon put his arm under her back and helped her sit up. She clutched the edge of the pallet, trying not to faint as he pulled out her IVs. When he was done, he helped her into her jacket, covering up her arms. He kneeled and put on her boots.

"You'll...have to come with me," she managed, slurring. "Not safe for you either anymore."

Pigeon nodded.

It broke her heart. "I'm sorry."

He stood, grabbing her hands. "Don't be. I don't know why you put yourself in this situation, to begin with, but I'm sure you have your reasons. I know you're careful and cautious. So I'm sure you knew the risks. I just wish... I wish you would have told me."

"Couldn't risk it," she swallowed. "I care about you."

Pigeon's face fell. "I care about you too, Dear. You remind me of my daughters."

Her heart flooded with emotion, and her chin fell to her chest. It was too painful to hear, to cry even.

"None of that now," he said, curling his arm under her shoulder. "Time to get you to safety."

He hauled her against his frame and guided her to the exit. He checked the corridor twice before leaving the medical lab.

She tried not to faint.

They managed to make it to the stairs, and from there she had to work up the strength to bear down on her feet and use the wall while Pigeon kept her upright. By the time they made it to the bottom, they were both sagging. Alexa peered down the long hallway ahead of them and the hatch at the other end.

They were never going to make it.

But it wasn't about her anymore, it was about Pigeon's safety too. Hysterian might have told her he'd never harm her, but he never said such words to any of the other crew... Not that she knew of.

Hobbling along the wall, she and Pigeon made it to the armory, the menagerie. She looked into her work space for the last time as they drifted by. Her eyes landed on the male locust curled up sleeping in his enclosure on the other side. Alexa turned away. They made it to the hatch.

Pigeon set her against the wall, and she slid down as he

moved the panel to type in the ship's security code. She tried to catch her breath.

We're going to make it. Hope and fear, and another dose of misery, filled her.

The hatch opened.

Hysterian was on the other side.

"Captain..." Pigeon said, straightening.

Alexa's eyes fell on the Cyborg blocking their path. Tall and decked, with his white hair once again perfectly held away from his face—she didn't need to see his mouth to know he wasn't happy.

"What's going on here?" Hysterian said cooly. "What in the ever-living hell do you think you're doing?"

"I was taking— That is— Alexa needed some air—"

"We're leaving," she whispered. She wasn't going to let Pigeon take the fall. This wasn't his battle. It was much too late for lies.

The next thing she knew, she was in Hysterian's arms, and he was carrying her back into the ship. "Like fucking hell you are."

"Captain!" Pigeon chased after them. "Please."

Alexa wrenched her eyes closed when Hysterian spun to face him. Sweat poured from her brow.

"You're fired, Pigeon. Get off my ship."

"But—"

"Now!" Hysterian roared. Teal light burst forth. "Unless you want to spend the next few months in the brig!"

Alexa gripped him weakly. "You hurt him, and I'll never forgive you," she gasped, catching his glowing eyes. She held them through the pain.

Something in his gaze shifted. Frustration?

"Get out of my sight," he warned Pigeon though he

stared at her while he said it. Hysterian swiveled and took her back to medical. He laid her back down on the pallet, and the machine hooked her up. Tears rushed from her eyes, knowing what was about to happen.

She caught sight of Pigeon in the doorway, watching on in horror.

"Why the fuck were you trying to leave?" Hysterian demanded, pulling off her boots. There was a heavy thud when they hit the floor. "What's possessed you? You need to rest. Do you know how close you came to dying?"

"Hysterian," she tried to stop him.

"I'm this close, Alexa, this close"—he put his fingers together—"to ripping off every head on Libra, and you're trying to take a fucking stroll?"

"Stop—"

He leaned over her as the needles slipped back into her arms. Her chest constricted.

"You can't die," Hysterian said. "I won't allow it. If I have to rip my skin off and give it to you for that to happen, I will."

"I'm not human..."

Alexa fainted.

TWENTY

HYSTERIAN PACED THE BRIDGE, examining Alexa's medical records. He had the medical equipment rerun all its scans for him, take her blood, all while he denied what she'd uttered. Then he had them all deleted and removed from his systems, only to do it all again.

It was all right there.

The abnormalities. She had T-positive genes, and her blood type? Nothing any full-blooded human could ever have.

He scanned the records he had on file for her and the ones from his lab. If he could convince himself it was impossible, maybe he could convince the systems inside him that urged him to waste her. For a split-second, he'd nearly touched her.

Hysterian palmed his face.

He couldn't deny the evidence, and he couldn't deny the conversation that happened between her and Pigeon before they tried to leave his ship. No matter how hard he manipulated his coding, it remained the same. Better Cyborgs than him had tried and they couldn't do it.

How could he be so easily duped?

He thought about Alexa's hair dye, her sweet-smelling blood, and how she was always cold. The sweat, the dampness of the bedding after they'd had sex. Perhaps even why she tried to fight him every step of the way...

He missed every sign. His hands clenched.

Alexa was a half-breed.

She held the enemies' blood in her veins. And he'd fucked her? Took her virginity?

He may have not killed countless Trentians like other Cyborgs had, but he'd still killed many. Even now, the codes —the first ones, the ones that were nearly impossible to remove from his systems—urged him to swat her life out like a bug. Or to hand her over to the authorities.

They demanded he remove her from the equation, because the only good equation didn't have aliens in it.

She could be a spy.

Why else would she infiltrate his crew knowing the risk?

Hysterian turned to the porthole and stared at the stars as the *Questor* flew farther and farther away from Libra. He'd kept them docked for nearly a week while Alexa recovered, but now that she was on the mend, he wanted to be as far from the port as possible. Far from the shit that happened there, farther still from his own stupidity.

He could outrun it if he tried.

Was it insanity, flying out into space with your enemy? Each time Hysterian tried to leave, or thought about dropping Alexa's sick body off for someone else to deal with, he couldn't do it. Because each time he tried, he knew he'd want to kill anyone who got close enough to try and take her away from him.

She lied to me. He scowled.

And I wanted to protect her, was willing to hunt down her enemies and tear their spines from their bodies... He turned from the porthole and stormed out of the bridge, heading straight for the gym's bathroom. He stripped, turned on the cleaning unit, and stepped under the hot water. His nerves thrummed.

How was it that he started with a crew of five, and now he was down to one, and in less than two months' time?

How was it that he had an alien sleeping in his fucking bed?

Because that's where Alexa was now, locked in his room, away from all the medical equipment she could use to create a weapon or hurt herself with. He made sure there was nothing in his room she could use—if that's what she planned now that she'd been found out.

He needed to keep her close until he figured out what he was going to do with her.

Hysterian rested his palms on the wall as the water washed over him. *What the fuck am I going to do with her?*

The heat comforted him, took some of the pressure away, and he wanted to laugh because it was heat that could kill Alexa. *The same fucking heat I crave.*

How was it that he'd spent his life fantasizing about a hot-blooded woman, only to fall for the first cold-blooded one he came upon?

He pushed off the wall, denting the metal.

She won't fucking talk to me. Part of him wanted to wring her pretty little neck for that alone.

After he had Horace drag Pigeon to the brig—because the guy wouldn't leave—Hysterian sat by Alexa's side until she woke and was well enough to move on her own. Even if he was the most dangerous being to be around her, the part of him that was human needed her to get better.

He needed it more than his next breath. Hysterian clawed at his skin, scrubbing his secretion off with his nails. He hated it. She nearly died because of him, because he'd let his guard down.

It hadn't even been his skin that poisoned her; it had been her underwear.

He'd left the pair in his bathroom after he had changed. He left them there after they'd been wrapped around his cock all day. They would've been dry by the time she'd showered and found them.

She'd put them on, and whatever poison that had absorbed into them had been enough to penetrate her flesh and fill her with the destructive nanobots within it.

If he hadn't discovered the poisoned underwear and removed them sooner, she'd be dead right now.

Hysterian slammed his fist into the wall. The metal echoed through the shower unit, paining his head.

He shut off the water and stepped out of the unit. He dried, dressed quickly, and was outside his quarters moments later.

Alexa was lying asleep on the sofa when he walked in.

He was about to grab a blanket before he stopped himself. *She's a fucking Trentian. She won't want a blanket.* Blankets would just heat her up. The room was frigid for a human, but for her, she looked more comfortable than she had been the entire time she'd been on his ship.

His hands fisted.

She looked so innocent sleeping. She hadn't looked like a Trentian at first after he'd found out. But then again, she was only a third. Whether it was her father or her mother who was a half-breed, he wasn't sure yet.

Raphael hadn't gotten back to him, and Hysterian was

sure as hell not going to be asking another Cyborg for help now.

They'd tell him to eject her from the ship, at worst. At best, they'd want him to hand her over to the government. She did lie to them.

She'd been on Earth.

Trentians—half-breed or pure—weren't allowed to step foot on the home planet, regardless of how much they had. A crime punishable by life in prison.

And if Nightheart found out Hysterian had a Trentian spy on one of his ships? Working for him? Privy to classified information? Hysterian tensed.

Hysterian hadn't decided whether he was going to tell his boss about this problem they both faced, but he now thought it would be better if Nightheart didn't know.

She doesn't look like a spy...

Hysterian crept to the sofa and kneeled.

He'd verified Alexa's educational credentials; she hadn't lied about that. She was at least qualified for the work she was doing. He also knew she had access to information, and to him, more than she should have. And if she was out to steal secrets, or to kill him, why the hell would she sleep with him?

She'd let him strip her naked, leaving her at her most vulnerable, had given him her virginity, and if she'd pretended she hadn't known about her heritage, he might have believed her.

He'd had her screaming in his bed as he sank deep inside her.

Me. Trentians hated Cyborgs more than Cyborgs hated them. Being programmed to hate was different than full-on, natural hatred. She had to have known before she even applied for the job on his ship that she was a half-breed. She had to have known who she'd be working for.

Did she want to die?

It made no sense to him why she was here on his ship. He didn't deal in governmental secrets or technology development. His weapons were mostly standard-issue, and those that weren't were locked up in places she'd never be able to access without him.

So why the fuck is she here?

Her dark hair fell softly upon her cheek where it had escaped from her hairband. Her hands were cupped under her face, and soft breaths slipped past slightly parted pale lips.

He imagined her with translucent white locks.

Hysterian licked his lips.

Was it sick that he wanted her still? After knowing what she was, what she'd done. It was absurd.

Why did she sleep with me?

Was she trying to get close to me? If so, she'd done a fine job at it. *Maybe she was waiting for the right moment...*

I probably killed some of her ancestors.

Her eyelids fluttered open. Once her eyes focused on him, she tensed and shot upright. His audio picked up an adrenaline surge from her—her heartbeat skyrocketed. Her cheeks flushed pink.

"Why?" he asked.

Alexa slunk away from him.

"Why?" he asked again, lower this time.

He sat back when she refused to answer. "You will tell me. You'll never leave this room otherwise." When she remained silent, he scowled. "You had to have a good reason, half-breed. How could you not? It must've been hard, no doubt. I wonder if this was your plan all along, getting on my ship, getting close to me? Or was it just the luck of the draw? You saw an opportunity and took it?

"Maybe you have a good reason? Someone found you out during training and is now blackmailing you? Is that it? Threatening to reveal your identity? Or is there someone you love in danger?"

He hoped she was being blackmailed. He prayed—fucking prayed—it was something so easy to forgive.

"Tell me!" Hysterian shouted when Alexa still refused to speak.

She didn't even flinch. It was like she'd shut down.

"Why the fuck are you here, Alexa? Are you here to hurt me, kill me? Why!?"

He surged to his feet before he did something he'd regret. This was all too close to home for him.

The pads of his fingers slickened with poison. He could make her speak and tell him all her dirty secrets. He could make her delirious with a single touch. He could make her addicted to him, giving her little doses of heroin, or worse, until she was mindless and broken. And all she thought about was pleasing *him*.

He could have all his answers and so much more.

Anyone would spill their secrets rather than go through excruciatingly painful withdrawal.

But this was Alexa, not a war criminal. She wasn't some desperate, addicted club whore easily used and discarded.

"I will get my answers from you," he said. "Whether you want to share them willingly or not. I will get my answers."

He strode from the room and locked the door behind him.

TWENTY-ONE

Days passed, and each time Hysterian visited Alexa, it was more of the same. He would watch her, she would watch him back, and he would threaten her. He never touched her, never allowed himself to get close enough that she might try and touch him back.

And each day, she drifted farther and farther away.

He brought food, made sure she ate.

He set it on the table beside the sofa, where she spent most of her days.

On the third day, he was half-crazed. He yelled, railed, tore up the bedding, destroyed the room all while she stood in the center quietly watching.

Once, he could get any living being to talk, to spill all their secrets, but not with Alexa. Every time he came close to using his skills on her, disgust filled him and he stormed to the gym's shower and boiled.

He wasn't getting through to her, and he needed to make a choice with what needed to be done. He couldn't, wouldn't, not until he knew all the information. His threats weren't working.

Fear wasn't working.

Three days and he was fucking exhausted by it all.

When he went to fix her food next, he took his time—like he always did—but researched the general fare aliens enjoyed eating. He had his replicator create some for her.

He placed it on the table by the sofa when he returned to his quarters.

She came out of the bathroom when she heard him.

His eyes took her in.

She was wearing the same clothes as days before and was just as beautiful. He was beginning to think, the longer this went on, she only got more beautiful to plague him.

"Are you ready to talk?" he asked.

No answer.

"That's fine. I'll be back later to pick this up." He stood and indicated the food, turning for the door. Better to leave now before he made things worse.

The next morning, he found her back on the sofa staring at her hands. The food from the night before had been picked at. He replaced it with the new tray he brought with him.

"You need to eat," he said. "You need to regain your strength."

She stared at her hands.

He hated this. He hated being shut out.

He missed her.

She hadn't tried to escape since that time with Pigeon, and he wasn't sure if he hated that the most. It was like she'd given up and was just waiting for him to finish her off.

"We'll be arriving at Atrexia in a few days," he said just to fill the silence, to get a reaction, anything from her. "After that, we're due back on Earth."

She didn't look up.

He couldn't take it anymore. Hysterian was in front of her within the next second. She jerked back with a gasp.

It was something. It was fucking something.

"Tell me, Alexa. I'm begging. If someone is blackmailing you—"

"No one's blackmailing me!" She snapped to her feet and fled to the upper half of the room.

He stilled. It was the first time he'd heard her voice in days.

"Then why?" he asked cautiously.

"You might as well kill me and get it over with."

"I don't want to fucking kill you. Let me help you."

Her laugh sounded hollow with defeat. "Help me? You don't want to help me. You want to shout and threaten, and get your way."

He stormed after her and grabbed her arm. She tugged but he wasn't going to allow her to get away.

"Why did you sleep with me?" he asked.

Her face fell.

"Tell me!"

She looked at the ground.

He had half a mind to crawl under her so she'd be looking at him instead. He cursed, dropped her arm, and left.

The next time he came back, she stood in front of the mirror in his bathroom, pulling at her hair with tears in her eyes.

He grabbed her hand before she yanked her hair again. "What are you doing?"

"I want them to stop," she cried. "I want them to stop!"

"You want what to stop?"

She sobbed. "The thoughts."

Hysterian pulled her into his arms. She hit him with her

fists as she cried. He stayed still, keeping her trapped in his embrace.

"I can't make the thoughts stop, but I can help you. Let me help you," he urged. "Let me *help* you."

"Pigeon," she gasped. "I want to talk to Pigeon. Only Pigeon."

His voice hardened, "Pigeon tried to take you away from me."

Alexa wiped at her face with her hands. It broke his damned metal-encased heart. She was deteriorating, and he didn't know what to do. He wasn't equipped for this. He watched her dry her tears and slip back into stasis.

Later that night, he stared at his own hands, sitting on the sofa. Alexa was curled up on his bed, just within his sight. She was watching him.

Sometimes it seemed like she was about to speak, but then she'd turn away and shut him out all over again.

He'd lied to her. He could help take away her thoughts. At least for a time.

He could make her happy, delirious. He could reconfigure his poison into something else for her, something that would shut off her mind completely. Hysterian tugged off his glove and unfurled his fingers. With a single touch, he could make her smile...

Had he ever made her smile? He couldn't recall. There were no occurrences of it in his memory.

Had he ever made anyone smile that wasn't with the use of drugs? He rubbed the moisture between his fingers.

Tomorrow, they would arrive on Atrexia and deliver the locusts. He had Horace managing the lab, and Hysterian needed to check in on his second soon. Time was running out. He couldn't keep Pigeon locked away forever, and eventually, the lack of contact from his crew with the EPED was going to be questioned.

Yet he'd gotten no closer to why Alexa was on his ship.

If he handed her over to the government, he'd never see her again. It was either keep her captive forever, or...let her go.

She hadn't actually hurt him, not physically. She hadn't done anything wrong as far as Hysterian knew.

Except lie. Except be something she's not.

Killing her was out of the question. Despite his codes urging for such a fate, he wasn't like other Cyborgs; he'd been made to be used against *humans*. The codes were still there, but he was managing them, and even so, half-breeds were a jumble in his mind.

He'd been around many over the last decade, having only ever killing a few. Domestic aliens and half-breeds were viewed as lesser threats than Knights and their religious zealot warriors.

A sad laugh flitted through his head. It never reached his lips.

He could ignore the urges because he'd spent the last ninety or so years doing the same with the codes forcing him to secrete. Sadly, those codes were far harder to keep under wraps than the ones urging to get rid of Alexa.

The fact that they were there at all disgusted him. He didn't want to hurt her.

But convincing her of that was going to be hard. Perhaps the hardest thing he'd do in his miserable life. *And I started by threatening her...* Recent history proved that there couldn't be anything between them. Her kind was born to hate his kind, and vice versa.

"My skin is dangerous," he said, unsure if she was even listening. "Few people know that about me, though it's no secret. It's easier not to talk about it." Why he was telling her this, he wasn't sure. As far as he knew, she might already know this about him. She hadn't questioned it so far which had been odd.

"The reason you ended up like this was because you put the underwear on in my bathroom that night. There were traces of opium and batrachotoxin left on them that hadn't fully dismantled. It takes hours for the nanocells in my poison to dismantle, and longer still if I'm nearby.

"I can't get close to people—I can't touch them—without worrying that I'll kill them, or have them become addicted... to *me*. It's why I cover my mouth. When people touch me, their body heat triggers my glands to open, releasing whatever toxin I so choose, and if I don't, whatever my systems choose for me. I'm trying to control it."

Hysterian sighed, kneading his brow.

"Alexa, I'm the captain of this ship because Nightheart offered to find me a cure—a way to remove the codes, to replace them, or perhaps destroy that part of me. To burn it out like cancer. I wouldn't be here at all if there was another option left. The last hope I had died, and it took parts of me with it." He forced the words out. "Parts of me I gave away that I never meant to..."

His past clutched his throat and squeezed.

"I've done terrible things that go far beyond my time in the military."

He didn't want her to make the same mistakes he once made.

Alexa sat upright, clearly listening to him. The wires in his chest thrummed from the simple act. Was he getting through to her?

Would she come to him?

His fingers twitched, glimpsing her through them.

Her lips parted and his world stopped.

"Terrible things?" she asked.

"I went numb." Hysterian dropped his hand before he clawed the skin of his brow off. "I turned off. I shut out my humanity and every part of me that made me human when I last lost hope. I've killed more allies and friends than I care to admit. At first by accident or misfortune, until it was on purpose. I aligned myself with an evil fucking piece of shit who used my numbness to gain power, and I let him, all because he relished my sociopathy. He made me feel like I belonged in this universe even when there was no war left to be fought. That I could do what I wanted, to whoever I wanted, and—"

"Is this what Raul meant by—"

His lips twisted. "Don't say that name to me. If you say anything at all, tell me how disgusted you are, how I deserve to die, and that you're here for that reason and that reason alone. But not another man's fucking name."

She pushed the blanket she clutched aside. "Why are *you* here?"

The very same question he had of her.

"I'm here so I can someday touch another without worry. I crave it, endlessly. This need for touch, for companionship, to know what it's like to embrace someone and not worry about killing them. I crave contact. Perhaps because I can't have it. I've never told anyone my reasons before. Despite what you are, or why you're here, if it has something to do with me...

"I need you to know that I'm sorry."

He closed his eyes and exhaled.

"What are you?" she whispered.

"A frog. A golden poison dart frog. An amphibi-ous...creature that's been extinct for centuries. A goddamned fucking frog. And do you know what the worst of it is? I can't shift. I have this *need* to be what I am, but I can't. All I can do is endure."

"A frog?"

"I lied to you before. If you want your thoughts to go away, Alexa"—his soul shriveled—"I can...make that happen."

"You can't control it? At all?"

It's the most she had said to him in days.

"Yes, it's how I do most of my killing," he said. "And control it?" He growled. "I can to a point. I spend my night shifts boiling in water, draining my body of all its resources. Only to be forced to replenish and do it all again the next night."

Her brow furrowed. "Do you remember..."

"Do I remember what?"

"Nothing." She looked away.

He stood. "Do I remember what, Alexa?" *Don't shut me out.*

Her face shuddered. "It doesn't matter."

"What doesn't matter?" he demanded. "Give me something, anything."

"I want to talk to Pigeon," she murmured, turning away.

Pigeon? Again? Another man's name.

His glands opened. Had he been worrying about Raul all this time when he should've been worrying about the seventy-year-old mechanic? Anger coursed through him.

Hysterian gritted his teeth. His tongue shot out to coil and slide around, rubbing against them.

"I meant it when I said I'll never hurt you," he said. "I know I already have, but I still mean it." Devils, he had to believe it was true. "If you don't want to come clean to me, I'm going to have to turn you into the authorities. I can't risk you giving information to our..." He cleared his throat, trailing off.

The word *enemies* was left unsaid in the air.

She didn't respond.

He stormed to where she sat, grabbing her shoulders and shaking her. "Why are you giving up? Just fucking tell me, Alexa. Make me understand!"

She jerked out of his grip, and he let her go. Cold. There was nothing but coldness.

"Fine," he sneered. "Have it your way."

With one final look, he memorized everything he could about her—the woman who'd snatched his heart from his chest when he wasn't looking—and strode to the door before he did something he'd regret.

"Goodbye, Dear."

If Alexa was done, so was he.

TWENTY-TWO

THE DOOR to the cabin closed with a resounding *hiss*. She scrambled to her feet and ran to it, only to stop once she got there.

Pain burst in her chest, her heart shattering.

What was she supposed to say? He wanted her to tell him what he wanted to hear. That she was forced to come aboard his ship and pretend to be something she wasn't. It wasn't true. She came of her own volition. She came to kill him.

That was her only objective. That was her goal.

To make him answer for his actions.

If he hadn't planned to kill her already, he was certainly going to if he found out the real reason she was here. How could he not? They were enemies, even if he wouldn't say it aloud.

And now that she knew about his time with Raphael... His reasons. It made her sick. She pitied Hysterian. She'd always known Raphael wasn't a good man. The owner of Dimes was known on Elyria as being awful, but she had no proof of anything, only rumors.

And what Hysterian did? What he *could* do?

What he could've done to her?

Those weren't rumors anymore.

As long as she'd kept her mouth closed about her reasons, she could bide her time, wait for new information. So she'd waited and slept when she could. She'd waited with nothing but her guilt to keep her company.

Alexa pushed away from the door and sat heavily on the sofa because deep down she knew that it didn't matter how much time passed, nothing was actually going to change.

Because she loved Hysterian so much it hurt.

She shuddered.

She needed to talk to Pigeon. She needed someone to tell her what to do.

She needed her dad. She wanted to know why he'd been involved with Raphael and Hysterian at all. She'd always wondered, but it had been eclipsed by his murder. She'd convinced herself that he'd been killed out of cruelty, malice.

That he'd been a victim of a hate crime or that he'd been in the wrong place at the wrong time.

She needed Pigeon. Alexa shook. But she wanted Hysterian.

Alexa pulled at her hair and groaned.

He kills people when he touches them... Was that how Hysterian killed her dad? And a frog? She had no idea what a frog was. She assumed it was some Earth creature they didn't have on Elyria. Still, she wished she had her wristcon so she could look it up. Of all the things she'd learned, out of all the training she'd had to get where she was right now, she realized how very little she actually knew.

Alexa untangled her fingers from her hair. Hysterian

had given her a reason to forgive him, and she held onto it because, to her surprise, she was still alive.

He *seemed* to care. That he'd told her all he had because he was trying to earn her trust. She wanted to believe he cared just as much as she wanted a reason to forgive him. But once she gave him what he wanted, would he change and kill her then?

Was it all an act?

Didn't he just say he was a master at getting people to speak? That he was specifically created for the intention of covert warfare and punishment?

Why else would he tell her about his skin? His animal? His time on Elyria? He'd told her more just now than what she'd gathered about him all these years she'd obsessed over him.

Is he biding his time? Are we both?

She hadn't killed him yet; she hadn't even tried.

The door to the cabin opened, and Alexa swiveled. Pigeon appeared, exhausted.

"Pigeon?" she whispered, taking a step forward, not sure if what she was seeing was real. "Hysterian let you come?"

Pigeon glanced to his side at something she couldn't see beyond the door and stepped into the room. He shut the door behind him.

She rushed forward and threw her arms around him. "I'm glad you're safe! I've been worried."

He hugged her back, patting her hair. "Now that's a dumb thing to go and do. No need to worry about me."

"Why didn't you leave when you had the chance?" She was so happy to see him. Alexa held onto Pigeon as if he might slip from her arms. For a moment, he was her dad. The scent of Elyrian sands and Sunwater flowers filled her nose.

For a few more moments, he remained her dad.

"And be stranded on Libra?" He huffed, patting her head again. "I think not. Anyway, I wasn't going to leave you with him knowing what you are. Especially when you were so sick." He pulled from her arms, grasping her shoulders so he could look at her. Alexa wiped her cheeks. "You look well, if not tired. Has he hurt you? Are you okay?"

She nodded. "Yeah. I'm okay. I'm better now. I'm just so glad you're here."

"Good. Captain told me you were asking for me." Pigeon squeezed her shoulders then dropped his hands. He followed her to the seating area and sat down next to her. "I don't know how much time we have," he said, lowering his voice. They leaned into each other. "He's been keeping me in the brig."

"I know. I'm so sorry. Has he hurt you?"

"He hasn't yet. I made my own choices, Dear, but I'm worried about you. Never saw someone so sick before. It's been bothering me. You were fine at Termites. What happened?"

"I..." Her tongue suddenly felt too big for her mouth. Pigeon didn't know it had been Hysterian who made her sick. She still didn't know how she felt about that herself. "I must've caught the flu on Libra."

"Nothing I've ever seen. I may be a mechanic, but I've seen my share of illness. That wasn't the flu."

She shook her head. "I don't know what to do."

"About what?"

"Everything."

"Now don't do that. I'm sure the captain would have done something to you by now if he was going to hurt you. He's probably deciding whether to turn you into the authorities once we get back on Earth. I'm sure if we both try we can convince him not to. We'll figure this out."

"That's not it."

"It's not?"

"I love him," she blurted out.

Pigeon went silent. Unable to look at him, she dropped her hands to her lap and stared at them.

"That's a problem," he eventually responded.

"I know." And that wasn't even half of it. "I don't know what to do. Tell me what to do."

"Have you told him?"

"No."

"I'd start there."

"He's my enemy." He'd just said it, though not out loud.

"And you knew that and still took a job working for him? For *them*." Alexa knew Pigeon meant Cyborgs and humans in general. "Is he really your enemy, or just an asshole? Because if he was your enemy, I don't think you would've spent the last couple months in his company."

A laugh burst from her throat. "I wish it were that simple."

God, if only.

Pigeon placed a finger under her chin and tilted her head so she had to look at him. The wrinkles on his brow deepened.

Old eyes searched hers. "Why did you take the job knowing what you know? Are you in some trouble?"

"Why does everything think that? I'm not in any trouble."

"Well, knowing the history of your—umm—alien ancestry, it is a strange choice to make. It's dangerous enough for you to be around humans, but Cyborgs? You'd have to have a reason, unless you enjoy the risk. In the time I've known you, you're not a risk taker, Alexa. It only makes me believe it more that you're not here of your own volition."

"That would be easier, wouldn't it? If I had an excuse."

"You're saying you don't? You risked yourself for nothing?" Pigeon shook his head. "That's not the Alexa I know. Despite your reasons, you've been found out, and now you only have two choices."

"Beg him to save me? Or face my fate head on?"

"Tell him the truth."

"I can't."

"Why not?"

"There's some things I can't explain because they're too hard to put into words. If I try, I find myself drowning..."

"You're scared."

Her breath hitched. "I'm scared," she agreed. "I'm scared that if I tell him everything, the world will end. I'm scared that he knows I'll break—I'm breaking—and that if he waits me out, I will tell him everything, and then what? He may kill me then, take me to the authorities. Or worse... I'm scared that if I tell him, he'll look at me with disgust and break my heart."

"I see. I don't think the captain will hurt you...if he hasn't already, but I'm not sure. He was" —Pigeon rubbed his mouth—"a mess when you were in sickbay. He rarely left your side. It was exceedingly difficult to hide any abnormal indicators on your readouts. It was only possible because he was so focused on you that he wasn't aware of anything else. Not even me, the job, anything. But if you think his feelings for you have changed because of your blood...?"

"I can't tell him. I can't."

Pigeon slumped. "Dear, if you won't tell him how you

feel, and you don't think you can fully trust him, then you need to do the next best thing for your safety. Leave."

The air fled from her lungs. But on her next breath, they expanded, and a calm came over her. *Leave.*

"The sooner the better," Pigeon said. "Before anyone else finds out what you are. We're due to arrive on Atrexia tomorrow, I'm told. Horace has been bringing me my meals and keeping me updated. Atrexia is an unregulated planet. It isn't privy to the same laws as Earth, or one of the main colony planets. It's small. Private sects of people live on Atrexia, mainly those in research and resource harvesting. You'll be able to find someone to help you at the port. There will be private and personal ships. Go to the terminal desk and see if anyone is willing to take on an extra passenger. It might be your only chance."

Alexa's heart raced. "What about you? I won't leave while you're locked up. You're there because of me."

"I don't think I'll be locked up much longer, so don't you worry about that. When I'm out, I'll lead him astray if he doesn't just let you walk out on your own, and I'll do my best to destroy any evidence you leave behind so he'll have nothing to give to the authorities."

"He's a Cyborg, Pigeon. Hysterian is probably watching us right now. I won't leave without you, I can't."

"Let him, and you can, damn it! If he harms me, he's never met my daughters, but he will, and it won't be pretty." Pigeon visibly shivered. "I'll be fine. I've lived a long life anyway, seen a lot of things. Had too many kids. If he's got an inkling of good in him, and you've done nothing wrong but keep a part of you secret that isn't hurting anyone else, you won't come to any harm, especially if he feels the same about you as you do him. I think he might."

Her throat constricted. Wouldn't that be something?

Even so, he wouldn't feel anything for her if he knew what she knew.

"Please," she breathed.

"Pigeon! Time's up," Horace's voice came from the doorway just as it opened. Horace found them but wouldn't look her in the eye, keeping his gaze on Pigeon.

Pigeon stood, worry etched on his face. He opened his mouth to speak, but she shook her head, stopping him. Alexa rose and wrapped him in a hug. It may be the last time she would ever be able to do so. He embraced her back, just as hard.

"Be safe, Dear," he whispered.

"Don't make me come in there," Horace warned.

"Remember, Atrexia is the next day shift," Pigeon said against her ear. Alexa gripped him harder. "I'll do what I can for you on my end."

"Don't," she pleaded, but he was already pulling away.

There was a sad smile on his face as she drew back her arms and hugged herself instead. She watched him walk to Horace and out of the room. The door shut, and she was alone again.

Alexa stared at it for a handful of moments before going back to the sofa and curling up. She was going to leave tomorrow, and she was going to leave alone. She'd been stuck in this room for days—she'd lost count. For once in her life, she didn't want to be alone.

It's for the best that I am...

She couldn't kill Hysterian. She just couldn't. She tried; she had thought about it a lot those first days. She was done with the guilt and the shame. She may not be able to trust him, but that didn't stop her from giving him her heart on a platter to be served back to her by sharp knives. She couldn't stay, not now that her secret was out in the open.

Alexa decided.

She had one last night. One night where she could be with him and not alone. She needed to say goodbye.

TWENTY-THREE

SHE TENSED, heat coiling in her belly. God, how she wanted Hysterian. She had always wanted him. He was her very own fallen angel.

Alexa combed out her hair with her fingers, letting it fall in damp waves down her back. She stared at her face in the mirror. There was nothing remarkable about her that would lure in a man like Hysterian...

It'll have to do.

Alexa frowned. She wanted to look nice.

She wished she had her bag of clothes from Libra. She hoped Raul hadn't rifled through them, and that they remained untouched on her old bunk. And Raul... Alexa's head clouded.

She hadn't seen or heard of him once since Libra.

Alexa ran her hands down her shirt. After tonight, she was never going to see the *Questor* or anyone on it ever again. If she didn't encounter Raul, she wouldn't have to break things off with him or explain anything. Maybe it was better that way.

She left the bathroom and went to the bed. She straightened the bedding out for the hundredth time. When the sheets couldn't get any straighter, she stepped back.

It's time.

She looked around the room. There was nothing left to do, nothing else she could do.

She still searched for an excuse, because after she called Hysterian, he was either going to give her what she wanted, or not. Wistfulness gripped her heart. She was going to miss the *Questor*. Even this room. The last few months had been better than she thought they could ever be.

She cared about more than just her revenge now.

In doing so made her fail. She fell in love with the one being she vowed to end. Now it was time to leave before something worse happened. Alexa wouldn't let anyone else get hurt on her behalf.

Heading to the door, she braced for what was about to come.

"Hysterian," she said his name, a little hesitant at first. She'd never called out for him before. "I'm ready to talk."

It was a lie, and he would know it was, but it was the perfect bait.

I love him. There was nothing wrong in pretending for a little while that everything was perfect, right? Tonight was for her, and no one else.

There wasn't any shame anymore.

She didn't have to wait long before the door to the room opened.

Hysterian, perfectly handsome, exceedingly dangerous, walked into the room and straight toward her, stopping a foot away.

"You came," she breathed.

He glared at her, pinning her to where she stood. He was mad. As he should be.

"Not by choice," he said, his voice low.

She straightened. "I know you're upset—"

"Why did you call for me, Alexa?" he growled. "Speak."

"I..." Now that he was here, nervousness stole her courage. He was so beautiful, so overwhelming. Why did he ever want her in the first place? Alexa gritted her teeth and shut the thoughts out. If she failed this time it was going to be because she put her full effort in and he denied her anyway.

She knew he very well may be lying. That he might not actually care about her at all, but whether he cared or not, whether he was manipulating her or not, she was going to do her best to manipulate him right back.

"Why am I here?" he asked again, curiosity now edging his tone.

"I wanted..." She licked her lips. "I, uh..."

"If it's not to tell me what's going on in your head, then say it."

"I wanted"—he swallowed, her cheeks flushing—"to be with you."

Her heart hammered.

His eyes searched her, and she tried not to wither. She wished she knew what he saw in her. She wished she wasn't a half-breed and he wasn't a Cyborg. That they were two normal beings.

She prayed he still wanted her as much as she wanted him.

But as the moments passed, and he continued to stand silently before her, embarrassment wiggled its way into her head. "This was a stupid idea—"

"Strip."

"What?"

"I said strip."

Hysterian's eyes flashed teal for a split second and he pivoted, striding to the sofa. He sat down and crossed his boot over his knee.

Had she heard him correctly? "Strip?"

"I gave you an order." There was no softness in his voice.

Alexa shivered and wiped her palms on her pants. This is what she wanted, she reminded herself. She wanted Hysterian, even if he didn't actually want her back. She was doing this for herself and not for him.

She faced him and started tugging off her shirt.

"Slower," Hysterian said.

She paused midway and inched the cloth up her torso. When it slipped over her bra, she bunched the material up in her hands and drew it off, letting the shirt drop at her feet. She fanned out her damp hair behind her shoulders.

He sat back. "Now the rest."

Something dark and delicious invaded her soul. Her eyes flicked to the bulge that appeared between Hysterian's legs. She knew what was under his uniform, and the ache that awaited her if she got what she wanted. The all-encompassing heat. The blissful lightheadedness while being in his arms. She could feel the heat coming off him already and she was feet away from him.

"Now, Alexa," he commanded when she took too long. "I gave you an order."

She turned to the side and unbuckled the snap of her pants and wiggled them down her hips, knowing this was going past the point of no return. She hadn't put underwear on after her shower. She wasn't making that mistake again.

Alexa took a steadying breath and let her pants drop, revealing her crux, her legs.

She heard Hysterian groan.

She stepped out of her pants and toed them and her shirt aside.

Mostly naked now, she faced Hysterian again.

He was leaning forward, elbows on his knees, his eyes glittering with flashes of light. They flicked over her body, twitching, bulging in that way she'd only seen a couple of times before. His tongue pressed against the cloth of his mouth, pushing it out.

She wanted to see his face.

"Will you lower your mask?" she asked, shifting from one foot to the other.

"You don't get to ask anything more of me, Dear. Not until you come clean. That ship has fucking sailed," he said, rubbing his mouth. When his hand dropped, it was normal again. "Fuck, you're glorious. Your skin practically glows. How did I ever want something different?"

Her skin prickled from the compliment.

His eyes finally met hers. They'd gone dark with heat. "Take off your bra."

Trembling fingers went to the clip between her breasts. She unsnapped it and let her last bit of covering fall away.

Hysterian stared at her.

"Come here," he said.

She shivered and took a step toward him.

He reached forward and grabbed her, dragging her on his lap to straddle him. His bulge pressed into her. She gasped, it was almost hot enough to burn her.

"Is this what you want?" he asked, his hands on her hips, fingers pressing into her skin. "You want me? You can have me, little alien. But know I'm not easy to take, nor will I ever be. I'll break you."

Good thing she was already broken. "I know."

His eyes glinted. "Don't touch my brow, Alexa. Or hair."

"All I want to do is touch you..." she whispered.

He gripped her harder. "Bad, bad girl. Playing with fire."

Her core knotted, and she shifted on him.

"Take it," he urged, hunger lacing his voice. "Take what you want. Your captain is waiting."

His hands slid up her body and cupped her breasts. His gloves were rough on her skin, and she loved it. He pinched her nipples, and she jerked on his bulge.

"Yes," he hissed, tweaking her peaks. Pleasure surged through her. She flattened her palms to his chest.

She moaned, pushing down onto him. Emptiness bloomed within her, and she was starving to be filled. Hysterian pinched her nipples, and she squeaked, her knees locking. He pinched them harder. She moved on him, bolstered by his attention.

"I love the sounds you make, *Dear*."

He was still furious.

She grabbed his wrists and pushed her breasts into his palms. He moved his hands up and wrapped them around her neck. His thumb rubbed her throat. "Someday, I'll feel this," he murmured.

She didn't respond. It would break her heart if she did.

"Your skin?" she whispered.

His eyes shot to hers. Faster than she could conceive, he was on the other side of the room and she was left sprawled on the sofa. She scrambled upright.

"Don't move," he warned, leaving the room.

What?

He was back before she could even react, carrying something under his arm.

His suit. Any thought that he was going to reject her fled.

He wanted her just as much as she wanted him.

Excitement filled her just as much as fear. She wanted to touch him, to feel his skin under her fingertips. Hysterian grabbed her hand, tugging her off the sofa as he strode to the bathroom.

"What are you doing?" she asked.

"Exactly what you asked for," he said. He released her hand as he went into the bathroom, and stripped. "But this time, we're going to do this right. Stay out there. I want to look at you."

She stood awkwardly on the other side as he pulled off his jacket, yanked off his boots, and stripped for her like how she'd stripped for him. Her mouth dried up as he pulled off his tight mesh undershirt, revealing his lean, muscled body. His beautiful face.

She'd never seen him in the light. Curves of hard muscle, ropes of tendons, and smooth, scarless skin revealed themselves. His waist tapered to a deeply toned pelvis that vanished under his pants. The outline of his cock was flush inside them.

It was long.

She'd forgotten how long and lean Hysterian was. His limbs were sharp despite the muscle wrapped around them, like they could coil if they wanted to. He'd always been tall —so were many men she'd met along the way—but he was built and it showed.

The dryness of her mouth eased as saliva pooled.

How had she ever thought she could kill this being? Even without armor, he could probably take out everyone on Libra within an hour.

Hysterian unbuckled his pants and pulled them off, revealing his cock.

It was hard and roped and long—as perfect as the rest of him.

It wasn't fair.

"I want to touch you," she said, her voice barely audible.

"No. You don't," he said, straightening.

"Your skin doesn't look dangerous..."

How could something so alluring be such a trap? She eyed his hands, his arms, his lips—

His mouth opened, and his tongue shot out, hitting the side paneling of the door.

She started, confused at what just happened. "Was that...your tongue?"

Hysterian did it again. His tongue shot out so quickly she couldn't get a good look at it before it hit the wall next to her with a thunk and vanished back within his mouth.

Alexa's brows furrowed. "I thought you couldn't shift."

"My body," he said. "I'm still an animal. Even if only a part of me is."

"Do frogs— Do they have more than that? A long tongue?" she asked, searching his body.

"A long tongue, a long jump, an enormous amount of power, but not much else. My skin is where the real danger lies, Alexa. If you really think you want me, you need to see for yourself."

He reached out his hand and spread his fingers under the bright bathroom light. She looked at it, trying to see what he was showing her. Slowly, his hand changed. Little by little, tiny droplets formed, like beads of sweat but smaller. As she watched, they got bigger until one dripped off the side of his finger to land on the ground.

She noticed more droplets appearing elsewhere on his body.

"I can't control it, not entirely. I can't make it stop, at least not for long. I can't weaken it, only changing the quantity I give my enemies. My body reacts based on natural cues from my environment, and those who created me... brought me into a dangerous world. I can manipulate the nanobots within my poison to reconfigure it based on other toxins I've ingested—I can copy them—but trying to dilute it..." Hysterian sneered. "Just makes it turn back into something called batrachotoxin. A highly dangerous poison to humans as well as animals. Do you still want to touch me?"

She licked her lips. Was it terrible of her that she still did?

Hysterian fisted his hand and gave her his back. The shower turned on, and he stepped under the water. Alexa collected herself as he washed, dried, and threw his uniform into the laundry receptacle, and picked up his black suit to dress.

"Why are you telling me all this?" she asked as he stepped into the suit. The material embraced him like a lover, but she wanted him—*him*—not a barrier.

"So you'll trust me," he growled. He snapped the mask over his face as he said it, leaving just an obsidian outline of everything she wanted to explore. "I've never told anyone what I've told you. You know more about me than anyone in the universe does. Do you understand what I'm saying to you, Dear?"

She shook her head. He grabbed the doorframe and leaned toward her.

"I'm sharing with you what makes me vulnerable." His eyes flashed. "So you'll be the same with me."

"I can't..."

Tension filled the space between them.

"Why did you sleep with me, Alexa?" he asked softly. "Why did you give me your virginity?"

She swallowed. "Because I wanted to."

He stared at her for a moment before releasing the frame and cupping her cheek. She stilled.

"I hate that I don't understand you," he whispered.

"Kiss me," she begged.

He pushed up against her and brought his other hand to cup the other side of her face. Her lips parted. The coiling warmth in her reignited as he slowly leaned down.

She closed her eyes. He pressed his mouth to hers.

She felt something hit her lips, and she knew it was his tongue beneath his suit. She clutched him as she moved her lips against his. Heat burst between them and Hysterian grabbed her back.

He picked her up and carried her to the bed, laying her flat upon it, deepening the kiss.

She felt his tongue move against hers, fighting the suit between them as the fervor built. Desperation and desire burst inside as she tried to tear the barrier with her teeth while he pressed his body against her, lying atop her on the bed.

Alexa hooked her legs around his hips and arched up. Hysterian ground his member between her thighs.

Sweat slipped down her brow, and she pulled back.

His eyes locked onto hers. He slipped a finger over her brow. "We both can't control what our bodies do." He eased off her. "But I can at least make sure you don't hurt yourself."

She was done with talking. The night was only so long.

Alexa climbed onto Hysterian's lap and straddled his waist. His hands slid up and down her body, petting it. She curled her fingers around his cock and squeezed. Heat returned to his eyes, and this time there was also softness. The softness hurt. She didn't know how she could handle him being soft.

He brushed her hair behind her shoulder, and unshed tears of goodbye put pressure behind her eyes.

She lined herself up with his cock and lowered herself upon him.

Her lips parted.

He held her tightly as she worked her body to accept him, letting her take the lead. She was already wet, empty, in need. She'd been that way from the start.

But as she pushed down a little upon his length and popped back up, the ache returned. Her breaths deepened as she stretched to accommodate his size. Hysterian marked her, branded her, from the inside-out like only he could.

He lay back on the bed, gripping her hips, helping her move.

Alexa sank down on him, taking him fully into her.

"Sweet fucking hell," he groaned.

She clenched and he groaned again, so she did it once more, urging her body to accept him and the branding. She wanted to remember this forever, however long that would be for her. She wanted to take with her one last good memory.

Because like her time on the *Questor*, she didn't expect to live through what came next. And she wasn't going to bring anyone else down with her.

Alexa rose up and sat back down.

Her fingers curled against the cloth on his chest, and she wrenched her eyes closed. His heat rushed through her.

"Fuck," Hysterian growled. "Use me, Alexa. Take what you need."

She gave in. Hysterian's hands squeezed her hips, helping her rise and fall, building in tempo, increasing in speed. Each time she took all of him, the stretch of him sent her nerves into a frenzy, the emptiness inside her grew. She was at her limit, and yet she needed more.

Gripping his hands on his hips, she rode him hard. The bed shook, bedding shifted. Hysterian's eyes brightened with each undulation.

Power filled her. Completion. She took what she wanted and gave nothing in return. Alexa dug her nails into his suit, wishing she could make him feel pain for her as much as she pained for him.

She wanted his strength, his godliness. She wanted to scream and hit him, she wanted him inside her always, not just in her head. She needed him to be consumed, to meet her obsession head on. A moan broke from her lips.

Her body slickened with sweat, only driving her closer to the brink. She squeezed and rocked, becoming an animal, riding Hysterian, chasing the high. When she panted, her head falling back, he stole the power back and moved her hips for her.

"Alexa," he gritted through his teeth. A curse.

Alexa fell back upon him as he thrust up into her, lying on his legs. She swayed her hips and slid her hand over her clit, thrumming it.

Hysterian grabbed her hand and replaced it with his.

The next thing she knew, he was above her, holding himself up with one arm, thrusting into her hard. He filled her vision, and there was nothing else to see, not even the ceiling. He was everywhere.

"Make it hurt," she begged, letting her hands fall above her head. "It already hurts so much how badly I want you."

He slammed into her, sliding her body up the bed. His

fingers and thumb rolled and tweaked her clit, sending her body reeling.

Alexa thrust her chest out, possessed. Pleasure exploded through her, and Hysterian pummeled his hips to hers, pounding madly. Her core constricted, gripping him. Cries tore from her lips as the emptiness in her expanded and then filled.

Finally.

Waves of intense pleasure surged into Alexa's limbs. Her joints locked; her mind blanked. Movement, heat, wetness, male, hardness was her entire world for a blissful moment, and she screamed his name.

He fucked her through her bliss, and she clawed at his suit.

She was growing more sensitive with each thrust, yet he gave her what she needed. Euphoria. Alexa managed to open her eyes as the tension inside her built all over again.

He stared at her like she was the sun and he'd just spent an eternity in the darkness.

She came again.

Hysterian didn't stop. He finished what she started. He moved over her, inside her, pulling her atop him, only to flip her again and take her from behind. Even still, he continued. She didn't know how many times she'd lost her mind to pleasure when her body finally gave up and she couldn't lift her head anymore.

They were on the floor and he was kneeling between her legs, dipping his tip in and out of her. She was slick with sweat, swollen, and...happy.

Alexa smiled. She couldn't remember what it was like being happy.

She watched Hysterian as he stared between her legs.

One was hooked over his shoulder. She wanted to sleep, but she didn't want this time with him to end.

"Hysterian," she whispered as he pushed inside her again.

His eyes tore from her sex. "Have I hurt you?"

She shook her head.

He slipped out of her, and she moaned. He pressed his thumb into her mouth and rubbed her tongue. "I can't get enough," he murmured. "It's nothing like I imagined. Even with the damned suit."

She didn't know what he was talking about. "Imagined?" she mumbled dreamily.

He withdrew his thumb from her mouth, moved out from between her legs, and picked her up. He brought her back to the bed where the bedding was damp but chilled, and it eased her limbs. She curled into it. Hysterian slipped in next to her.

"We both have our secrets," he said, pulling her against him.

She hummed. The wonderful ache was back between her legs, but she wasn't going to let anything ruin this for her.

She settled her head on his chest. "Is this safe?" she asked after considering their position for a few moments.

"As long as you don't touch my eyeballs."

Ick. "I don't plan on it."

"I'm paired with the nanotech in the suit. As long as I don't get too hot, the pressure can be sustained for a time. And you—"

"Run cold," she murmured.

"Run cold," he repeated, petting her back.

She dozed for a while, but couldn't fall all the way asleep. She didn't want to miss a single moment. Alexa knew how precious this time was. The night couldn't be much longer, which meant they were probably in Atrexia's orbit by now.

He was going to leave and fulfill their final mission during this run. And while he was distracted and off the ship, she was going to get out of this room and leave. She was going to go somewhere he wouldn't be able to follow, nor would he want to.

Alexa shuddered, rubbing her cheek against Hysterian's chest. She was doing this for both of them.

Even if he did want her now, it didn't mean he'd want her a week from now, or a year. What then? She'd be lost, working for a man who didn't want her, who'd also hurt her worse than anyone. She knew her love for Hysterian was never going to end, but she couldn't take the chance that he would ever feel the same way about her.

Even if he was telling her the truth, that she could rely on him. Even if he forgave her. Just because she'd forgiven him meant nothing.

Her heart fell. It was safer to leave and finish what she started.

Even if the ending is not what she imagined.

Hysterian brushed his fingers through her hair, soothing her to sleep.

Alexa awoke far too soon, with him shifting out from under her. She fought the sudden need to grab him, pull him back into bed, and keep him with her.

"Sleep, Dear. I'll be back soon," he said.

"Atrexia?" she asked, digging her knuckles into her eyes.

"The locusts will be out of our lives today," he grumbled. She watched him saunter to the bathroom, turning on the shower. A dark fiend, rippling with muscle, dressed in black. He walked into it fully dressed when a cloud of steam poured out from the sides.

Her eyes slanted to the door.

A moment later, the shower turned off and the vents sucked up the steam. A very naked, built Cyborg appeared, hair dripping and plastered to his skin. He caught her eyes and held them as one of the *Questor's* bots came into the room and delivered a fresh set of clothes. He dressed into his uniform as the bot left.

He was everything she wanted and more.

Alexa brought the bedding to her chest, almost unable to believe she'd just spent the night in his arms.

When he came back into the room, he wasn't Hysterian, the Cyborg who ruined her, but her captain, the one she longed to please. Her eyes drank him in, putting every detail to memory. Sorrow threatened to erupt inside, and she clenched the bedding tightly.

He walked toward her, slipping his uniform up his face.

"Please be careful," she implored.

"I like the way you look in my bed, *dear*."

"You do?"

His eyes glinted. "Once I'm cured, I won't be leaving it. Not while you're in it."

"Hysterian..."

He leaned down. "I'll be safe. I always am, little half-breed."

She nodded.

He reached out and curled a tendril of her hair around his finger. "When this is over, we'll figure out what this is between us. If you're scared because of what I am—"

"I'm not. Not anymore," she burst out.

He rose up, letting her hair go. "Good." His eyes lost all

their softness, going hard and steely. Numbers flickered across them, and he looked at the door.

She'd seen him this way before right before a mission.

"We just received access to land," he muttered. "I need to get to the bridge. Need to get the locusts prepped."

"I can help?" She sat upright. It would get her out of this room. "Let me help."

He turned his face back to her, and his eyes regained focus. "No. I want you just like this when I return."

"I can do the job, my job." She frowned. "I'm not a spy."

His eyes searched hers. "I believe you."

"Then let me help?"

He remained silent, and she tensed, knowing he was reading her. She wasn't going to lie to him—that was idiotic, he would know immediately—but she could omit the truth.

"No," he decided. "We need to finish talking first, you and I. Until then, I can't let you leave. I won't let you leave," he said, his voice hardening.

"Tonight," she forced out, bringing the covers up over her shoulders. "We'll talk."

A burst of teal filled the room, but it was gone a moment later. Hysterian growled. "Tonight, Alexa."

With one last look between them, Hysterian strode to the door. He caught her eyes once more when he reached the threshold. "Tonight," he warned.

The door closed, and he was gone.

TWENTY-FOUR

ALEXA WAITED, staring at the shut door. Adrenaline coursed through her, erasing her exhaustion and some of her sorrow. Her heart was shattered, but it had been that way for so long. The pain of loss was a long, lost friend having returned once again.

Hysterian's voice came out of the intercom. "Landing to commence in fifteen minutes."

That was her cue.

She scurried from the bed and pulled out her duffle from under the bed. She grabbed her dirty clothes off the floor and stuffed them in, checking the room once more for anything else she might need to take with her.

There was nothing. Not even something of Hysterian's to steal. The room literally had nothing in it—not even something she could use against herself, and she cursed him for it. Her plan would be much easier if there was something in it to use...

She ran to the shower and quickly cleaned up, scrubbing her swollen sex, letting the cold water rinse the smell of sex from her skin.

Alexa was dressed and sitting on the bed when the ship's lights flickered and the ship's gravity changed, indicating descent.

Now to wait.

Once Hysterian was gone, all she had to do was hurt herself enough that she'd need medical attention, and the door to the room would open. The *Questor* was built with AI technology, and AI technology could be manipulated if it wasn't specialized. As far as she knew, Hysterian hadn't done anything with the AI in the last few months. It would respond to her...

If it didn't, something was bound to open the door and feed her soon.

Alexa pushed her bag back under the bed when the lights stopped flickering and the gravity changes ended.

We've landed.

Her fingers went white as she clutched the bedding. She waited a few minutes, but Hysterian didn't come back. She waited a few minutes more.

When she was certain he had to be off the ship, she snatched her bag and went for the door.

Right as she was about to figure out how to hurt herself, it opened.

Horace stood on the other side.

Alexa recoiled.

He stepped into the room.

"What are you doing?" she gasped. She hadn't expected to see Horace.

"Getting you out of here," he said, looking around the room. His eyes landed on the bed. He cursed. "Didn't believe Pigeon when he said the captain had you locked up in here, keeping you prisoner. Thought you were just recovering." His eyes went to her. "Sorry, Dear."

She went to correct him but stopped. "It's okay…"

He grabbed her bag. "Come. We gotta go." He turned and made his way down the hallway.

Alexa stood, confused for a moment, before chasing after him. She caught up to him as he was going down the stairs. "What about Pigeon?"

"Bastard won't leave the brig, says he needs a free trip back to Earth anyway. He can suit himself."

It was then she noticed Horace had a second duffle.

"You're leaving too?"

"I ain't staying here after crossing the captain. I'm not stupid like Pigeon. I know what Cyborgs can do, what they've done, the power they wield," he said, speaking quickly. She'd never seen Horace like this before.

Was he scared?

"I thought Daniels vanishing was odd, but now that Raul's gone, too, and there's no trace of them being fired on the servers…" He shook his head. "I'm not willing to stick around and find out what really happened to them."

She caught her breath when they stopped at the hatch. Wait. Had she heard that correctly? "Raul's gone?"

"Never saw him again after we landed on Libra. Boss said he quit. I'm not so sure anymore."

"What do you mean?"

Horace shook his head. "Raul needed this job. Even if he and the captain didn't get along, Raul was drowning in debt, and loan sharks were after him. He wouldn't give up the pay, couldn't from what he told me. Jobs like this don't come around often. The pay's enough to look past a lot." Horace dropped the bags and started typing something in on the panel beside the hatch. He glanced at her. "But not everything."

Alexa licked her lips. The hatch opened before she

could respond. Horace grabbed their bags and they entered the pressurization chamber. The inner hatch shut, the chamber recalibrated, and the outer hatch opened. Horace leaned out, looking right and left.

"Thank hell there's no cameras out here," Horace muttered.

Bright desert sunshine blasted Alexa's eyes. She hadn't seen anything but stars, metal walls, and outer space for weeks, even before Libra. When her irises adjusted, a golden haziness met her, as well as swirling dust and rows upon rows of ships with cement buildings between them. She curved her hand to shade her eyes, peering out.

In the distance was a single large mountain, and surrounding it was a swirling dark cloud.

Not a cloud.

Millions of locusts.

Alexa dropped her hand as Horace walked down the ramp. She remembered the male locust and how it watched her. How it made her uncomfortable, nervous. She hated it.

Feeling exposed, she ran after Horace. He went right, carrying their bags with him. Ahead were a bunch of ships and people and androids loading and unloading them.

"Where are we going?" she asked.

He faced her, and she stopped before she ran into him. "We're not going anywhere. You and I split here." He dropped her bag.

She reached down and picked it up, throwing it over her shoulder. Horace walked away several steps, stopped, and came back to her. He fished something out of his pocket.

"Here, I almost forgot. I snagged it off of Hysterian's console this morning after he left." He handed it to her.

My wristcon.

Alexa put the band on her wrist, clutching it gratefully. "Thank you."

"No need. It's the least I can do after letting him lock you up," he said, his chest rising and falling. "Good luck, Alexa. I never thought I'd have to question a Cyborg's honor. I'm sorry it came to this."

"He's not..." She swallowed, deciding what he believed about Hysterian was for the best. "Bye, Horace."

He grumbled and turned. She watched him walk away.

When he was gone, Alexa scanned the ships around her. She needed one that was leaving today, right now preferably. She hoped Hysterian wouldn't come after her— that he'd be happy to be rid of the burden—but dread wormed its way into her soul and she wasn't sure anymore.

If he caught her before she could escape, he would lock her back up. And knowing him... If he wasn't going to forgive her now, he wasn't going to forgive her later.

She may not be a spy, but she had come to kill him.

Someday, he was going to figure that out.

Alexa spun full-circle, twirling her wristcon over her wrist. There were so many ships on the tarmac that she didn't know where to begin. She caught sight of a small passenger ship with a group of people hanging outside it.

She straightened her shoulders and made her way toward them.

TWENTY-FIVE

HYSTERIAN FOLLOWED the security officials working for the research group taking in the locusts. Tranqs had put the females asleep, but the male fought inside his crate, unaffected. The crates were loaded on the back of a truck and strapped down in place so they couldn't fall off.

The male still tried.

The locusts had been dosed and locked up for months, being manipulated and stimulated by machines since they didn't have the freedom to move. Hysterian felt for the creatures but was ready to be rid of them. Atrexia was far from the main spaceway channels, and days of light-speed away from the nearest port or colony. It was a perfect place to hide if he were a criminal, but it was also a crapshoot for the same reason.

Everywhere he looked, detritus filled his vision. The buildings were made of worn stone, their metal infrastructure rusted out. There were as many dead, broken ships lingering on the tarmac as there were working vessels. Scrapper and scavengers removed pieces from them to reuse or sell.

In the distance, he could see the locusts swarm Mount Etta. The mountain was the one other thing Atrexia was known for besides its unusual inhabitants.

A vehicle awaited them at the edge of the tarmac where the ships came to an end. A man walked over to greet him.

Hysterian barely heard what the man said as he unstrapped the crates. His mind was on Alexa.

His mind was always on her these days. It should've bothered him, but it didn't, at least not anymore. He'd decided.

She was his woman. There was no one else for him. He didn't want anyone else. He hadn't, not since she'd walked into his life and onto his ship. He thought he'd wanted a woman made up of all the attributes a red-blooded male could ever want, but that was until Alexa tore his fantasies to shreds and replaced them with something else: her.

She wasn't afraid of him or his skin. She touched him wanting him, not wanting what he could give her. He could see it in her eyes, in the way she reacted.

Her actions were sincere.

She may be lying about her reasons, her past, omitting information he wanted desperately to have, but when it came to their interactions... He knew she wanted him as much as he wanted her.

Hysterian was ready to peel back her layers and discover all the little secrets she kept buried inside. He wanted to sink inside her soul and curl up. He kept replaying the way she'd screamed his name when he'd brought her to climax.

He wasn't a red-blooded male. He was a stone-cold Cyborg who had the power to change the color of his blood to suit his needs. He had control. He had Alexa in his bed.

Whatever she wasn't telling him, he was going to find out eventually.

Hysterian could wait. He was fucking good at waiting. He'd waited his entire life for her; he could wait a little longer.

He had to wait anyway so he could finally touch her, feel her like he needed to feel her. The first thing he planned to do once he was cured was kiss her. His nostrils flared. He'd always fantasized taking a woman to bed, but kissing them? Never. Now it was all he wanted when it came to Alexa. He was going to kiss every inch of her body, coat her body in his saliva. There weren't going to be any barriers between them ever again.

The man talking to Hysterian stopped and moved away. The security guards circled the first crate containing the female locusts and lifted it slowly. Too slowly.

Hysterian stepped between two of the men and picked up the crate in its entirety, deciding to speed things along. The guards backed off when they realized he didn't need any help.

"Payment's been sent," the first man said. "Sad to find their DNA can't be spliced in animals on Earth." He shrugged. "Maybe Earth isn't equipped for animals again after all."

Hysterian loaded the last of the three female locusts on the man's truck. All that was left was the male. The crate was still as he approached it.

"Glad we're changing shifts soon," the man continued. "You got here just in time."

"In time?" Hysterian feigned interest as he circled the male's crate.

"Yeah. The female locusts are about to enter their heat. They've been gathering around Mt. Etta for the past two weeks. People have been arriving from all over to see the event."

Stupid fucks. "Isn't that dangerous?"

"Yeah, but they don't care. Most can view it from their ships, but this"—the man indicated the clear sky—"isn't going to stay this way for much longer. The swarms will continue to grow until the sky's blotted out. If anyone's out then, it'll be a bloodbath. Locusts will eat anything, even each other, during this time of year."

Hysterian grabbed the male locusts' crate, braced his legs, and lifted it in his arms.

"Try and leave tonight if you can, like me. Ships are leaving hourly," the man said.

Hysterian glimpsed Mt. Etta in the distance as he hauled the crate to the truck. A comm pinged his audio, alerting him he had received a direct message to his systems. He stopped, bringing the message up. He never received direct comms unless it was from another Cyborg or his ship's AI.

It was from Raphael.

The wires in his chest vibrated, and his fingers dug into the hard edges of the crate. Hatred for his ex-boss arose swiftly, but it was soon replaced with dread and curiosity.

The crate shook in his arms.

He stared at the comm behind his eyes, debating whether or not to open it and download the encrypted message. What would Raphael have for him? Had he found information about Alexa? Her past? Had she been hurt? Was she being bribed?

His anger returned the longer he stared at the comm. His glands opened up and poison bubbled under his suit.

Maybe he didn't find anything out at all. Hysterian hoped there was nothing on Alexa, that she was just...

concerned about him being a Cyborg and she was a half-breed. She didn't know about the codes that ran deep in Cyborgs, urging them to destroy Trentians.

They were nothing compared to what he'd been dealing with his entire life and his skin.

"Are you okay?" the man accepting the locusts asked.

A growling came from inside the crate right before it rocked in Hysterian's arms. His hand slipped and the crate fell, crashing to the ground. Wood, metal, and straps broke and snapped. Two large wings burst from the sides as the male locust's growls crescendoed into a roar.

The security guards backed off, and one yelled, grabbing his gun from his belt. The intake man shouted, stumbling back, falling before scrambling to the door of his vehicle. The crates containing the females started to shake.

Screams filled his ears. Hysterian opened the comm.

The male locust shook off the debris from the crate, baring his teeth. Large wings flapped, readying for flight. It didn't see Hysterian glaring at the security guard who was backing away. Four large arms stretched out, claws elongating, growing sharp.

Hysterian took out his gun and shot it point-blank in the head.

The male locust crashed to the ground.

"That's for scaring her," he said, pivoting toward his ship.

He knew everything.

Alexa's father. Her history. Everything. He scanned the comm from Raphael a hundred more times by the time he saw his ship in the distance, memorizing every sentence, every bit of punctuation. The screams followed him for a time but quieted the farther he got away. His audio cleared it all out as a chilling dread filled him.

I killed her father.

Xavier Lyle Dear.

He'd known the name on Raphael's comm before he even had a moment to question it. He remembered everyone he killed. The last name Dear wasn't a common one, but how was he supposed to make that connection? He had met countless people since his creation. Many shared names, first and last.

Hysterian cursed as power surged through his systems. He picked up speed, sprinting now, needing to see Alexa. He never thought in a thousand calibrations that he was the reason for her pain. That time in the lounge that night... *She fought me. She thought I was going to kill her.*

She came here to get revenge.

The air left him, and his throat constricted.

She'd come to kill him.

It made sense.

Another streak of electricity coursed through him. He bore down on his feet and sprang into the air, jumping the rest of the way to his ship. The tarmac cracked when he landed, and dust plummed in the air. He connected with his ship before he made it to the hatch. Sirens went off in his head as well as his ship.

Xavier Lyle Dear had been a known half-breed, a junk worker brought up in the Elyrian slums where most half-breeds lived. Xavier had fought Raphael when Hysterian's ex-boss sought to buy the land where he and many other half-breeds and the poor lived. Thousands of humans, aliens, and half-breeds would've been displaced. Xavier protested, riled up others to protest, and sought to stop Raphael from taking the land and developing it.

No one told Raphael what to do and lived.

It happened nearly fifteen years ago now. It was during

that time Hysterian had encountered Raphael for the first time and Raphael had offered to help him. Hysterian's last venture into finding a solution to his skin problem had failed miserably. The head scientist who'd had a hand in Hysterian's creation died, and with his death, Hysterian had lost all hope that he would ever be fixed.

He'd gone numb.

He'd turned off his emotions and became nothing more than a walking, talking machine, with the added weirdness of his animal.

Going numb was the only way for him to accept the loss, to cope. Not only for a solution, but as a way to avoid grieving for the one person who was the closest Hysterian would ever have to a parent.

It had been a dark time. He'd gone to Dimes, practically living at the club for weeks before Raphael approached him. Before that, everyone left the 'Cyborg' alone for fear he'd turn on them.

He'd never hid from others back then. People would touch him and faint or get blitz from the highest high of their lives. People gathered around him, wanting to touch him and take the risk. They paid him for bottles of his secretion.

In his numbness, he found a cult of addicts.

Raphael noticed how much money Hysterian was making him, how people from all over the city flocked to Dimes to touch the Cyborg. He'd become an attraction, and while he was emotionless with loss, Hysterian enjoyed the distraction. He'd enjoyed letting men and women take his hand, hold it, and give him the warmth he'd always craved.

Some lasted for minutes before falling.

He hadn't enjoyed them dying at his feet, though. It still left a sour taste in his mouth.

But the touching, the warmth, even the fucked-up companionship he'd received from his followers had given him a lifeline. And then Raphael had approached him and solidified the deal.

Raphael convinced Hysterian that he had the money and resources to help Hysterian with his problem, but if he was going to help, he wanted something in return.

Hysterian's loyalty.

Back then, he would have done anything for Raphael. Hysterian wasn't proud of it, especially now as he looked back, but he had enjoyed it for a time. There'd been no rules, no need for control.

For a being who'd been created to be controlled... It was like breathing for the first time.

But Raphael was a calculating and cruel man who only cared about his own pleasure. A psychopath and an unhinged, emotionless Cyborg made a great but devastatingly merciless team.

Whether Xavier knew who Raphael was when Xavier went up against the crime lord, Hysterian had no idea. All he knew was when he'd killed Xavier, Hysterian had broken into the man's apartment and took his hand while he slept. Hysterian had been cruel for so much of his life—torturing information out of war criminals—but he couldn't be that way to innocent people, even if they had crossed Raphael. He'd never questioned why Raphael had asked him to kill Xavier. Hysterian had been hired to kill people in the past. But during that time...he'd just been numb.

I killed her father.

Hysterian broke into his ship and ran to his quarters. He scented Alexa's smell the second the hatch opened. He scented Horace's as well. A glimpse at the security feeds showed him they'd left.

Horace too? He couldn't fucking trust anyone. Every person in his crew had betrayed him.

Twenty fucking minutes ago, they'd left. His nostrils flared as he slammed his fist into the wall and turned back.

She lied to me.

She seduced me into bed, and for what? To distract me?

To give me hope only to steal it away?

Rage boiled, building, eclipsing reason. His codes urged him to blight out Alexa's existence, knowing she'd only come here to kill him. *She's an alien.*

She's my enemy.

His hands clenched as he stormed back out of his ship. He needed to find Alexa. He wanted to punish her, make her feel what she forced him to feel.

To have everything you've ever wanted given to you only to be snatched away.

If this was her plan, she fucking succeeded. She didn't need to kill him to destroy him. He practically handed her the keys to his ruin. He'd told her everything. She'd turned everyone against him and stole his bloody metal heart right from his chest. If she thought she was going to get away with it and live, she had another thing coming.

Hysterian strode off his ship, scanning the shipping tarmac. He knew she couldn't have gotten far.

Twenty-two minutes ago, she was where I'm standing. He closed his eyes and seeded into the wireless connections and electrical currents all around him. He fell out with a curse, finding it devoid of security and cameras.

Hysterian jumped atop his ship, surveying the horizon, but dust clouds obscured much of the field. His eyes flicked upward. The swarms around Mt. Etta had grown larger in the past hour. Several ships took off or readied to take off around him. He heard the rumble of a ship landing in the distance. Something flew past his head, sending his hair flying—a female locust. His eyes flicked to the sky, finding hundreds more heading for the mountain.

He cursed, recalling what the delivery man had said. Below him, people scurried for cover and ships closed up. Some people cheered, some laughed, others jeered, striking his nerves. His facial recognition software didn't recognize any of them.

Hysterian checked his gun, sliding it back into his belt, knowing he was going to have to search on foot. He didn't have much time if what the man had said was true. If the locusts were going into a breeding season, time was short.

He needed to find Alexa before that happened.

He was going to have his revenge. No locust was going to take that from him.

The flapping of wings filled his audio as he surged forward, picking a random direction, sniffing the air. It only served to remind him how inadequate he was compared to others who had animals that were naturally good hunters and trackers. A frog couldn't hunt or track.

All the more reason to get his hands on Alexa and make her pay.

He stalked through the ships on the tarmac, searching groups of people, demanding answers from them. Hysterian found no sign of her or Horace. More ships readied to take off, more still closed up for the day.

Worry set in. He hurried his steps.

Where the fuck is she?

He missed her by mere minutes. She couldn't have gotten far.

A group of people rushed by him, ducking with their arms above their heads. He grabbed them and checked each one, sending them fleeing in terror soon after.

The sky darkened.

This time, when he heard shouting, he didn't ignore it.

He came upon two men arguing. They were alone. Hysterian gritted his teeth, turning full-circle. Wind swept past his ears, and dust got in his eyes. His brow dripped.

"Alexa!" he roared.

No one answered.

Another ship took off. Hysterian watched it break through the locusts, killing hundreds, sending body parts flying everywhere. Still, Alexa was nowhere to be found.

Fear took hold.

When the ship vanished, he stared at the place it had been.

He couldn't have lost her. It was impossible. She was in his arms hours ago. *She was...*

The dust swirled around him.

I'm coming for you.

TWENTY-SIX

Alexa wiped the sweat from her face as she washed her hands in a puddle. Her grimy complexion stared back at her as the water settled. Her roots were showing, revealing her naturally translucent, shimmering hair. She hadn't dyed it in over two months.

She no longer cared if people knew she was a half-breed. There wasn't a reason for her to care anymore.

On Elyria, half-breeds were all around her. This was the only real home they had, so this was the place they congregated. Regardless of the crime or the destitution, despite the animosity they received or the lack of prospects, Elyria was all they had. Even with the sweltering desert heat, Trentians and half-breeds made it work. She trapped some water and poured it over her head.

"Share the wealth," someone muttered.

Alexa stood and moved away as a young man, a full-blooded Trentian, kneeled and did the same. Unlike the Trentians that lived on Xanteaus, this one's hair was cropped short around his face.

To survive the heat, no doubt. He didn't have the luxury to keep his long locks if he worked under the Elyrian suns.

Alexa made her way through the parking lot, leaving the adolescent behind, and toward the tenement housing beyond the lot. Litter and sand were everywhere. The rolling dunes of Elyria had been flattened a century ago to expand the ever-growing Oasis City, but the sand was still everywhere. It got in people's houses, and when it was windy, it made the sky hazy. When there wasn't wind, it laid in dirty piles in alleyways. Sandy trash heaps. You never knew what you might find in a sand pile.

It was a favorite game for unwatched children.

At least in the slums.

In the distance, the sky towers, the skyscrapers, and the buildings of the wealthy rose up like spikes. Those buildings reached for the stars, while the ones she aimed for currently... were forced to stay near the ground. The slums didn't have infrastructure like the main locales of the metropolis, nor did it have the flashing lights, pounding music, and neon mess.

Like Dimes.

She could see Dimes and its large dome several blocks away. It glowed gold, catching the suns against its metal adornments. The dome was always gold during the day. It was only at night when it erupted into a tacky riot of colors, but the music from the club was a constant. The heavy bass bled into the streets and could be felt from blocks away.

She'd lived in the domes and Raphael's shadow until she'd stripped herself from her past, changed her appearance like everyone did in Oasis City, and applied for school.

Alexa hadn't been back home since, clawing her way out by her broken, dirty nails. They were dirty now, but no longer broken. Some things never changed.

She made her way past groups of people loitering and toward the poorly manufactured homes where she used to live. The smell of meat, cooking oil, and grease filled her nose as she passed by home after home on her way to her destination.

Alexa saw a vendor selling water as she went. She bought a bottle, sucking it down to keep from overheating.

Her chest tightened. *It's been too long.* More than a decade.

She didn't recognize any of the people. She was certain no one would recognize *her*. She also couldn't believe how many more people there were. The slums had been crowded before, but now? It was bursting.

Alexa dodged two women walking in the opposite direction, nearly colliding with them.

Saddened, she sped up. The apartment of her childhood home appeared a short time later.

A young girl stood in the dirty window looking out. The same window Alexa used to look out and watch the people on the street below when she was the girl's age. Alexa waved, and the girl turned away.

Alexa's heart fell.

Why did I come here?

She knew why as she continued deeper into the slums.

She needed to say goodbye, to remember, because tonight...she would face Raphael for the first time.

She landed on Elyria a week ago. During that time, she had familiarized herself with the locals near her old home, asking questions, staying low. She asked about Dimes and Raphael, gleaning she could that would help her. She visited old haunts, hoping they would snap her out of her grief.

That she'd remember why she left in the first place, why she was back here at all.

Revenge.

She'd learned that Raphael would be at Dimes tonight. That today was his birthday, and the bastard was celebrating at the club. This was her chance to get access to him, to get close enough to kill him, for her dad, but also for Hysterian. If she didn't act tonight, she didn't know if she'd get another chance.

Raphael was a rich and powerful man. According to locals, he wasn't hanging out at the club often anymore, having set his sights on other properties he managed.

Alexa felt the hard outline of the gun she'd bought second-hand at a pawn shop near the port, resting in the lip of her jeans. Her shirt hid it from view. In her pocket, she had an extra clip, just in case, but the gun was loaded and ready.

She just needed to get close enough to her target.

A short time later, she was at her destination.

The columbarium, where the ashes of her dad were. She swiped her wristcon, paying the fee to enter—because everything on Elyria demanded a fee—and made her way down the stark aisles of slots where urns of the dead rested. The *poor* dead. Flowers and stacks of mementos dirtied the ground, and she had to pick her way through.

Resting two feet above her, she stopped at her dad's slot. Alexa stared at the nameplate.

The sun lowered as she stood there, darkening the aisles to gray, shifting the shadows to elongate the lettering.

She parted her lips to speak but quickly closed them.

She tried again and failed. Again.

I'm sorry. The words whispered through her mind.

I'm sorry I wasn't there. I'm sorry you were alone. I'm sorry I...

She trembled. *I'm sorry I fell in love with your murderer.*

Alexa reached up and flattened her palm to her dad's slot and closed her eyes. *May you be with Xanteaus in the halls of rebirth. May your next life be better. May I not be in it.*

She turned away and left.

LATER THAT NIGHT, she was dressed in clubwear, wearing a little dress she'd found in one of the local thrift shops, watching the crowds gather outside Dimes. Strangely enough, most of the crowd were made up of androids and sentient robots. She thanked the odds because it would only make it easier for her. Her gun was strapped to her thigh, under the folds of her dress, giving her even more courage. She loaded the mirror on her wristcon and checked her makeup.

She had stripped the remaining black dye from her hair, and the translucent strands, which were still drying, clung to her shoulders. Humans may openly hate her kind, but in the dark, they fantasized about them. Especially the men. Trentian women were so rare now, if a half-breed or even a human could pass off as one, you'd get noticed.

People noticed her.

Her hair had always been a curse, but tonight? It was a blessing.

She didn't have to wait in the lines outside the club long. One of the bouncers pulling real women from the lines saw and came directly for her, shuffling her in.

"Master Raphael awaits you inside," he said, eyeing her.

She tensed, waiting for the bouncer to check her for weapons.

Instead, he flicked his gaze over her several times. Alexa smiled to distract him. He eventually shook his head, and she walked where he indicated for her to go, following several other women who'd been pulled from the lines by other bouncers.

Alexa held her breath until she was inside.

She'd never been inside Dimes before. Someone thrust a drink at her, and she offhandedly took it, captivated by the vibrancy of the party raging before her. It was big, bigger than it seemed outside even, with a huge open center and floors upon floors above. People, androids, and guards walked the rails, talking, dancing, and laughing. The guards wore large black wings and carried guns.

Fallen angels.

Like Hysterian.

She shook her head, dropping her eyes from the rails.

A cold sweat broke out on her skin as pounding music blared and switched. Someone pushed her toward the dance floor. Hands grabbed and groped, and she fought her way out of the moving thrall of people. Someone pinched her ass, and she nearly lost it, dropping her cup and fleeing.

When she made it out from the crush, she tugged her dress down and caught her breath.

She couldn't fail. She couldn't let her nerves get to her. Not again.

Alexa swallowed, letting her heart settle, and searched for Raphael. She walked toward the stairs since the glass elevators were thronged with patrons.

I wish Hysterian were here. She stamped out the wish as soon as she'd thought it.

She was never going to see him again. It was hard to think about him because all she wanted to do was contact him, or find him on the network, and either action would only hurt her further.

He wasn't on the network. And she was certain only two courses of action would result in contacting him: one, he'd either ignore her, or two, he'd trace her comm and come find her.

She didn't want to be his captive again, nor be handed over to the authorities, and she couldn't face him knowing what was between them. She would always want Hysterian and only Hysterian. It'd only ever been Hysterian for her.

But she was a liar, untrustworthy. She held the blood of his enemy in her veins.

Her broken soul had never been more complete than when she was with him. Ever since she'd fled Atrexia, buying her way on the nearest transport vessel, she'd been hollow. Empty. Numb.

She had seen him from the porthole of the ship ascending from Atrexia, watched him running across the tarmac searching for her, shouting her name. She had wanted to scream for him as the locusts swarmed the sky and the dirt drifted up to his boots. It had been easy to leave him up until that point, that moment when her sight of him was about to end. Alexa hadn't expected to see him again after that morning. She hadn't been prepared to see him screaming her name.

She'd cried for him, her heart shattering.

Since then, she'd been numb, putting all her focus on getting back to Elyria and finishing the job she set out to do fifteen years ago.

Thinking about Hysterian only hindered her. He was

like an alluring whisper in the back of her mind telling her to stop what she was doing and go back to him.

Alexa was afraid that if she gave in and did, she'd just walk right onto his ship, straight to the brig, and bunker down, a willing captive. Just to be in his presence.

If he dragged her and tossed her out of his ship, she wouldn't even have her pride left to keep her company. That's why she couldn't let him into her head anymore. She'd already been his captive for far too long.

If that wasn't reason enough to keep her away, knowing her dad's real murderer was walking scot-free, drinking it up, and whoring—killing others while destroying lives. It brought her back to her senses.

Alexa caught sight of Raphael on the opposite side of the club, surrounded by more men dressed as angels and several scantily clad women. One mostly naked woman was bobbing her head between his legs as he sipped his drink and laughed.

Raphael wasn't a hard one to locate once pinned. With his bright spiky hair and his extreme jubilation, he commanded attention. If it wasn't the jubilation that gave him away, it was the giant tiered birthday cake on the table behind him. The cake was large enough to feed the whole club and then some.

Disgust crossed her face.

The fat, meaty fucker was about to meet his end.

She straightened and headed for Raphael, threading her way through the partygoers. She pushed her hair over her shoulder and licked her lips, stopping at the barrier that kept Raphael and his minions away from the beings party-ing. Seduction wasn't her forte, but she hoped...

Alexa swayed and smiled at one of Raphael's guards, catching his attention. An attractive man, perhaps a few years younger than her, walked forward, his eyes zeroing in on her hair.

She twirled a damp strand of it around her finger.

"You a half-breed?" he asked.

"I am, unfortunately."

His eyes shifted to her face. "Not unfortunate tonight—if you're willing to put out?"

Alexa kept her disgust inside this time. Her eyes hooded and she saw Raphael and the woman licking his small dick like it was the best tasting popsicle she'd ever had.

"I am," she said a little bluntly, forgetting to purr.

Thank god the guard didn't seem to notice. He typed in a code on his wristcon and unbuckled the strap between them. He ushered her inside. She started to head for Raphael when the guard grabbed her arm.

"Not unless he wants you," he warned, pointing her toward a private bar where several other women were hanging out. Another angel approached them and led one of them over to Raphael. Raphael pushed the woman licking his dick out from between his legs and told the new one to take her place.

Bile rose in her throat. The first woman was handed a pill. She jumped for joy, wiping the saliva from her lips, gulping it down. One of the guards threw her over his shoulder, making her laugh and kick her legs. His fake black wings flapped. He slapped her ass and carried her through a door behind the birthday cake.

"Everyone can have a good time on my birthday!" Raphael bellowed, laughing, pushing the new woman's head down into his crotch.

"Go," the guard next to her said. Alexa jumped and made her way to the other women still waiting by the bar.

What would Hysterian do if he saw her right now,

about to subject herself to his ex-boss so she could get close enough to shoot him? It was a terrible plan if she wanted to survive, but she was done waiting.

It was now or never.

It could be months before she had Raphael pinned down again.

Alexa waited for her turn.

It wasn't long before Raphael looked up and caught her eye. He smiled, called a guard over, and spoke in his ear. The guard came straight for her shortly after.

"He wants you," he said.

Alexa calmed. She prayed she had the courage to go through with her plan.

She smiled her brightest smile and followed the guard toward Raphael's smirking form.

TWENTY-SEVEN

After weeks of chasing her, hunting her, and reaching out to Nightheart for help after swallowing his fucking pride, Alexa was finally before him, and all Hysterian wanted to do was throw her over his shoulder and fuck her into loving him.

With her startlingly beautiful hair, she was an ethereal goddess, a mesmerizing blend of both her species. Hysterian stared in awe. Gone was the cold crew hand who used to work for him, replaced by a sprite.

He'd had no idea Alexa was so goddamn beautiful. He swore an oath he would personally destroy all the dye in the universe. Alexa in a dress, lips glistening with clear gloss, made his systems frenetic, made him ache in only the way she could.

He hadn't been in her presence in nearly six weeks.

Six weeks of utter hell. Six weeks of nothing. Six weeks of scenting her all over his ship, of being stuck in memories of their time together. It was a curse and a gift to have internal databases that recorded everything.

He'd been furious, worried, running about and shouting

her name as others watched on. Fear had stolen him even when he'd known she was gone. He had battled through the locusts, invaded other people's ships, and had threatened the controllers, stopping all travel off of Atrexia.

Alexa was long gone by then, having left hours prior on a ship she'd bought her way onto with all the money she'd made working for *him*.

To make matters worse, the *Questor* had been land-locked for days as the locusts bred, feasted, and then bred again.

In those first dark hours, he hadn't been sure if he would have strangled Alexa had he found her, or tied her to his bed and forced everything he'd wanted to hear out of her throat. Hysterian had been out of his mind from her recklessness, her idiocy.

What being in their right mind thought they could take down one of his kind? It took more than a bullet or a sharp edge. It took planning, the right equipment, and a fuck-ton of luck. It took calculation, precision. A weapon used on one of his brethren might work well on that specific model, but that same weapon might do nothing to another of his kind.

She had come to kill him anyway, and then she'd left him, having done so much worse in that small act.

She'd left him.

She'd left him without saying goodbye—not that he would have let her. She made him feel for her, made him want her more than all others.

Once he'd gotten through those first dark hours, those first days on Atrexia with no one but Pigeon to listen to him while he had raged, Hysterian eventually calmed.

It would've been far more merciful for Alexa to have killed him. No, she had to take his hope and wring them out. No one did that to him and not pay for the crime. No one fucking dared.

And then he found the bag of clothes in her old quarters —the lingerie she'd bought—and the whole process started all over again.

This time with his cock in his hand, trying to jack out the rage and confusion.

He took to the stars on a mission to get her back.

Seeing her now, in a little black dress that was still slightly too big for her, swaying absently to bad music, made him forget everything—all the desperate nights he spent worrying. It made him excited.

I found her.

Now that he had her, he wasn't going to let her get away again.

After Hysterian found out Alexa was on Elyria, her funds verifying it, Hysterian knew what she was going to do. He'd warped through uncharted space to get to her before she risked her life.

It was then he realized she loved him.

Because she hadn't killed him, she hadn't even tried.

He rewatched every second of video feed of her and found she'd never even made a single fucking attempt. His ship was dry of resources, having pushed it past its limits so he could get to Elyria sooner. All he could do was watch old footage of her.

No wonder she fought me. It all made sense.

But going after Raphael? That was suicide.

His ex-boss's laughter filled his audio.

Hysterian hadn't been in the presence of Raphael in almost a year. The fat bastard was enjoying his usual power trip—the birthday notwithstanding—having his guards bring him women to worship him orally.

It was Raphael's kink. He preferred women's mouths over their cunts. He got off on beautiful girls kneeling at the altar of his ego. The younger the better.

And Alexa was in line.

Hatred washed over him. Raphael was untouchable, even for someone like Hysterian. His ex-boss had way too many powerful contacts, knew far too much information, had more money than God. He also had a very rare and expensive shield around his body. One Hysterian partially designed...

But if he touched Alexa, none of that would stop Hysterian. If Raphael hurt her, the devil wouldn't be able to hold Hysterian back. Death would be the last mistress to lick Raphael's dick as Hysterian blasted his ex-boss's brains all over his fucking cake.

Hysterian sensed his pupils brightening and adjusted his illusion to hide them. If Alexa got wind he was here, she might run. He wasn't going to risk it.

As he stormed through the throngs of dancers, the bartender slid Alexa a drink. Hysterian pulled out his gun, switching off the safety.

She shook her head, denying the free offering. Good. He wouldn't have to kill another tonight. The bartenders drugged all the drinks. One sip and Alexa would be giggling, horny, and high, a pretty little naïve offering, ready for any of the countless men to descend upon. They could have any other woman, just not Hysterian's.

One of Raphael's guards moved toward her.

Hysterian pushed through another group of dancers.

The guard led Alexa to Raphael.

Hysterian's systems thundered. He shoved the throng of clubbers out of his way.

Alexa reached under the lip of her dress. Hysterian saw the gun just as she yanked it out and aimed it at Raphael.

"No!" Hysterian shouted. He sprang the rest of the way across the room just as a shot was fired, his boots cracking the floor upon landing.

An ear-splitting *boom* blasted through the club, stunning the dancers out of their revelry. One of the guards slammed into Alexa, forcing her to the ground. Hysterian's illusion dropped.

He yanked the guard off her, wrenching his arm. The guard screamed as Hysterian kneeled and picked up Alexa's shaking form. Others aimed their guns, running to the scene.

"Stop!" Raphael bellowed, making the entire nightclub pause. "Hysterian, is that you?"

Hysterian rose and faced him. Raphael shimmered as the invisible forcefield around his body settled back into place. Alexa's bullet never even got within a foot of the fucker.

Hysterian scowled. "Raphael."

Alexa was stone cold and still in his arms. He didn't dare look down at her.

Raphael yanked up his pants and laughed, clapping his hands. "What a surprise!" He spun, looking wildly around. "Who set this up? This was fabulous!" The angels glanced at each other uneasily. "Come on! This couldn't all be Hysterian's work." Raphael turned back to him, cheeks flushed. "What a fine little actress you have," he said, eyeing Alexa with newfound interest. "She is for me, right?"

"Hysterian?" Alexa said, so low it was barely audible. "Kill him." The order was a tickle in his ear.

Hysterian's eyes glinted.

How could he deny her? He'd hurt her so much, finishing the job was the least he could do.

But he was going to deny her.

Raphael wasn't his to kill.

"Why don't we go somewhere quiet to chat?" Hysterian said, smiling at his old boss. "This one is all yours." He set Alexa on her feet, taking the gun hanging limp in her hand. She looked up at him in shock.

Hurt crossed her features as he pushed her toward Raphael. She stumbled forward before catching herself. One of the angels came forward and grabbed her arm.

Raphael beamed. "Yes. Let's go somewhere we can chat." He flicked his fingers, and the club resumed as if nothing unusual had just happened. The angels went back to their posts.

Raphael led them to the private rooms at the back of the club—his special rooms, he liked to call them. The guard followed, dragging Alexa, while Hysterian trailed behind them. She looked back at him. The pounding music of the club vanished as they left it and was replaced with screams. Not all were screams of pleasure.

Memories rose like weeds in his head. His glands opened, releasing poison to slick under the friction of his suit.

Hysterian had spent a lot of time in these rooms.

He'd been evil. Cruel. Uncaring. These rooms, though he'd been away from them for a long while, brought back his time working for Raphael as nothing else had. They were once his home, his haven. His place to be numb, finding camaraderie with others who were like him. Beings who also wanted to be numb.

Hysterian's fingers twitched.

They entered one of Raphael's favorite lounges, a place

with numerous pillows and screens covering all the walls, displaying anything he felt like watching at the time. They were currently streaming what was taking place in the adjoining rooms.

"Come, sit," Raphael said. "Have a drink, a whiff, a pill. Hysterian, should I have one of your favorite girls brought in?"

"Are they equipped with the latest software?" he asked.

"Yes, yes. All the bots are," Raphael scoffed. He waved at the guard holding Alexa. "Let her go. Give her to me," he ordered, already unzipping his pants.

Hysterian stopped his eyes from bursting. He kept his face clear of emotion as the guard pushed Alexa toward Raphael.

"You were brilliant, dove. Just brilliant." He grabbed Alexa's hands like a grandfather would his granddaughter. "For a moment there, I thought you sought to kill me. I've never had quite a surprise like that before."

Alexa stared at Raphael with nothing but disgust and hatred.

Raphael was too secure in his own importance to notice.

She spat in his face. "It wasn't an act." She yanked her hands out of Raphael's as he slowly reached up to wipe the spit from his face.

There it was, clarity. The gummy man who liked to party morphed into the cruel bastard Hysterian once admired.

But he touched Alexa, and even if Hysterian hadn't already decided to give Alexa what she wanted, Raphael had doomed himself to die.

"Dove," Raphael's voice had lost its exuberance, "it would've been much easier for you if you'd just played along."

Hysterian stood, walked to the door, and locked it.

One of the guards grabbed Alexa from behind and threw her onto the couch. She shrieked and struggled as the guard yanked up her dress and tore down her underwear.

"Hysterian," Raphael said. "You don't mind if we speak later?" They had been close once, but never this close.

Because deep down inside, Raphael was afraid of Hysterian. Even though Hysterian had once vowed his loyalty to Raphael, and a vow from a Cyborg was eternal. It mattered in many circles. It mattered to Raphael, but Hysterian had vowed other things as well.

Like protecting the one he loved.

He strode forward, pulled down his mask, and tore the guard off of Alexa. Hysterian spun the guard to face him and slammed his mouth to his. Stunned, the guard didn't fight him as Hysterian filled his mouth with poison.

Raphael recoiled, tripping to the other side of the room, sliding into the corner before Hysterian finished the kiss and flung the guard away. He stalked toward Raphael as pounding fists hit the locked door from the outside.

"Hysterian, what are you doing? Please!" Raphael cried. "It's my birthday!"

"Alexa, are you ready?" Hysterian asked.

He slammed his hand into Raphael's forcefield without waiting for an answer. Electricity exploded, overwhelming his systems, setting him on fire. Hysterian pushed through, melting the skin off his fingers, his hand. His suit sparked, catching the electricity. The smell of hot metal and meat eclipsed the old stench of sex in the room.

Alexa screamed.

"Not yet," he gritted.

"Hysterian, what happened? I don't know what I've

done to anger you, but we can work this out, can't we?" Raphael begged.

Hysterian winced as Raphael's shield repelled him.

"Like the old ways, right?" Raphael continued. "I know what makes you happy, what helps take away the pressure."

"Shut up," Hysterian growled.

"I can bring you girls. I can drown you in them. Money, too. I need someone to help me manage my business. You could do that job. We could rule Elyria together!"

Hysterian shifted his feet and braced his legs, feeling his hair curl and crisp around his ears. A crackle split the room, and his hand jerked forward.

Raphael startled, pushing into the corner. Hysterian's fingertips brushed Raphael's cheek.

"I know how to cure you!" Raphael screamed.

With a grunt, Hysterian sprang up and slammed the entirety of his weight down on the shield. The forcefield shattered, and he spun and coiled his body around Raphael, stopping the inevitable blast of electricity from reaching Alexa.

It hit him instead.

Hysterian seized and tore off Raphael before he killed the fucker with his own gore.

"Alexa," he murmured, jittering with each spike of electricity. He dropped his arm with his gun, uncurling his fingers from it. "It's time."

TWENTY-EIGHT

Alexa stared at the half-burned body. One eye twitched, the other was bloodshot and sparking. Organic matter sizzled, bubbled, and melted off metal plates and wires. With his hair half gone, Hysterian's scalded eyes rolled her way.

He'd found her. Her throat clogged.

She could barely believe he was here at all.

"Alexa, it's time," he croaked, his arm falling outward, his fingers unfurling around a firearm. It snapped her out of her daze.

She rushed forward and snatched the gun. She aimed it at Raphael.

Blubbering, staring outward, Raphael didn't see her or the gun. She pulled the trigger. The blast eclipsed the pounding at the door, the music. Alexa closed her eyes, dropped her arm, and sighed.

It was done.

He's dead.

Then the ringing in her ears stopped, the pounding, screaming and music returned. Her eyes opened to find

Hysterian struggling to rise to his feet. She rushed to his side.

"Don't!" he ordered, holding out his hand, stopping her. "I'll kill you."

She halted, staring helplessly as blood and other unknown liquids squirted out of organs and tubes. "What can I do to help? Oh, God, you're hurt. Why did you do that? Why did you do that?" Alexa could do nothing but watch as guilt choked her. She'd never felt more useless.

Hysterian, pressing his hand to the wall, steadied himself. "I would do anything for you." His mouth smoked as he said it. He blinked, and his eyes miraculously cleared. They cut to the door. "I'm fine, but staying that way will be hard if they get through."

"Fine?" she warbled. Hysterian looked closer to death than anything resembling *fine*.

Nervously Alexa glanced at the door. The middle cracked like something large was being thrust against it. *Thud. Snap!*

Her hand squeezed the gun still in her grip. "What do we do?"

"There's a hidden passage." He stumbled toward a table off to the side where a crystal decanter and glasses rested untouched. "There's only three more shots in that gun," he bit out.

She glanced at the weapon and nodded. "I'll make them count."

"Yes."

Hysterian picked up one of the glasses and handed it to her. "Push the top into the groove," he pointed to a textured bit under the table.

Quickly, she took the glass from his hand and pressed it in. A staircase appeared behind the table.

It was empty.

"Go," he ordered, spitting.

Alexa dashed past him and entered the small space. The wall snapped back into place as the shouting from beyond broke through the outer barrier.

For the next few minutes, she ran. Hysterian shouted directions, telling her where to go and what to do as he brought up the rear. The strength in his voice returned with each turn. The thumping bass of the club music pounded the walls.

"Alexa, drop!" he ordered, springing past her fast enough she only caught a blur. Landing a few yards ahead, Hysterian shielded her as men appeared in the hallway ahead, guns swinging. "Shoot them!"

Using Hysterian as cover made her sick, but she aimed anyway. Hysterian took the guards' bullets like the metal wall he was as Alexa took them out. Something splashed her skin, and she yelped, wiping it off.

The guards hadn't even fully fallen before Hysterian twisted and saw what she was doing.

"I got some of you on me!" she cried.

"Calm down," he growled. "Let me see."

Sucking in a breath, she stilled as he leaned forward and scanned her arm.

"Hysterian," she whispered as he studied her skin, liquids still pooling out of flickering, rent joints. It hurt her soul to see him in such a way.

Fear threatened to take over. If she was poisoned, that was it. It filled her with terror knowing Hysterian would never leave her behind. Not if he'd come all this way for her.

He would stay by her side as Raphael's army swarmed them, fighting to the bitter end.

His eyes flicked to hers just as the lights overhead went red, and the music stopped somewhere far off.

"Fight it," he said, amplifying her emotions. "Fight it, Alexa. For me. Go!"

He threw his body against the wall for her to pass.

She bit down and sprinted, counting the seconds in her head, already sensing her world teetering.

Once they were through a door, they were finally back within the main part of the building. Hysterian surged into the air as more guards met them. He dropped atop them one by one, crushing their bodies. Below them lay the main floor of the dance room as people charged to the exits. Fleeing.

They blurred as she stared at them.

It wasn't until Hysterian landed in front of her that her eyes cleared to focus on him.

"Fight it! Go," he yelled, pointing to the right.

Alexa ran, blinking, finding her world growing fuzzy. Her fear, her worry for Hysterian vanished. When they broke through a large, metal door and the night sky—Elyria's cloying heat—met her, she fell to her hands and knees.

Screams filled the night. So many bright neon lights filled her eyes that she smiled.

She was lifted uncomfortably off the ground, her dress strangling her body like a vice, feet dragging behind her, and she glimpsed Hysterian above. He was clutching the back of her dress, almost ripping it to lead her to a hover-craft on the roof.

For a time, Alexa knew nothing else but a spinning, vibrant world.

A beautiful world where her nightmares couldn't get to her because they were dead.

And she laughed. She laughed and laughed until her throat went hoarse and she tasted blood in her mouth. She couldn't stop even when her ribs hurt, and her stomach cramped. Bile bled into her mouth, mixing with her blood, and she vomited.

"I love you, Hysterian! I love you. I love you," she wiped her mouth. She heaved again.

She laughed.

TWENTY-NINE

She didn't know when her mind cleared, only that she woke to having water and broth trickling down her throat time and time again. Clarity returned more with each meal. Exhausted, Alexa groaned, rolling over in the soft bedding. Bedding she knew well. Her brain strained, trying to break from the cage of her skull. Her eyes snapped open.

Hysterian sat beside her, watching her.

It took her a moment to remember Dimes, Raphael's blood on the walls, and Hysterian's broken body. It all came back to her as they stared at each other.

He was clean, dressed in a uniform she knew all too well, and only the slight char to the tips of his usually perfect hair gave any evidence of his state at Dimes. He'd made a full recovery, at least from what she could see, and Alexa sprang forward, wrapping her arms around him.

She didn't care if he held her back, or if he even liked her. She didn't care if he planned to take her to the authorities and make her face her crimes. All she cared about was that he was here, whole, and she wasn't alone.

His arms came around her to hold her back. Gloved fingers tugged at her hair as they threaded through it.

Tears slipped over her lashes as she held him, needing more.

She didn't know how to say it—she didn't want him to deny her—but with her soul finally clear of all the grime covering it, Alexa tore at Hysterian's pants, fumbling to open them.

It had been so long.

To hell whether she could touch him or not, she needed him inside her. Her fingers shook with her desperation.

He released her to help her unveil his cock, straining to break from the nano mesh covering that hid it from her view. Alexa gripped it, rising up. She wasn't wearing her dress anymore but a large shirt and cotton underwear—he'd changed her—and as her mind fumbled with that notion, his fingers tore her panties from her body. She lowered onto him.

A cry tore from her mouth and her head fell back as her body struggled to open for him. The heat of his turgid tip burned her. The burn, the ache was perfection, and Alexa refused to let it beat her, impaling herself fully onto his length. Wet, she gloved him.

His grunts filled her ears, his heat branded her flesh. Nearly suffocating on it as she rode him like her life depended on it. She fucked him through the madness in her mind. His power poised between her legs, she filled herself with him until she couldn't.

The orgasm that hit set her soul on fire.

Hard fingers dug into her hips, taking over when her strength faltered. He jerked her body up and down, rutting her through the waves of her bliss until he found his own.

She felt him expand, his body tensing, and then a bright

flash of teal blasted the room, shooting from his eyes as he roared her name, plowing higher. Her feet swung as she bore down on him, wrapping her limbs around his large frame.

They stayed that way, limbs locked together for hours, refusing to acknowledge anything else.

Only each other.

Everything else was dust. She couldn't let it in.

When she was naked, wrapped back in blankets, and gulping down her third cup of water, she knew their moment of heaven had come to an end. She watched as Hysterian straightened his uniform and tucked his cock back into his pants.

"Rest," he said. And then he was gone.

Alexa had no reason to fight him. She fell asleep.

When she woke the next time, she was alone. There were food and fresh clothes beside her. She ate, rose, and showered. The door to Hysterian's quarters was open when she left the bathroom.

She made her way out of the room and found Hysterian sitting alone in the bridge. Quietly, she made her way toward him. He stared out the porthole of his ship, and as she looked at the view, she discovered they were still on Elyria. He hadn't taken her to the stars.

Or to Earth.

To be taken prisoner.

He'd helped her, saved her. She owed him everything.

Alexa licked her lips, knowing the fight had left her back at Dimes. "Whatever you decide to do to me, I won't fight it."

"Is that so?" he purred.

He could do a lot to her, a lot more than just turning her over. Alexa straightened. This was her penance. "Yes."

But she hoped he had an inkling of mercy—

"You're mine, Alexa," he said, rising. The captain's seat swiveled as he turned and faced her, staring her down.

She wasn't sure if she heard him correctly. Her brows wrinkled. "What?"

"Say it."

She stared at him, surprised and confused.

He took a step forward. "Say it." A wildness touched his eyes.

"I'm yours."

As the words left her, she felt them blanket her skin, becoming a part of her.

Now in front of her, his hands cupped her head. Teal eyes searched hers. "Say it again."

"I'm yours," she whispered.

And just like that, she killed him.

She saw it happen, the change that came across his face, just what she could read above the lip of his mask. Hysterian softened, his cold layers defrosting. The hard edges, the taut frame, the bulging muscles relaxed. The sheen of his secretion on his brow dried up.

"I love you," he said, his fingers spanning into her hair. But then his softness fled as his fingers tangled into the pale strands. "Never leave me again." It was a warning. A threat that if she did, worse things would happen than what already had.

Alexa shuddered, grasping his hands. "I'm a half-breed."

"And I'm a fucking frog, princess."

She closed her eyes as he clutched her to his chest. "It won't work."

"We'll make it work."

"And your skin? My dad? Everything else?"

Hysterian's arms banded around her like chains. He wasn't ever letting her go. If she hadn't wanted to stay, it would've been terrifying. But as it was, she settled.

"Tell me what to do and I'll do it," he said, surprising her. "These last weeks without you have been torture. Why didn't you tell me?" He growled, squeezing her. "Why didn't you say? I'm furious." His voice cracked. "I'm..."

"You can hurt me if you want," she breathed.

He jerked back. "Never."

Her eyes flooded with tears. "I love you."

Hysterian drew her back into his arms as she cried.

The next few hours did hurt. He railed, yelled at her, destroyed a bridge that, to her surprise, had already been destroyed. She took it all, was happy to do it, because the more he unleashed, the more she realized they were going to be okay. Their pasts weighed heavy. They clung to every word spoken, every glance they gave each other, but as the minutes turned to hours, and the Elyrian suns descended the sky, the tension was slowly exorcised.

At least she thought it had been.

Pigeon arrived with a plate of food for her, and Alexa lost it, begging for forgiveness all over again.

Not from Hysterian this time, but from Pigeon. And unlike how she cried with Hysterian, she sobbed against Pigeon. She didn't eat that night, clinging to him as he and Hysterian tucked her back into bed. She felt like a little girl again. Pigeon sat by her side and told her stories of his daughters until she slept.

Hysterian readied the ship for takeoff.

He'd been keeping tabs on the local networks, and although the attack at Dimes was front and center when it came to Elyrian news, it never mentioned Raphael's death or Hysterian. But the news did mention Alexa, showed pictures and requested information about her because she was wanted for the murders of eight men.

She wasn't going back to Elyria, not for a long, long time. It wasn't until Alexa awoke in space the next day that she realized it.

She said goodbye to her home, quietly, alone, under the blankets. She let her memories flick through her head. Alexa rose again alone. After she showered, she made her way to the lounge, ate, and went to the laboratory.

She found a spare crew uniform in storage, tugged it on, and got back to work. Later, when her fingers were aching, she looked up to find Hysterian.

Always.

He was always there, always in her head, always just a breath away. It used to frighten her. Now, it made her feel safe.

"Where are we headed, Captain?"

He pushed off the door frame. "Earth."

She shuddered.

He strode to her and twirled a curl of her hair with his finger. "We have vaccines to deliver, remember?"

"Yes." She glanced at the closed door of her old quarters. "I should dye my hair if we're going back."

"Like hell you are."

"Half-breeds aren't allowed on Earth."

"Mine is."

The smug assuredness of his eyes had her believing him. Still, even if she believed him, she wanted reassurance. Life had just begun to right itself, and she was still afraid that maybe it was all a dream, that she was going to wake and be back at Dimes.

"And the other Cyborgs?" she asked.

"Your records show you're human, Alexa. No one has to

know, especially them. Unless you tell them outright, they won't immediately know."

"They'll know when they see my hair," she deadpanned.

"They'll assume you like the look. No Cyborg would ever willingly work with or for a Trentian, that's what they'll believe. You will be with me, under my protection. No male or female of my kind would go after you for that reason alone, despite what you are."

"Are you certain?"

"Yes. And there's more," he said, changing the subject. "There's a coder who might be able to..."

Her scalp pricked when his fingers tugged on her hair.

"To help you?" she offered for him when it looked like he wasn't going to finish.

"I won't hope," his voice lowered. "Not again."

Alexa squeezed his hand.

Though she feared going back to Earth, she knew if she stayed with him, she would have to go back to the humans' home planet time and time again. It went with the job. She wanted to keep her job. She earned it. It paid well, and she really liked her captain.

But handing her life over to Hysterian was something she couldn't do all at once. She was willing to build a life with him out in space, on this ship, but she needed the same from him.

She decided she wanted something in return. Pigeon made her happy. Hysterian had promised to forget that Pigeon helped her escape. Could he forgive Horace as well, and the others?

She coveted the precious moments that made her happy, and despite trying to keep away from her old crewmates, they'd made her happy.

She missed her family.

Hysterian was petting her hair when she asked for the gift. "I want the crew back. All of them, even Daniels, even Raul."

His fingers stilled. "Why?"

"I miss them." She didn't know how to tell him how she felt. It was strange, and a little sad. This *need* to have them back, to have everything the way it was before she... Alexa swallowed.

"I killed Daniels."

Her heart skipped a beat. "Why?"

Hysterian watched her closely. "He was here under false pretenses and he threatened you."

Alexa shuddered.

"Don't kill any more of the crew," she said. Hysterian had killed many people long before they had even met; she knew being with him that he would kill many more.

His eye twitched.

"What did you do?" she asked.

"Raul may or may not be alive."

She threw her hands up. "You killed Raul?"

He caught her hands in a vice-like grip. "No, but I may have touched him and left him to the whores on Libra."

Alexa's mouth went slack. "We have to go back! We have to make sure he's okay..."

Darkness flooded Hysterian's gaze. "He doesn't deserve your worry."

"Raul isn't a bad man... He's my—"

"Your fucking what, Alexa?"

"My friend."

THIRTY

THEY STOPPED at Libra and picked up Raul. Raul, shouting obscenities at seeing Hysterian was dragged aboard the *Questor* while Alexa watched aghast. She could have her friend, but only under Hysterian's rules.

They were never to be alone unless they were working in the menagerie, and even still, Hysterian made sure to let Raul know he'd be watching his every move. Raul, in the middle of filing a complaint with the authorities about being attacked by Hysterian, dropped them when Hysterian paid off all the man's debts.

Neither of them were entirely happy about the situation, especially Raul, who had become very aware of Hysterian and Alexa's relationship. Still, he stayed.

The money was too good.

Horace was easier. As Hysterian's second-in-command, Horace only needed to have a drink with Pigeon to be convinced to come back.

Alexa got her family. Hysterian made sure of it.

He would make sure of it...

In return, he not only won more of her trust, but also

her happiness. She smiled more each day. And during the night shift, the morning shift, the evening shift, he relished in her, happy knowing she was here, on his ship and in his arms.

But he hadn't been able to touch her.

Not in the way he needed to, that they both needed him to. He always wore his nanocloth covering now to protect Alexa when she forgot he was dangerous, when she was so desperate for affection and comfort that she touched him.

For a time, he wondered if she was addicted to him. But she never sought his bare skin, and so he refused to dwell on it.

With each passing moment, Hysterian's need for *her* affection grew. She was the fantasy in his head that played out on loop, but with each play, his hands were upon her body. He would take her mouth and drink her down. He would feast on her flesh, slide his tongue over her curves, and spread her pale thighs.

He would kiss her there, lick her, stretch her with his tongue, and then he would secrete all over the lavatory shower unit, climaxing at the same time as the water burned off his flesh.

Sweetness bloomed from her, scenting the air, and it made him ravenous. Even if it was just in his mind.

It was all he thought about when he wasn't lavishing her with gifts.

Clothes, jewels, stones, guns, fresh fruits, fresh coffee, and chocolate from every planet. The crew. Even Raul was a gift—one Hysterian hadn't wanted to give.

But she wanted the one thing he craved as well: his touch, his kiss, untainted by poison. And it was the one thing he couldn't give. They'd been lucky so far with her recoveries—she'd never gotten a full dose of him, thankfully—but if she ever did, she might not survive the third time.

He was adamant that would never happen, although Cyborgs could still make mistakes.

So as the weeks rolled on, and Earth remained billions of miles away, he'd begun to avoid her for fear that he'd lose her all over again.

Alexa's smiles wavered when she realized what he was doing.

It had taken a lot longer to get to Earth than he originally planned...

Hysterian clenched his hands as a cybernetic doctor, and his team of coders, peeled off the skin on the back of his neck and plugged him directly into a supercomputer. A computer made specifically for the very task of correcting the hundreds of millions of codes in his systems. For the first time since his creation—as the cryoliquid pooled around him to keep him from overheating—his mind went blank.

The last thing he saw was Alexa the first day he met her.

He awoke three months later.

Disoriented, his systems surging to life, Hysterian slumped forward onto the ground as the liquid drained. He gasped as three months of information poured into him instantaneously. His fingers curled against the metal floor.

Naked, wet, and cold, he immediately thought he was secreting profusely— like he had when he'd awoke the first time, killing one scientist and putting another in a coma— but after a moment, sense returned and he wiped the cryoliquid off his face.

"You're awake," a voice he knew all too well said.

"No kidding," Hysterian spat. "Where's Alexa?"

Nightheart grabbed his arm and helped him rise. "With

the rest of your crew, housed in the EPED suites. How do you feel?"

Hysterian glanced at the doctors, scientists, and even the coders who'd helped build a supercomputer strong enough, fast enough to take on the webs of codes and DNA that made him who he was. Cypher was among them.

Of course he was.

Hysterian looked down at Nightheart's hand on him.

Hysterian waited for his glands to open, to release poison he didn't want to be released, but as the seconds passed, nothing happened.

"Hotter," he demanded.

Nightheart heated his hand.

Hysterian's glands remained closed.

It wasn't until he forced them open that he secreted, and even then, what pooled from his body was anything but poisonous. It was as benign as water. Something his poison didn't do unless it was out of range from him and out of his body for a length of time.

"Is it..."

Nightheart released him. "You tell me."

Hysterian ordered his nanocells within him to change. They did. He opened and closed his hand, his body jittering with excitement.

Years he'd waited for this. Years he'd searched. No one had access to the resources Nightheart had, and Hysterian cursed himself for not approaching his brother sooner. Instead, he'd made the best and worst mistake of his life...

Alexa.

He was out the door and seeding into the EPED's systems within the next moment. Voices called after him, but he outran them, heading straight for the one being in the universe worth waiting for. His body groaned, his joints springing, air breezed over his naked form, and he felt freedom.

Pure, perfect, delectable freedom.

He smelled her before he saw her. Entering the resident staff housing floor, gasps followed him as people and androids dodged out of the naked Cyborg's path.

"Alexa," he called.

She shot out of her room the second her name left his mouth.

She halted, staring at him, face etched with worry. He stalked toward her, threw her over his shoulder, and carried her back into the room.

It may have only been a blink since he'd last seen her, but a blink was more than enough for him to suffer.

Skin bare to all the universe, Hysterian laid her on the rumpled bed of her dorm and covered her with his body. She cried pretty little tears from seeing him as her fingers whispered sweetly over his damp skin. Starved, he gripped her hair and tugged her head back until their eyes met.

Her beautiful hair glinted teal from the light of his eyes.

He rubbed it between his fingers. It felt like heaven.

"You waited," he said, making her aware how trapped she was now, his legs and elbows caging her body under his.

She could have run again while he was out, and it had taken a lot of coaxing on her part to convince him to turn off. Even though he'd pulled away from her for fear of hurting her again, he had needed her to reassure him again and again.

Because he'd kill every last being in the EPED building, Nightheart included, if he awoke and she wasn't there. Alexa had laughed at the threat.

She had a lot left to learn about his kind.

"Of course I waited," Alexa said.

Her hair shimmered, clear around his fingers. "You didn't dye it."

"You destroyed all the dye. Nightheart said it no longer exists anywhere. I hate you both," she muttered playfully.

He didn't actually care if she dyed it or not anymore, as long as she stayed right where she was. Hysterian manually shut down his systems, the ones that didn't matter, and focused entirely on Alexa.

Her face softened as he took her in. He couldn't look away. She was beautiful.

"Alexa..."

Her tongue peeked out to swipe her bottom lip.

His mouth watered.

"Kiss me," she whispered.

"Yes, princess," he groaned and sank into her. Sensation erupted over him as her lips softened against his, opening to give him access to her body. A body he'd worship for the remainder of his days. A body that didn't seek his touch out of addiction, a body that didn't tremble in fear. Divine, refreshing like a cold drink of water slipping down a throat that had never experienced such pleasure, Alexa opened up for him.

Hysterian slipped his tongue in her and coaxed her ever further, mesmerized in the feel of her.

He ran hot. She ran cold. Together, they were perfect.

When she gasped, he rose up and undressed her, caressing the velvety curves of her body as he did, and when she was once again beneath him, as naked as he was, Hysterian spread her thighs like he'd done a million times in his head before.

Except this time, sensation pulsed through him, electrifying his senses.

He'd come the moment he saw her, his cock rigid as he

ran through the EPED. He'd come again when he threw her over his shoulder and he'd brushed her flesh the first time. And he did it now as he opened her slick sex with his fingers.

Twitching, bulging, reverence consumed him as he leaned forward and licked her long and hard.

Alexa buckled, screaming his name. He covered her in his saliva, he gripped her knees, and he aimed at her exposed flesh each time he came.

He preferred it this way, watching his seed trickle over her skin. He rubbed it in and hardened when it didn't affect her. It would never affect her.

Hours passed, and he was lost in the way Alexa's body felt, drinking from her mouth, between her legs. And when his little half-breed got too hot, he fed her water from his mouth.

He enjoyed her for hours as a man, not as a Cyborg, nor a frog. Or any other fucking thing he was in his black soul. He savored her because at the edges of his mind he knew he didn't fucking deserve her, or her forgiveness for what he'd done, or the pain he had caused her.

But he was ready to spend the rest of his life trying to earn her.

She thought she needed to earn forgiveness from him. It was incredulous. She had no idea what was in store once he convinced her who the real bad guy was between them. He was certain it wouldn't take long. Raul would have an accident one of these days that he wouldn't recover from...

A painful accident.

Alexa's eyes hooded with pleasure, and Hysterian lined up his cock to her opening.

Her eyes widened. She clutched the bed, panting. "Finally?"

"Finally," he rasped. "A child?"

A smile tugged at the corners of her swollen lips.

He shared her smile. If she wanted a family, he'd give her a real one.

She moaned sweetly as he pushed into her, spreading her where his fingers and tongue had just spent hours exploring. And still, she squirmed with a twitch of discomfort. It was sublime.

His mind exploded.

He came hard, roaring, terrifying her, filling her with his seed. Her and only her, forever. She writhed, her quivering sheath stealing his senses. Hysterian fucked her until her eyes rolled back into her head and her body was nothing but a mess of endless orgasms.

Until he was certain his seed took hold inside her. That it had trapped her egg as surely as he trapped Alexa beneath him. He connected to the nanocells in his seed, making her his completely.

Then he washed her hair, fed her, and worshipped every inch of her body.

Afterward, Hysterian put her to bed, and he held her flush to his chest while she slept.

He'd never been more content, not in all the years since he'd been brought into this world. He never imagined a heaven like the one he had lying against him.

Eternity without heaven to look forward to nearly destroyed him.

Alexa had come to kill him. Instead, she had given him the greatest gift.

A new life.

He sold years of his life to Nightheart for the chance to touch another without hurting them. If Hysterian had known what else he would find working for the EPED, he would have sold those years long ago, he would give up everything for Alexa.

He held her tightly to him, allowing hope to swim through his soul. Content. Finally.

"I love you," he whispered into the darkness.

"I love you too," she responded.

AUTHOR'S NOTE

Thank you for reading *Dark Hysteria, Cyborg Shifters book 8*, the princess and the frog. If you liked the story or have a comment, please leave a review! I love reviews :)

If you're excited and wondering when *Cyborg Shifters book 9* is coming? Click here!

And if you love cyborgs, aliens, anti-heroes, and adventure, follow me on Facebook or through my blog online for information on new releases and updates.

Join my newsletter for the same information.

Naomi Lucas

Turn the page for a sneak peek at Viper, Naga Brides Book 1... A sexy, dystopian SciFi romance with cunning alpha aliens who hunt down their human brides!

VIPER (NAGA BRIDES)

Long have we been alone.

Without brides, without females to warm us during the long nights. Without sweet mates.

But we see them, from afar, brides that could be ours. Kept away from us by walls and weapons. Females we long for greatly.

Obsessively.

Human females.

And the one with red hair? I want her. I saw her first. I will fight to the death for her.

She is MINE.

So, we'll come together and make an exchange with their men that will benefit us all.

After that?

To the winner goes the spoils...

Let the hunt begin.

But the red-headed female is MINE.

Buy Now!

Turn the page for a preview of the first chapter!

VIPER

NAGA BRIDES I

NAOMI LUCAS

THIRTY-ONE

CHAPTER ONE

THE PACT

Vruksha

"Our truce ends after they release the females," I growl, peering at the males around me. The King Cobra's mane flutters, the Boomslang nods. Others react; some don't respond at all. I take their silence as agreement.

We're the strongest of our kind. The oldest. The deadliest. We saw the humans' ship breach our sky and land within our forest.

We're also competitors. The fact that we've all come together for this—*for them*—is a miracle. It shows how much we want *them*, how desperate we are to have *them,* and that we would risk our lives to make a deal with *their* keepers.

Their puny males.

Males who do not deserve the warmth of a female. They don't realize how lucky they are to have females, so we will take their females and covet them, mate them, make them queens to the lands we rule. As is how it should be.

There are many wrongs that need to be righted, and many mistakes in our past that need to be fixed.

My fingers tighten around my spear as I scrutinize the nagas gathered today, sizing them up. Some of us won't survive.

Humans are different from us, at least from what I've seen, and it's more than the way they look.

We thought them long gone. A species that had been eradicated when we were born on this Earth. Neither me nor the other naga males around me have ever seen a living one, not once, until recently.

They flew down from the sky in a large metal machine. Machines like the ones here, but not overgrown with weeds, roots, and vines. Not ruined the way Earth was ruined.

No, this machine—this ship of theirs—came to us clean of the forest and landed outside the old ruins of a civilization long gone, deep in the mountains. Other smaller machines came out with weapons and cleared the ruins. They erected a barrier and cut down the trees.

The humans restored the ruins into what it once was: a military facility.

Meanwhile, I watched the robots from afar, from the shadows of the trees, and soon found other nagas watching them too. We didn't know why they were here, or what they wanted, but we are determined to keep our secrets...secret.

At first, there were only machines to watch. We didn't realize there were humans on the ship. The robots poured from their vessel in droves, destroying the terrain we once knew. The terrain *I* once knew. A growl tears from my throat at the thought. The robots left us alone, though, having one singular purpose, a purpose we nagas did not know until several weeks after their landing.

They were making the facility ready for human inhabitants.

When the humans first stepped out of the ship, I stared in awe, thinking it was only machines that had flown down from the sky, nothing else, nothing so exciting as *women*.

Thinking back on that day quickens my heart.

Her red hair. My fingers twitch. I can imagine the softness of it running between my fingers. I've never seen such a shade of red like my own tail...

Zaku, the King Cobra, went to the humans when we realized they had females among them. He made our presence known. He wanted to meet them, court them, mate with one... We were bigger, stronger, larger than their males, and thought that because of it, they should be ours.

I did too.

Perhaps we could offer our help in return? Who knows?

Zaku came back to us enraged. The humans turned their weapons on him, refusing his request. They told him this land was theirs, as it has always been, and as long as he —we—abided by that, they would not kill us.

Hah. I would like to see them try.

They have no idea what they're up against when it comes to us.

I know now that if I want my red-headed beauty, I'll have to fight for her, kill for her. And I'm willing to do more than that, but I do not want her hurt. And fighting? I've seen enough death to know accidents happen.

It wasn't that long ago. Days, maybe? Seems like an eternity. The other nagas came together after word spread of what happened to Zaku.

It wasn't hard to win me over. I would do anything for *her*.

When I first saw her, everything changed.

Gone was the bloodlust, the anger. Real lust took its

place. Red hot desire, with a wild mane of red hair to match. Transfixed, I stared that first day as she descended from the ramp, realizing something more miraculous than machines had fallen from the heavens. She stared at her surroundings with wonder and curiosity.

She had gazed at the sky and the clouds above. She had touched the grass at her feet. Her tongue poked out to swipe at her lips.

Her eyes had found mine, even as I hid beyond her barrier, in the shadows of the forest. From that moment, she was mine.

A human female, wondrous in her rarity, who with one look ruined me.

My female.

The way her eyes widened. The way her lips parted...

The fear on her face hadn't bothered me at all.

She was mine. I expected her to face her fear and come to me then, but instead, she turned away and rushed into the shadows of the facility, leaving me bereft, lusty, and angry.

But she had looked at me, had met my gaze. She saw me, and that was all that mattered. Now I know I am in her head. She will always remember the first time she saw me. For I am a strong male, a vicious one, and refused to be forgotten.

It would be dangerous to forget me.

My anger had returned after I lost sight of her, and my agitation at these human interlopers built. My need for this female stole my mind. Reclaiming the facility and this land meant nothing if I couldn't have her. I wanted both but only cared about the latter.

I saw her first.

She saw me first.

She was in *my* head. No other naga's head mattered unless they were hanging from a rope off my belt or lobbed off and impaled on my spear, decorating the entrance to my den.

But as whispers of human females spread through the forest—the mountains—the other nagas had similar thoughts. My female wasn't the only one, and nagas from far afield, males I have not seen in years, returned to see them, to steal them, to mate with them, and hoard them away in our respective nests.

The need to mate overcame us all like a storm. To conquer. These females came from the skies to be ours. We became very aware of our diminishing numbers, and with the threat of invaders from the skies on our minds...our biology altered against us, clouding our minds.

I wasn't the only one changed, nor the only one desperate to nest. A piece within us unlocked, and it can't be undone. Some nagas feared the change—this need to conquer—and fled, hoping the change would reverse.

Less to die by my hands. I hiss out a breath of air.

Azsote, a Boomslang, snaps his tail. "And if they don't release them?"

"We invade with our weapons and strike them down. They need to know this land is not theirs, not without a price," Zaku snarls. Some of the other males snarl with him. The King Cobra is out for blood, one way or another. A king, even though Zaku wasn't one, doesn't like being told what to do.

Zaku's only king in name, and he holds no more sway or dominion than the rest of us.

"They will pay for it with females," I say.

Azsote snaps his tail again. "Yesss."

"They want our technology, our land... We will give them a little for a lot more," Zaku agrees.

I eye the facility far, far in the distance, through the trees and across the shattered landscape, hoping to see her. A splash of red among the green. But she's nowhere to be found from our vantage point way up on the cliffs.

I haven't seen her in many days. Venom leaks from my fangs. I need to see her soon or I may do something crazed, like storm the humans' barrier and take on their robots for just a glimpse.

She is the same color as me. I never thought such a female existed besides my sisters. One with Viper in her blood.

No creature in all the verdant lands or the oceans of sandy waste has ever been the same color as me. She is mine because of this. Even if I haven't memorized her face, even if I don't know the sound of her voice, or her name, she is mine.

My hands tremble with the need to comb my fingers through her hair. My nose itches to burrow into her neck and languish in its warmth, in the scent of her skin.

"We give them nothing, and they won't be the wiser," I hiss, "while they give usss everything in return."

The other males beat their chests and hoot in agreement. The coming hunt excites us. I feel it in my veins, the way my blood pumps heavy. My member rises to the occasion. I slam my fist against my chest and hoot with them.

"How many females are there?" Vagan asks when we settle. "Not enough, last I checked." His blue scales and long, slender body are like mine, except he is blue where I am red. Vagan is of the Blue Coral clan, a ruler of the dangerous waterways. He may be brightly colored like me, but to face him near water was certain death.

Of all the nagas gathered, Vagan is the one I watch the most. Him and the Death Adder.

But Zhallaix, the Death Adder, is not here. He would rather kill us than work with us. An enemy to us all. He has no honor, nor allegiance. Ruthless and wild, he is probably fucking a mossy rock and spitting venom somewhere off in the hills. I have not seen Zhallaix since the ship first appeared.

"I have only seen three," Zaku answers. The King Cobra is fearsome, but I do not watch him like Vagan and some of the others. One bite and the Cobra could take out any one of us, but he has honor in his cold veins.

Honor I do not know if I have. But Zaku isn't just honorable, he's pompous and hard-headed. Everything is beneath him, and it shows in his inability to help anyone but himself, even in this. If Zaku could steal a female human for himself, he wouldn't have gathered us. Sometimes I think he's not honorable at all, just overzealous.

I keep an eye on him anyway. If Zaku doesn't win one of the females today, he's going to destroy the world. Or die trying.

As for everyone else? They watch me.

I tighten my grip on my spear, meeting their eyes.

"Three? Three is not enough!" Vagan shouts. "There are at least seven of us here, and more yet in these woods. How will three brides appease us all?"

"They won't," I say. "We will fight for them when they are handed over."

Some growl, some hiss in agreement. We size each other up, considering who we could off now before the humans arrive.

The Boomslang with the shimmery green scales slips to the ledge, his voice lowering. "Why not fight now? Until there are only three of us left?" Azsote suggests, waving his hand.

"Why not let the females choose who they want to mate with?" another offers. I look at the naga and bare my fangs. It's the Copperhead. He is a quiet one. I'm surprised to hear him speak at all.

"No," I snap.

"That won't work," Zaku says at the same time.

"We will not honor their choices," I add. If my female chooses another over me, I would kill him and take her.

I am not honorable, after all.

The Copperhead nods. He knows what I say is true. The females can't have the luxury to choose, not now that their very presence has created a strange fervor.

Our members have filled up with unspent spill, causing pressure, bringing us pain. When I first saw my human, my shaft flooded with seed, seed that has been dormant for years, and I have had to milk my prick nightly to relieve the pressure.

If I'm suffering, the other nagas are too.

"Three females is a problem," says Zaku. "But I have an idea. If we fight for mating rights to them, there is a chance they will run while we battle. It is paramount that the females do not come to any harm. Especially by us or our ways. They may be all there is, and we can't lose them. We must keep them safe."

We mumble in agreement. I love the red of my female's hair, but it is the only red I wish to see upon her. I do not want to witness her blood outside her moon cycle.

Zaku continues, "If they run, the animals could kill them, the pigsss. They could get hurt—"

"So what's your suggestion?" Vagan interrupts.

"I suggest we spread out when the human males hand them over. So we do not fight. I suggest they run, we follow, and we hunt them down. Whoever catches the females first wins nesting rights to them."

Silence hangs over us as we ponder Zaku's words. It is a good suggestion but not the greatest. My redhead is already mine. But the other male nagas will want proof, and a hunt —because I know I will catch her—is a good way to prove it.

"I like this idea," Boomslang speaks up first.

"Of course you do," Vagan snaps. "You are a hunter of the forest."

Azsote shrugs. "I am. That does not change that this is a good suggestion."

"And what about me? What about Syasku? We fare best in the water. A hunt over land cripples us."

Nobody cares about Vagan or Syasku, but I don't say that aloud. "There is water nearby, a lot of water. If the females head for it, then you have an advantage."

"And if they don't?"

I turn back to the facility, not caring enough to answer.

"I will accept a hunt," says Syasku of the Cottonmouth clan. *Good.* If the other water naga accepts a hunt, then Vagan has no grounds to argue it.

Vagan scowls.

"It is settled then," Zaku declares. "We will hunt for nesting rights to the females."

Another wave of shouts soar in the air. I lift my spear and release a bolt of electricity to the sky. I like this. I will win. I have destiny on my side. Vicious, red destiny.

The other males pound their chests, and some release their well-hung and hard members from their scales. Tails coil and thump the ground. For a frenzied moment, excitement and real camaraderie return to us. It is a rare thing. We are deadly as a group.

We are deadly alone, but together... The world would tremble with fear.

But the excitement does not last. I turn back once again to see if my bride is outside, if she's being gathered with the other females to be handed over.

And for a second, I see her. My heart stops.

She's being led to one of the flying transport machines. Another female is fighting, kicking, and screaming behind her. She's lifted off the ground and hauled to the machine.

My female goes calmly.

She knows her fate. Knows who awaits her

Me.

Venom fills my mouth. My heart revs back up.

The others have gone silent, and I know they are watching as well.

"She is the one I want," Azsote rumbles. My eyes flick to the Boomslang watching my female, and I slam my spear into his side.

I attack him, striking out with my tail, knocking him over. He evades my speartip, rolling away before I can plunge it into his gut.

"She is mine!" I roar, fury surging through me. "Mine!"

How dare he want her. How dare he even look at her! Azsote strikes back, hitting me with his fist, slicing me with his claws across my bicep. The sting of pain erupts, but I barely notice, needing to see his blood splattered across the ground.

Hands grab us, pulling us apart.

"Enough!" Zaku shouts.

Fighting his hold, I spit venom in Azsote's direction. He

pushes his capturer away and shrieks a battle cry. Furious, only his blood on the ground and his spine in my hand will appease me now.

"I sssaid enough! They're coming! Do not let them see us fighting." Zaku shoves me away, getting between us. Growling, I rise to fight the King Cobra as well, but he's facing the horizon.

Behind him, the humans' transport vehicle is heading our way. It glides soundlessly through the air.

All thoughts of Azsote and the others fall from my mind. My female is heading for me.

In mere moments, I will see her up close for the first time. My body tenses to not only fight, but to fuck as well.

"Present the technology," Zaku orders.

Vagan hands Zaku a small metal box. A data collection. An ancient thing left here by aliens. Both this technology and the humans once shaped this world, but for countless years, both have been ours. Times have changed and now the technology is wanted by these humans that have returned from the sky.

I don't care about the technology. I have my den, my weapon, and enough resources to last me into old age. These trinkets that we are giving the humans is nothing compared to what we keep hidden.

The transport flies past us to land on the clearing behind. Some of the males scatter, readying themselves for the coming hunt.

When the transport opens, the only ones left are me, Zaku, and Vagan.

I will not lose this chance to finally see my female up close.

My fangs drip. A male dressed in a powersuit steps out.

My spine stiffens when another man follows after.
Where are you, little female?
My hands clench.
Then I see her, and my mind blanks.

WANT MORE? Click here!

ALSO BY NAOMI LUCAS

Naga Brides
Viper

King Cobra

Blue Coral

Cyborg Shifters
Wild Blood

Storm Surge

Shark Bite

Mutt

Ashes and Metal

Chaos Croc

Ursa Major

Dark Hysteria

Wings and Teeth (Coming 2022)

The Bestial Tribe
Minotaur: Blooded

Minotaur: Prayer

Stranded in the Stars
Last Call

Collector of Souls

Printed in Great Britain
by Amazon